BEYOND

STORIES BEYOND TIME, TECHNOLOGY, AND THE STARS

Scott Overton

No Walls Publishing

SUDBURY, ONTARIO, CANADA

Scott Overton/No Walls Publishing
Sudbury/Ontario/Canada P0M 3C0
www.scottoverton.ca

Publisher's Note: This is a work of fiction. Names, characters, places, and incidents are a product of the author's imagination. Locales and public names are sometimes used for atmospheric purposes. Any resemblance to actual people, living or dead, or to businesses, companies, events, institutions, or locales is completely coincidental.

Book Layout © 2017 BookDesignTemplates.com

Beyond/ Scott Overton. -- 1st ed.
ISBN 978-1-9993860-4-7

CONTENTS

NO WALLS

I ALMOST DIED the first time I learned that I could walk through walls.

At least you no longer laugh at the concept. That's progress. But then you know better. My guards do not, so they laugh. Of course they laugh. They've never seen me do it. If I could do it here I would have escaped long before now—that much is obvious to anyone.

You know better because you've seen it, used it. Used me.

I'm not bitter anymore. Without you and your Institute I'd never have had a scientific explanation for what happens to me. I might still believe that I'd permanently slipped a cog and was living in some schizophrenic hallucination. (I never tried to spend the money from that bank, you know. Part of me couldn't believe it was real.)

I was desperate for an explanation—you can't know what it's like. At least Pearson's theories about interpenetrating universes offered one possible means of rationalizing the irrational. A straw I could grasp. Your Dr. Storck simply said the model fit the observable facts in my case. But I know he was glad he didn't have to try to convince the rest of the scientific community. Give up on their precious Einstein? I don't expect to live to see it. But then I don't expect to live to see tomorrow.

And that first time it happened I didn't know anything about the parallel universe theories. I just knew that I turned the wrong direction in a thirteenth floor office suite and instead of slamming into a triple-paned window I found myself in the open air with one foot on a ten-inch ledge and the other on...nothing. Nothing of *our* material universe, anyway. Maybe in that other place it was the protruding end of a two-by-four because that version of the building was still under construction. I don't know. In the bright sunlight I couldn't see it. I couldn't see anything but thirteen floors' worth of empty space between me and the hard pavement. If I'd stopped for even a moment, I would have lost my balance or fainted. Instead, my automatic reaction was to step backward, without thinking of what my right foot could be pushing against. And then I was back inside the room. Behind the glass. The whole thing could not have taken more than a few seconds.

I knew I must have been hallucinating. The mind can't accept something like that and just reject the construct of reality, built up over a lifetime.

It happened again a couple of weeks later. I've told you about that one. I desperately wanted to read my boss's analysis of the report I'd just given him. My career hung on it. Some of the report was going to make him look bad, and I'd need to defend myself when we brought it to the Board. I even made an excuse to stay late that night, hoping against hope that he'd leave his office door unlocked. He didn't. But as I leaned on the polished wood, trying to plan my next step, suddenly I was inside the office, and the papers were lying on his desk.

I couldn't explain it—didn't even try. I had what I wanted and that was all that mattered at the time. It was later, calming my nerves at a bar down the street that the first incident came back to me, and I began to try to make the pieces fit.

I felt like a God that night. I wasn't rational, I know that. A heady mix of hubris and eight ounces of Scotch led me to a way to test my theory at the YMCA next door. The attendant was busy watching TV as I made my way to the swimming pool area. The men's shower was unoccupied, as I'd hoped, but I could hear water running in the women's shower next door. On the other side of one thin wall. I had no control over my ability yet. I thought it somehow responded to desire, and I had plenty right then. Maybe too much—nothing happened. But as I began to wonder why, I sensed the change. A moment out of time. An orphan instant. My heart sometimes skips a beat—it was like that.

I slid through the wall and steam surrounded me. Four naked women were soaping their slick bodies and pivoting slowly in the hot spray. Two of them were white with athletic builds, smooth skin and small breasts. The third woman was black and heavier but with ostentatious curves. I've only reconstructed the scene from memory (and more often lately, in this god-forsaken place) because the reality lasted only seconds. The fourth woman began to scream.

Of course she saw me. Thanks to the alcohol it never occurred to me that incorporeal didn't mean invisible. And in my shock the walls stayed completely impenetrable, too. I was just damned lucky that the adjoining pool area had an outside door, and no pursuers were fast enough to follow my wet footprints.

Now you're laughing.

#

The guards have arrived. Two of them. The first few days they mainly ignored me, except to turn the lights on for different intervals at all hours. To mess up my time sense, mess with my mind, I know. I've read my share of spy novels. They're trying to 'soften me up'. For the same reason, I never know when my next meal's coming either. At first I tried not to eat anything—afraid of drugs, or something disgusting they might have put in it—but you can't keep that up.

One of them comes into the room. I'm sitting on the floor, so he just stands over me, staring me down, not speaking. Five minutes. Maybe ten. Then he unzips his pants and pulls out his manhood. I think he's going to piss on me.

At the last moment he diverts the stream and it hits the floor beside me. I can still feel the warm spray, and turn my head in shame.

When he's finished, he bends down near my ear and whispers, "Say your prayers. Soon you will die." They are gone before I can bring myself to look up.

#

I never read any physics until this happened to me, and afterward I could still only stomach the popular treatments: Hawking and Feynman digested in small pieces while riding the commuter train to work. They couldn't provide the answers I needed, though. I thought about Everett's ideas of duplicate universes being created every time a moving particle has to make up its mind which way to go. Does anybody really buy that? Unthinkably complicated! And anyway, it didn't explain how my body could suddenly be able to ignore solid matter. At the Institute, the scenario Dr. Storck painted for me was elegant in its simplicity, and as plausible as I was likely to find. Even high school dropouts know that atomic structure is mostly empty space, so the idea of other universes of matter coexisting in the same space as ours, but at an incompatible frequency of energy (or wavelength—whichever is the case doesn't make any difference to me) didn't seem impossible. It was either that or believe that I was already a ghost without realizing it, like the guy in "The Sixth Sense". That thought crossed my mind a lot in the early days. It didn't appeal to me at all.

Besides, Storck's explanation fit what I experienced. He said the other universes 'interpenetrating' ours were like the frequencies of the radio band, but our bodies were set to 'tune in' only one frequency and ignore all others. The atoms of my body had somehow forgotten that lesson. Sometimes they could tune out the home frequency, and no longer recognize a solid wall or other object as being a barrier. Picture conga lines crossing at a party: our atoms mutually agreed to allow each other passage through the gaps between.

It feels like that. It feels like I'm mentally 'tuning' across a range of options, until I hit on one that works. And I'm convinced that it involves more than just one overlapping Earth. I have no idea how many. As I'm *tuning out* the frequency of our universe I must be tuning *in* the frequency of another. That's obvious, isn't it? Otherwise I'd drift out of position, or sink into the floor, but I don't. I'm still walking on something that's recognized as solid by the atoms of my feet. The only reason I can go through walls is that I tune in a world *where those walls don't exist*. Where the building has a slightly different layout, or doors that are often left open. Or where there is no building at all.

You didn't know that, did you? I don't think Storck did, either. I figured it out for myself.

My captors don't know it. They just got lucky.

After the fiasco at the 'Y', I was scared to try my ability anywhere but around my own home. The house was only five years old, so maybe that's why it was easy to tune in an otherworld version of it with no walls. A few times I even miscalculated and ran into two-by-fours of the building frame, but I soon learned to predict where they were and avoid them. Plumbing hurt more.

Yes, that was a joke, but also true. Think of the pitfalls of an ability like mine. At a certain stage buildings don't have walls, but before that they don't have floors either. I learned to be very cautious.

I never told my wife or daughter. My wife and I were always on the verge of divorce anyway (did you feed her some kind of story about my disappearance, or does she think I'm dead?) And my daughter? Well once I had a beautiful little girl. Then one day I woke up to find there was a stranger living in my house: a stranger with dyed black hair, Alice Cooper makeup, and pieces of metal hanging from every body part that wasn't already stained by ink. She once caught me coming out of her room. Somehow the fact that the door had never moved didn't register on her brain. What registered was that I'd invaded her privacy, and the screaming exchange that followed was the last conversation we ever had, if you can call it that.

You know what's funny? I think my bizarre behaviour those last few days at home actually brought mother and daughter closer together. They'd always been like oil and water before, but despising me gave them something to share. I'm a man who can walk through walls. But only the physical kind.

#

The guards are back. This time I think they mean business. I don't know how many days it's been. I'm sure they're only leaving the lights off for two hours at a stretch—no more than that. I'm in a daze most of the time. The horrible food leaves me feeling sick, too.

There are shackles anchored in the wall. Two sets: high and low—I'm sitting right between the low ones. My captors have never used them on me, until now. I feel like vomiting as the metal bands lock around my wrists.

The guard that almost pissed on me bends over me and smiles. The other has stepped out of the cell.

"Why did they send you?" the first guard asks. The second one returns with something in his hand. It looks like a piece of shielded electrical cable.

Oh, God, no.

"Why did they send you?"

What can I answer? Do I try to pretend I'm innocent? Do I say I'm a spy?

Do I tell them I was sent because I can walk through walls?

I try to clear my throat, but I'm too late. The cable slices through the air.

Oh Christ! Oh Christ Jesus! I never knew anything could hurt like that! My battered feet instantly go into spasms.

"I'm not anybody!" I scream. "I'm not a spy! I'm a civilian. A civilian for Christ's...."

A whip crack.

My back arches off the dirt. I've bit my tongue—I can taste the blood.

"I can't...I don't know what to say! *What do you want me to say?*" Red spittle sprays my chest.

The air hisses in protest.

My head snaps against the rock hard wall, and my eyes dim, flooded with tears.

The voice says, "Why did they send you?"

"*I can walk through walls! I can walk through walls!*" I babble.

There is the sound of their laughter. And then the whip scrapes across the floor, coiling to strike again.

#

Think about this: What would the average person do with a 'gift' like mine? Is it good for anything but larceny?

After a while I tried breaking into other homes on the street, just to see if I could do it. I was still a chickenshit—I wouldn't risk it unless I was certain no-one was home. Even then all I did was look around. I rifled through drawers and found valuables in absurdly obvious hiding places—one time even a stack of hundred dollar bills in a fake stereo speaker. But I couldn't take them. Couldn't steal them. Not just because it felt wrong, but because it felt...petty. I had an ability that no-one else in the world could claim. Was I going to use it to become one of the bottom-feeding scavengers I despised so much? A contemptible sneak thief? The truth is, my only real thrill was when I mistakenly thought my lawyer neighbour's wife had gone out, and instead found her entertaining a young delivery man with his special package in her living room. I watched for about twenty minutes, then quietly made my way to the front door, slammed it, and yelled, "Jessica, I came home early."

I hid in the bushes long enough to see the man run naked from the back deck, then scrambled away myself.

Strange, how I could reject the vocation of burglar but embrace the role of voyeur. Freud might have been able to explain it. I didn't bother.

It wasn't that I couldn't physically steal things, either. Objects touching me travel with me. One of those small mercies. You've read or seen some version of the "Invisible Man" story—we all have. The poor bugger always had to leave a trail of clothes behind! A modern DNA lab would have a field day with that. At least I didn't have to put up with the inconvenience of nudity. Maybe that's why I finally decided I could get away with robbing a bank.

Anyone can tell you that a man who wouldn't dream of snatching an old lady's purse doesn't have the same scruples when it comes to knocking over a bank. They deserve it. I told myself if I could make one big score I could immediately retire from both bank robbery and my usual form of thievery: brokering stock.

The thing about robbing a bank vault is, you have to defeat all of the security systems, get into the locked vault, and then get away clean. If you can't disable the security cameras you have to make sure you can't be identified. And if you can't be absolutely certain you won't trigger an alarm of some kind, you have to be able to beat it before the security guards or cops show up.

I picked a bank that was built a couple of years ago. It was planted on an outcrop of rock, so they weren't worried about tunnels, and it stood on its own about a hundred feet from the other buildings in the strip mall, and seventy or eighty feet from a Greek restaurant and a row of connected townhouses that shared the same back alley. Driving by at night I never saw any signs of life: no guards and thankfully no dogs. So that left the video cameras I could spot and a few hidden ones, plus I assumed an array of various motion detectors, probably sensitive to body heat too. I couldn't avoid any of those things and I didn't have a clue about hacking them by computer, or even hacking away at a box of wires somewhere. I only had one advantage. But it was one they couldn't have foreseen.

I walked six blocks to the bank that night, after parking on a residential street with lots of other cars. It was a little after midnight, so the streets still had some traffic. The alley behind the building included a couple of large garbage bins for the Greek restaurant. I hid behind one of those for a while, working up my nerve and pulling the balaclava over my face, then walked up to the wall of the bank and through it without stopping. I'd been practicing.

No doubt I triggered the alarms right away, but I went straight into the vault, reached into the special cabinets for the cash, filled a black canvas bag with it, and exited the same way I'd come in, clutching the bag tightly to my chest. Then I went around the corner of the first townhouse, out of sight of the bank cameras, and ghosted my way through walls and hallways to the far end of the row a block away. I was dressed in nondescript dark work clothes, padded with newspaper to make me look fifty pounds heavier for the sake of the video, so at the last house I disposed of the newspaper and put the money in its place around my body. The balaclava too. By then a couple of cop cars had gone by. I wasn't too worried. I'm sure by the time they figured out that nobody was going to come out of the bank vault, and looked at the security videos, I was safely in my bed. Thanks to her usual four vodkas, my wife never knew I'd left the house.

Do you remember Storck's assistant's name? It's Amber. You probably only remember her 36-inch C-cups. I do too, don't get me wrong. But she genuinely wanted to help me, so I think of her often. You only asked, "What can you do? How do you do it?" Amber thought to ask, "How do you *feel* about what's happened to you?"

When drunk, I felt like a god. When sober, like a freak. I was rarely sober. I drank because it was better than crying.

The worst part was the nightmares: I dreamed that the change grew steadily worse until one day I simply dissolved into a shadow and never came back.

Amber was in the room one time when I woke up with a scream. She told me the 'overlapping' worlds theory might explain some of our dreams. Maybe a lot of psychic phenomena, too. It might be that mediums tap into the parallel worlds with their minds, believing them to be 'higher planes of reality' that we go to when we die.

I can't testify to any of that. Not yet. But sometimes I can see the other places, in dim light, and I suppose people there might also be able to see me. So maybe I am a ghost after all.

#

The guards left me alone for...it feels like several days, though I still can't stand for long on my mangled feet. Now they've come back. This time the whip man carries two cables: electrical cables, stretching from somewhere beyond the door. There's a motor sound: a generator?

Live electrical cables.

The talker shows his bad teeth, but doesn't waste any time.

"Why did they send you?" he hisses.

I try to shake my head, speechless with horror. The second man doesn't even wait for an answer...touches the bare wires to my torso.

I scream until my lungs are empty.

They're saying something, but I can't make it out. It doesn't matter. I can't work my mouth to talk. The wires touch my abdomen.

I'm hearing noises. Animal noises. They couldn't be from a human being. Couldn't be from me.

The guard touches the wires to my genitals.

When the blackness fades and I become aware again, the first guard is gone. The second sees that I'm awake and raises his arm. The electrical wires are gone. The flog of shielded cable comes slashing down across my ribs.

I want to die. *Please just let me die.* My life hasn't been worth living anyway.

I didn't even feel the third blow. Heard the crack against the floor but felt nothing.

Wait. I really did feel nothing. No contact at all.

I force my eyes open to watch. The cable slices toward my body...*and through it.* It strikes the floor with a snap.

The guard hasn't seen. He's not really paying attention—so inured to brutalizing his fellow man that he's bored by it. I have enough sense to mimic my earlier cries of pain, but he'll have to notice something soon. Notice that his victim's skin hasn't peeled like it should. That there's no blood.

They'll kill me. Once they understand what I am, they'll have to. They'll *want* to. It's what I thought I wanted too, only seconds ago. But now?

God, it's such a blessed relief to escape the agony.

But there might be a way to stay alive. And to do that there is a price to pay.

A whimper escapes from my throat as my body understands what's coming next. I will myself to become solid, and scream as the flail comes lashing down.

#

The superhero comics write about Kryptonite, but they never mention the truly fatal flaw of the powerful: *terminal cockiness*. I was more than human, therefore I was untouchable. I knew it was true because the alcohol told me so.

So I concocted the scheme to break into your headquarters.

Of course, my newspaper padding didn't fool your mass analyzers. My mask was no protection from your thermal imaging software. And it was child's play to track my car by satellite. Then I was a mouse in a trap.

You had both the carrot and the stick: I could be a patriot or go to jail. And the first few times I actually felt like a hero when you had me ransack the homes of those congressmen and senators in the interest of 'safeguarding democracy'. Then I read a few of those stolen files, and realized I was being played for a sucker.

You were even ready for that. I'd thought only gangsters would threaten a man's family.

That was a line you shouldn't have crossed. Remember that. You're going to regret it.

But for now the only thing that's burning your ass is knowing that you've squandered a priceless resource, a one-of-a-kind commodity. *Me*.

We both know it was madness to send me to the Middle East. The *jihadists* can sniff out an outsider. Or maybe you thought that wouldn't matter, because I had a talent for escape that Houdini would have given his right arm for?

Then it was just bad luck that you sent me against a terror cell whose headquarters was in a mountain cave.

Did you know that caves and mountains exist unchanged for thousands of years in this world...and the next? And in every world I've tried.

I've had no way to escape, and no answers the guards will accept as truth, to bargain my way to freedom. So there's not much doubt they'll carry out their threat to execute me tonight.

Will you lose sleep over that? Probably not. So how about this:

I convinced you that electronic equipment didn't function through the transition to and from the other universes. That was a lie. A miniature camera I bought worked perfectly. I just wanted a record of my 'assignments' to use as an insurance policy. Now I see it as a cleansing flame to sterilize a plague.

For the first time in a long time I want to live, if only long enough to make one phone call. One call, and a series of packages will find their way to several powerful (and uncompromised) congressmen. The top echelon of *Mossad*, and even the wealthy backers of my captors will all find the contents very enlightening. Your administration's time will be at an end, and a rift might even begin to heal. A carefully constructed *wall* might begin to crumble.

You can call me naïve. We'll see. If I fail, it means I don't escape a trap and you do. Either way, I have a feeling you'll get this message.

Don't even think about a reprisal against my family. It's far too late for that.

I can hear scraping noises at the door. The guards have come for me.

I've never tested it, but I have hopes that my transitional body can be convinced to deny the solidity of bullets and swords as well as walls and whips. The trick will be to maintain that state long enough to shake off any pursuit. The odds are against it, but I've had some time to practice. Maybe I'll even see Amber again.

If it doesn't work, well, I'm not all that afraid of Death anymore.

I've already been there.

\#   \#   \#

SHAKEDOWN

"**H**E'S A TEST PILOT FOR WHAT?"
"Video entertainment."

"He tests video games."

"They don't call them games anymore—they're too sophisticated for that."

Devon Kierkegaard grinned from behind the worn desk, showing a little wear himself from the six years since Truman Bridges had last seen him. And more than a little grey hair. Bridges fidgeted on the edge of the desk.

"How much did you say this project of yours cost?" he asked.

"By the time it's finished? A billion. Give or take."

"As a taxpayer, I know who's doing the giving." The ebony face wrinkled into a frown, then exploded with a laugh that showed very white teeth.

"Spare me the righteous indignation. You haven't been running a private psychology practice for at least five years. Who pays your salary now?"

"Which is why I am at your disposal." Bridges nodded his head in a mock bow. "And now you tell me you've entrusted your billion-dollar toy into the hands of a man who tests video games for a living. You *do* need my help—we can begin our first analysis session right away."

Kierkegaard laughed. "You haven't changed at all. I'm glad."

"But Devon, my friend, do you really mean you've spent a billion dollars to create a miniature submarine? And then what? Shrink this game-playing pilot of yours? I think I've heard this story before."

"Everyone says that. *Fantastic Voyage* was an entertaining movie, but physically shrinking something still isn't possible. What we've created is the next step in nanotechnology: engineering on the atomic scale. To perform medical miracles."

"A submarine with no crew?"

"You're thinking in the wrong terms. Let me explain."

The submersible known as the X4 was the size of a virus. Self-propelled, drawing its power from the ionization of atoms in the surrounding fluid. An assembly of *Buckminster fullerene* tubes made of Carbon 60, like long rolls of molecular chicken-wire a billionth of a meter in diameter with a hundred times the tensile strength of steel. No crew quarters, no cockpit. Only the smallest possible cargo space, capable of containing a microscopic payload.

"The X4 is controlled remotely, using virtual reality. Which is why we made what you consider such an unorthodox choice for a pilot. Its sensor array depends on atomic interactions and their byproducts, from which a supercomputer actually gives us a visual image and limited auditory information. It's a miracle of technology. Soon we hope to get enough data to produce *haptic* stimulus…the actual feel of the craft's motion."

"Like a carnival simulator ride."

"I suppose. But very convincing, I promise you."

"What if the pilot's experience is too authentic—enough to make him forget it's a simulation? A human being hurtling through a living bloodstream. Can a man's psyche survive that?"

"That's what I need you to tell me. We almost lost him."

#

Travis Li looked up at the white ceiling, trying to keep his mind as blank as that featureless space. Instead his brain treated it like a movie screen, displaying nightmare visions he was desperate to forget.

Protoplasmic projectiles…blind behemoths appearing out of nowhere and threatening to flatten him like a bug on a windshield. He hadn't signed on for that.

What had he expected? A joy ride? A chance to earn some easy money and notoriety? Or had the shrink at the juvie centre ten years ago been right? Was he still compensating for a childhood in Chinatown's Combat Zone? He had a scar on his left arm from a bad parachute jump, and a scar on his psyche thanks to a skinny frame and good grades. But he'd showed the bastards. These days he only returned to the old neighbourhood to show off his money. And sometimes treat the street kids or give his mother a cheque to help raise his orphaned niece.

Hell, the early trial runs had been a piece of cake. In fact, his first ride in the X4 had been the biggest thrill of his life.

Vertigo.

Powerful nausea. Warned about that. Something about the VR interface enhanced by electrodes at the temples and neck.

Grey...all shades. But twinkling. Like fireflies in peripheral vision. A virus-eye view of the world. X4 floating free in a test-tube ocean, filtered, sterilized, and filtered again to remove microorganisms.

Some angled bars in the bottom of the view. Computer's painting them a darker metallic grey: the craft's manipulator arms, with pincer ends crafted atom by atom, folded in a triangle around X4's nose. Incredible. Like something from a mech game, but the view is no game image. Softer, grainier, yet compellingly real.

Time to look around? What is there to see in a water column the size of Lake Champlain?

Treasure. Planted at the bottom of the test-tube. But which way is down? No feeling of gravity. No difference in light.

Give the pedals a kick. *Whoa.* Serious spin—instant response. Countered with too much force, too. Definitely going to take a while to get the hang of this. Ease the left joystick forward...yes, a sense of the nose dropping into a forward tumble. Damn. Nudge it back. Level again? No way to know. Orientation is only meaningful in relation to other objects.

So where are the other objects?

There. Hint of a different colour, maybe dark orange. How far on this scale? One kilometer? Ten?

Point the nose and ease the throttle forward with the right stick. The engine's always running, will never stop.

Whatever the coloured thing is, it's huge. Is that a curved edge or a horizon? Too far to go around. Best to head straight in and hope to gauge the distance right. Hate to dent the bumpers first time out.

The world becomes the colour of dull copper, with shadows of darker brown. Ease back on the throttle. Could be flying straight into a cliff face or in a suicidal dive toward the hard deck. No way to tell.

Sudden impression of hills on either side. Pull up! Craft responds too fast, the nose snapping up into a loop.

Level off, goddamn it! Get the adrenaline under control and use some finesse instead of overreacting like a rookie.

Better, much better. High walls, like a broad valley with a grooved floor. Another valley on the left. Turned too fast though—a sense of skid or drift. Of course: a fluid environment. Sim programmers have never been able to get it quite right.

The valley snakes around a little—a good chance to practice steering. Nearly perpendicular face on the starboard side. Whole thing is a series of rectangular facets as far as the eye can see. Flaked? Metallic?

Good God. It's a penny! A goddamned copper penny.

Picture a billion-dollar craft tracing the lines of Lincoln's face. Is the irony deliberate?

The view suddenly flashing red. A warning—must be. Are they going to pull the...?

Vertigo.

The wrenching nausea passed quickly, but he'd felt a surge of elation, realizing the historical significance of what he'd just done. His rational mind still thought that way, as he lay on the clinic bed. But the primitive core of his brain clung to a memory of a later journey: a lurid hell of demon projectiles run amuck.

His mouth filled with the taste of bile.

\#

Truman Bridges examined the model of the X4 in his hands: a single oversized propeller at the rear of a cigar-shaped fuselage, and four small fans on each side instead of diving planes.

"The motors are electric," Kierkegaard said. "And each propeller is independent. Much simpler than constructing gears or drive shafts at that scale. The oblong strip across the top is the sensor array. A series of paired atoms in an astonishingly complex order."

"How is the quality of the image?"

"Not high. Which is why we chose to...augment receptiveness to the simulation with electrodes in the VR helmet."

"Electro-stimulation of the brain?" Bridges' eyes grew wide. "The potential for serious side effects...."

"The headset accidentally produced a strong magnetic field during one of the first tests, and the results were amazing. We've seen no adverse side effects. I've tried it myself. It draws you into the simulation more and more, the longer you spend in the environment."

"In the environment. You mean seeing the universe from the perspective of a microbe." The psychologist drew his fingers through short-cropped hair. "Good Lord, Devon. It's an utterly *alien* environment, yet your pilot knows it is *real*. Not some game in which death simply means you have to start that level over again."

"Are you saying Li could believe he's in personal danger? I don't agree. Realistic or not, he still knows that his body is sitting in a chair in a laboratory, watching images in a helmet and listening to sounds you might hear underwater."

"And people watching IMAX movies sometimes get motion sickness. Simulator rides provide a rush of adrenaline from excitement and fear. Otherwise people wouldn't keep coming back. If the mind accepts it, that's what counts." Bridges leaned toward his friend. "You said that he was flushed and sweating with a rapid pulse, as if he'd suffered a terrible fright."

The leader of the Project slowly shook his head.

"We thought it was simply excessive stimulus. Li hadn't encountered obstacles before. The lab rat's vein was full of blood cells. They would have appeared to be coming at him at very high speed. Even allowing for the time dilation effect."

"The what?"

"*Time dilation.* It's a property of the nano-environment we hadn't expected. Time seems to stretch. The pilot may be hooked up for only fifteen minutes, but to him it feels like hours."

"That sounds like damned convincing evidence of subjective reality. I think you're the one who doesn't want to believe. Because it would make you responsible."

There was no answer to that.

"And what were you thinking, running a test in a lab animal so soon?" Bridges continued. "You should have trained the pilot for months in a controlled environment before doing that."

Kierkegaard's eyes lit with a dark flame. "Believe me, that was not my choice."

#

"We need your ship."

"You *what?*"

"Your miniature submarine. We need it."

The man in the grey suit had made the statement in the same tone of voice he would have used to say, "Pass the salt." He tossed an open wallet across the desk, but Kierkegaard had already checked the man's credentials: CIA, and with the backing of the Department of Defense at the highest level.

"I don't care if you're God Almighty," Kierkegaard said. "What the hell do you think we are?"

"You're a top secret research project funded by your government for hundreds of millions of dollars. It is now expecting a return on its investment." The voice sounded bored. "Please sit down, Dr. Kierkegaard. Histrionics will benefit no-one." The man casually took a seat himself. "The Prime Minister of Israel collapsed yesterday."

"I read about it."

"Impossible to keep quiet—it happened at an official function. Doctors believe it was a cerebral hemorrhage, caused by a blood clot." Grey Suit lowered his voice. "We believe it was enemy action."

Kierkegaard's mouth fell open.

"You can't be thinking.... That was a *movie, for God's sake!* Our machine cannot possibly find its way through the brain and destroy a blood clot. We have no shrinking ray, no miniature lasers. You're looking for *Hollywood.* We have only science."

"We're not asking you to destroy the clot. We only want an examination of the site to help doctors determine what treatment would be most effective. And to learn if this really was an artificially induced injury. The political ramifications could be...profound."

Kierkegaard sank slowly back into his chair, part of him cursing the day he'd given up a tenure at Harvard for a venture that could only be funded by the military. But when he'd lost Madeleine to cancer he'd learned that sometimes unconventional treatments were required to save lives. Even if you had to make a pact with the devil.

He stared into space. "The submersible hasn't even been tested in a lab animal, let alone the human bloodstream. It's never been subjected to a current, or moving obstacles. Good God, man, we only have course charts for the bloodstream of a *white rat.*"

"Do whatever you need to do," said Grey Suit, getting to his feet. "Doctors are keeping the Prime Minister alive for now, but his days are numbered."

The other also stood, pleading. "You can't expect us to produce a miracle dreamed up by Hollywood."

"Dr. Kierkegaard," the agent said, as he opened the door to leave. "If you and your team weren't expected to perform the things people saw in that movie, do you think you would ever have been given a billion dollars?"

#

Li had told them he was accepting the job out of curiosity. But he'd known that his ego was calling the shots. His cup had runneth over with cockiness from placing in the top 5 at the Cyber Gamers Championship in Vegas. He'd leapt at a chance to walk with geniuses, to be accepted as one of them.

Except he hadn't been accepted. His faded hammerloop jeans, hooded sweatshirt, and water mocs were a statement lost among men and women who were willing exiles from consumer society. A couple of techies tolerated him but never invited him for a drink.

So he threw himself into the work, determined to show them all. He recognized what he was doing, and hated it, but did it anyway. The X4 was the ultimate challenge. A few scientists had tried it out, and he'd made them look like monkeys. His skill improved every time he jacked in.

Then came a time when he realized that he preferred the *inside* world to the *outside*.

#

"Why do you ask about psychosis?"

Bridges and Kierkegaard kept their voices low, although there were only a few other people at the far end of the commissary.

"He became withdrawn," Kierkegaard said. "He volunteered for more and more time with the X4, though it exhausted him—a long day's work for the rest of us may have felt like weeks to him. Then even stranger behaviour. He kept his back to walls. Scouted a room before entering it. Looked startled when someone spoke to him."

"Paranoia?"

"He seemed to have trouble remembering how to navigate the building. Appeared confused when he entered a room. Finally I found him at the top of a flight of stairs, paralyzed with indecision. That's when I called you."

"That last incident is no great mystery," Bridges said. "Imagine having just spent a day in a place where there is no up or down. No gravity, perhaps not even any discernible inertia. What would you make of a flight of stairs?"

"His body forgot how to walk down steps?"

"Temporarily unsure, anyway. Like the way a sailor still swaggers after he's landed on solid ground. The mind soon adjusts. As for the rest...." He swirled the lukewarm coffee around his cup but didn't drink it. "Is he being treated with suspicion by the others?"

"I know there's a rumour circulating that he might be a plant from the intelligence community. But before you ask, no-one else knows about my conversations with the CIA."

"It sounds to me as if he's feeling isolated because he *is* being isolated."

"No more than that?"

"That is plenty, I assure you." The psychologist frowned. "Bad enough feeling like a fish out of water among you scientists. Think about the rest of his time. Imagine being the only one of your kind in an entire universe...."

#

Calm again. In control. The world as it should be.

The ship responds the way muscles respond to a nerve impulse. Reflex. No translation required. A body obeying its mind.

Visuals are still pretty primitive. Better than the early versions of "Doom" or "Descent", but not much. Enough to find new stuff tossed into the world. New *world*, even: a beaker-size ocean now. Room for whole new countries to explore. No longer just Lincoln Penny Island, but Metal Screw Peninsula, and even Silicon Chip Archipelago.

The spiral shape of the screw was good practice—finicky, with tricky magnetic fields close to the metal surface. Should have told somebody about that.

Might get around to it. Might not.

The computer chip was more fun. Like hacking a flight simulator so it'll let you take a JetRanger down to the deck on Madison Avenue. Dodge the skyscrapers. A few spooky moments with thermal currents and prop-wash bouncing back from the flat surfaces. Takes time to master something like that.

Lots of time, though. All the time in the world.

A virgin world, there for the taking.

All the property of the King.

#

Bridges was a master at putting patients at ease, but he found himself up against a wall with Travis Li. When he made his way to Kierkegaard's office to give a report, he noticed his friend's lopsided collar and tie askew.

"The CIA has paid another visit, hasn't it?" he asked.

"They're bringing the Israeli Prime Minister here the day after tomorrow," Kierkegaard said. "Ludicrous." He rubbed his eyes. "What about your patient?"

"Well, he doesn't trust me enough to open up. But there are some things I can infer. As I've said, the environment of the X4 is like another world to him. He's even possessive about it. But just when he thought he had it all figured out, you threw him a gigantic curve, injecting the submersible into a living bloodstream. That was frightening, even debilitating. It dealt a severe blow to his ego."

"His *ego*? Are you suggesting that he had a near breakdown because his pride was hurt?"

The doctor shook his head. "There's much more to the ego than pride, Devon. It's our whole concept of *self*. Who we are as a person. The sieve that sifts the universe for the elements that relate to our lives, and filters out the rest. We act and react according to our life experience. But Travis Li has entered into an entirely new realm, with the X4 as his avatar. In that realm his experience counts for nothing."

"I suppose he's not used to failure," Kierkegaard said.

"I don't think you give him enough credit," Bridges said. "He didn't just run afoul of a game with some new rules. This game violated the parameters of every system he's ever encountered. It shattered his confidence. In himself. In his world. It will take time to pick up the pieces."

"I don't have time," the other snapped. "We have to get him back in that chair at the peak of his abilities in two days."

"Have you heard anything I've said?" Bridges' face was a thundercloud.

"Of course I have. But what if we were able to give him back his self-assurance? Augment his abilities so he could handle the challenges of the bloodstream. Wouldn't his confidence reassert itself?"

"Do you have some powerful voodoo I don't know about?"

"Look, Truman, I brought you into this because you know as much about the workings of the brain as you do about the mind. I'm talking about enhancing his brain's processing of the VR input—giving him a fighting chance to keep up with the sensory overload. There must be drugs that would do that."

"Most of them illegal, and for good reason!" Bridges raised outspread fingers in supplication. They trembled with anger. "Even if you were to chemically stimulate the parts of the cerebral cortex associated with the senses—which are in several different locations—or the thalamus, the brain's gateway for all of the information, you'd intensify other brain responses as well. Hallucinations. Even the paranoia you believe this man already suffers from. You can't condemn him to that. Where is my old friend, the one who had a *conscience?*"

Kierkegaard's face was grey.

"I never wanted this, Truman. But if Li doesn't come through we may be condemning another man to death. Maybe many others in the bloody aftermath. And everyone else who might ever be helped through this technology." He looked into the eyes of his friend. "I won't sacrifice one man's sanity for another man's life. I just hope to God it doesn't come to that."

Bridges shook his head. "Hope that God will make a place for himself in the X4 with Travis Li."

#

The compound's small smoking area was outside a far corner of the building. The place was empty because of the late hour. For that Li was grateful because he didn't smoke cigarettes, and he was sure Kierkegaard would frown on his preferred substitute.

He never smoked weed when he was in a competition. It slowed down his reaction time and dulled his competitive edge. But *damn*, he needed a touch of mellow right now.

The thought of going back into the bloodstream scared the piss out of him. It was like jumping from the beginner level of a first-person simulator to the final flat-out phase of a multi-player space battle, with a handicap setting to keep him from seeing attacking missiles before they were too close to miss.

He held the high-grade smoke deep in his lungs, until he could feel his neck relax. Magical. The stars made pretty patterns overhead. Maybe he'd just lie on the tarmac and watch them for a while.

Pretty, pretty patterns.

#

The phone jolted him from sleep.

Six o'clock?

Goddamn! How could they have moved the schedule up? He had to hope a scalding shower would drive the last traces of fog from his brain.

As he jogged into the control room the members of the support team were all too busy to pay attention to him. Or maybe they were trying not to—embarrassed for him after what had happened during the last test. Just as well. It wouldn't do for anyone to look too closely. He slid into the chair, doing his best to ignore cold fingers that clenched at his stomach.

Devon Kierkegaard stood off to the side. Nice old man, but clearly under a lot of pressure. Did he think his presence would help somehow?

Li shifted his weight to get more comfortable, and flexed his fingers. The helmet settled onto his head.

Vertigo.

Familiar floating feeling. Everything calm, quiet. Soothing grey.

Still in the hypodermic. A few minutes to wait while the needle is inserted into a vein. Get into Game Mode. Deep breaths. Oxygenate the nerve endings. Bring the reflexes to a keen edge.

Movement now, sensed rather than seen.

Fast. As fast as the bloodstream? Soon find out.

Black tunnel ahead. Night falls. Tunnel walls not visible, but the body feels them. Hairs rising on the back of the neck.

Liftoff.

The world is the colour of dark honey with flashes of red.

Immediate turbulence. Not supposed to feel that. Not part of the interface yet. Has to be imagination, seeing the ship pitch and lurch. Got to feather the fans and line up with the current. Spun left—too fast. Still spinning. Counterthrust. Counter the spin, goddamnit.

Concentrate on steering. The King is in command.

Crap. Something hit us. Can't see what. Facing backward. Kick the right pedal.

Shit! Gone into a roll...now tumbling. It's the cross currents, or maybe the wake of passing blood cells. Cells the size of—*Holy Mother of God*—the size of Yankee Stadium. Maybe all of the Bronx.

Too fast. Everything. Way too fast.

Whales, blimps, ocean tankers appearing out of nowhere. Is that the vein wall or just a giant blood cell? No way to know. No way to keep from—*Shit!*—hitting it. Total chaos. Out of control.

No. Think. Nothing can hurt the ship. Nothing can hurt us.

Something's happened to the view. Sharper than before. Brighter. How can that be? See more, hear more, feel more.

Feel?

No doubt about it. Can feel the heaving, the wrenching. The slam of another impact.

That can't be. Not supposed to feel. *Not supposed to be here.*

Sudden flash of colour to the right. Something long, snakelike. Twisting like a leech through water. Keeping pace.

Another on the left, closing in.

Wolves running down a deer.

Got to get away. Shove the throttle to full. Can't see a goddamn thing anyway.

They're still keeping up. Moving in. Here comes....

IMPACT

Christ. Like a 300 pound linebacker. What the hell are those things?

Antibodies?

God, that's not good. Antibodies will call in the big guns.

The world fills with dull light. A sense of menace.

Where is it? Let me see what's happening, for Christ's sake.

The VR's not fast enough to keep up. Can't see. Like a hundred miles an hour on the highway in a bitching Boston fog.

God, no. White blood cell!

The iceberg seen from the Titanic.

Kick the pedals. Reverse the engine. Anything. Anything.

IMPACT

Can't run, can't dodge, can't fight, can't hide....

Another white cell behind. Like Thor's hammer.

Can't move, can't leave, can't *escape*.

No escape!

IMPACT

Get me out of here! Get me out! Get me out!

IMPACT

Getmeoutgetmeoutgetmeoutgetmeoutgetmeout....

IMPACT

IMPACT

Blackness.

#

"You fed him drugs, after I warned you of the danger!" Truman Bridges slammed his fist on the desk.

"I did no such thing," Kierkegaard snapped. "I told you I wouldn't sacrifice one man for another."

"I've seen the video. Something was wrong."

"He smoked a joint."

"*What?*"

"We just did the blood tests," Kierkegaard sighed, dropping into the chair. "There was cannabis in his system. Recent. God knows why. He certainly has never shown signs of it before."

"The poor bastard. THC would only have made things worse. He could never cope with the frenzy of the bloodstream in that condition."

"Exactly. And worse—it made the experience even more real to him. Horribly real." Kierkegaard looked up, an appalling burden showing in his eyes. "Will he recover?"

"That's more than I can say right now." Bridges emptied his lungs in a long release. "At the moment he's catatonic, his mind trapped within itself, with a terror we can't even comprehend. If there's any cause for hope at all it's that the trauma didn't last very long."

"I pray to God you're right." Kierkegaard's voice was little more than a whisper. "This could be the end...the whole Project and all of its promise. Maybe no human being will ever be able to safely pilot the X4."

Bridges shook his head. "You can't jump to that conclusion just yet. Perhaps he was simply wrong for the job."

"*Wrong for the job?* How do you find someone who can exist in two realities at the same time, and not go insane?"

#

The CIA man sat stiffly, not pleased to be back in this room.

"The Prime Minister is dead."

Kierkegaard barely reacted. There was no emotion left in him.

"Your Project has failed its patrons, Dr. Kierkegaard. In fact, it sounds like a rather complete failure at this point."

The man under attack bristled, then dropped his eyes. "Is there any way we can still learn what you need? With the Prime Minister's...."

"His body is being returned to Israel right away. They want to deal with it swiftly, publicly. There's absolutely no way to gain access to him."

Kierkegaard nodded. With the powerful current of the bloodstream stilled it might have been possible to navigate the X4. Within a short window of time. But it was a moot point. They had no pilot.

There had never been much hope that they could learn anything meaningful in time to treat a blood clot in the brain. Surely the CIA man knew that.

And then he realized that the man did know it. Had always known it.

"You were never expecting to save the Prime Minister's life," he said. "You were only interested in learning what killed him, so you could use it as an excuse to drop bombs on somebody. Or even adopt it as a weapon for our side."

The other man shrugged. "Are you expecting me to apologize for something, Doctor? Maybe you should face reality."

"*Reality*," Kierkegaard spat. "That's one word I've heard too many times lately. I'm not sure it has any meaning anymore." His head bowed, and he ran his fingers slowly through his hair, the silence forcing him to ask the question he dreaded. "Does this mean our funding has been cancelled?"

"Not yet," the man said. "The D.O.D. apparently feels your experiments still have a contribution to make."

"A contribution. Because you believe the X4 itself can be turned into a weapon."

"Come, Doctor." The other man actually smiled. "Without war, surgeons wouldn't have discovered the importance of sterilized instruments. Of anesthetic for operations. Penicillin would never have been perfected. How do you think most of today's important vaccines were created? While searching for biological weapons, of course. There's no need to be naive."

"Are we done?" Kierkegaard asked.

The CIA man rose from his chair.

"Reality, Doctor, is that death is a part of life, and it is war that protects peace. Sometimes sacrifices have to be made." There was no sign that he perceived the clichéd staleness of his words. Nor cared.

When he was gone, Kierkegaard left his office and walked the empty halls to the medical clinic. For a long time he watched through the glass of a silent room, where a bedridden man lay trapped in a reality no-one else could see.

#   #   #

THE LONG COMMUTE

SHON HOWARD LIFTED HIS BRIEFCASE, grumbling at the weight—the weight of time, of history. Some of the other reps could carry everything they needed in a false fingernail. He had to put up with archaic paper documents.

Jill straightened his tie and gave his lapel a tug. Her goodbye kiss was perfunctory.

"You should have picked up a few more of these old suits."

"No-one expected the job to go on this long. But I'll get another assignment soon."

With the usual twinge of envy that she could work from home, he stepped out into another overcast day. Far too hot for a suit jacket—he looked forward to the cooled air on the train.

It was already waiting when he got there, floating with a soft hum over the platform: sleek and bullet-nosed, clouds reflected in its mirror finish. A door hissed open and he stepped through the seal field into the cool compartment, looking around for a seat. A raised hand caught his eye.

"Morning, Raj. Where you headed? You're even more overdressed than I am."

A grey overcoat just reached the top of the man's black boots. The front of a white jacket showed under the open coat.

"The funding was cut for a key cancer treatment development at Sloan-Kettering. I'm supposed to see if I can give the test results a bit of a boost and change that." He showed bright white teeth. "But it's cold there. I hate the cold."

Raj's skin was as dark as Shon's own, the product of a Mumbai heritage.

"You still at the UN? The climate project?" Raj asked.

"Should wrap up the latest job today. The glaciers melted faster than those people moved, I swear."

"Important work, though. For all of us." When Shon just shrugged, Raj said, "You ever worry about getting caught?"

"Not really. Somebody would come for me. The New York drivers scare me more."

"I know what you mean." Raj chuckled then spoke in a lower voice. "Uh, you ever...think about staying? Staying behind? Not coming back?"

Shon was disconcerted at his friend's insight. Or his own transparency. He shifted in his seat. "Then the retrieval squad would come after me for sure."

Raj dropped his gaze and nodded.

"That's what they always say. Rumor has it that a lot of people have done it, though."

He sat back and his eyes glazed over—probably checking messages. Shon checked his own. His supervisor had sent yet another confirmation of the schedule for this run. There were a couple of queries from Requisitions about his expenses, as always. And Jill had sent a reminder about the parent interview that night with Alya's new tutor.

He frowned. Maybe he expected too much from his new daughter after only three months. This week Alya was mad at him because he'd missed her virtual introduction to her schoolmates and their families, and shown up late for her first music recital. Did every father screw up like that? He didn't know any others to ask. Jill always took Alya's side, insisting the girl was just lonely. Maybe the adoption had been a mistake. He didn't know if their marriage would recover. And when it got really bad, yes, he did think about staying behind—not returning home. But it wasn't so simple.

At those times he tried to remember that Alya was only five, and the doctors said she would never reach ten. The picture in his mind didn't include her breathing mask, only the shy, radiant smile that had won his heart.

Outside the broad rectangle of window the scrubby trees and sandy patches of his neighborhood had given way to sunbaked rock scoured by grit that swirled in short-lived dust devils. He could only see that because they were coming to the first stop. A couple of men across the aisle got up and pulled the loose white cloth of their robes up over their faces, knowing the sand would attack them the moment they stepped through the seal. The bright sun made him squint when the door opened. At least he'd never drawn that duty.

He shared a look with a woman a few seats away dressed in a well-tailored grey suit. She worked climate, too, but from the public relations angle and a stop or two after his. In a way, she was laying the groundwork for his team. One of these days he should introduce himself. The man beside her looked up and gave a nod, then dusted imaginary specks from his left sleeve where a V-shaped patch was attached. The jacket was a dull green and Shon thought it was a uniform from one of the early World Wars, although uniforms hadn't changed all that much even a hundred years later in the climate conflicts. The man clenched a cloth cap in his lap and occasionally slapped it against his leg to a rhythm only he could hear.

The next couple of stops revealed a landscape with more growing things and less rock. Then it was

Raj's stop. The windows were small and round now, and showed buildings of dark brick that made the snowflakes stand out. Not quite a blizzard, but he didn't blame Raj for muttering a few choice words before forcing himself through the door. Hopefully he didn't have to walk far.

Finally, it was Shon's turn. He hoisted his briefcase and stepped through the seal into the dank air of Grand Central Station. The smell of hydrocarbons nearly made him sneeze. He wouldn't miss that, but there were other things that made him envy the people of that era. He resisted the temptation of a donut shop but made a quick stop at a souvenir stand.

It was a good day for the walk down 42nd Street. The air was cool enough to show summer was over, but the wind was from Jersey and not too strong. He always enjoyed the view as he went under the overpass and the UN compound came into sight. The buildings showed their age, but the new renovations would make them look suitably impressive again one day, for a time.

The Secretariat Building cast a long morning shadow. He wished Alya could see it, imperious behind its guardian wrought-iron and legion of flagpoles standing at attention, the seven nickel-plated ornamental doors proudly proclaiming core tenets of the UN in bas relief. Or would these things awaken painful memories in her? He couldn't know for sure.

Sometimes he made a detour to admire the opulence of the General Assembly with its deep green carpeting, rich royal curtains and vast gold backdrop. And the wood—there was no wood furniture or trim where he came from. But he had no business in the public spaces this morning. His work was in the office floors of the Secretariat building and then the UN Environment Program's quarters across the street.

He surrendered his briefcase to a security guard and passed through a metal detector. The contents of the case were mostly camouflage: innocuous papers and file folders. The twenty-three document pages he needed were carefully placed to blend in with the rest. He pressed his thumb to a sensor pad and tapped a small disk in his pocket at the same time. The identity scanner bleeped its approval. If his pockets were ever searched, his Res-Ops field tool would look like a simple data storage disc of that time period.

He used the stairs. The wide hallways of the lower level, with their large-tiled floors and photography on the walls, gave way to the modest halls and small offices of the floors above. As he came to the first stop on his list he tapped the field tool again and heard a telephone ring inside the office. A moment later a man came out, putting on a sports jacket while he hurried away. The door swung closed, but that wasn't a problem. Another signal from Shon's disk opened the keypad lock.

The paper document to be replaced was in the lower right-hand drawer of the desk. He and his team had scouted these buildings for weeks to learn the most likely location of each hard copy, computer file, and backup disc that needed to be swapped or altered. To gather voice samples and assemble messages that would call bureaucrats away from their desks. To plan the most efficient access and escape routes.

The next day's summit would lay the groundwork for the Copenhagen Climate Council in December, and the substitute files he carried had to be in place for that, yet not early enough to be discovered prematurely. So it all came down to one day's intensive efforts, with no room for mistakes. You only got one chance at each intervention—no do-overs. That wasn't just a commandment from the Director of Restorative Operations. It was decreed by the laws of Physics.

The worst part was, you could never really know if an intervention would work until you returned home, holding your breath.

His field tool navigated through the directory of the desktop computer and replaced the required file. Then he checked to make sure he'd left no tracks and made his way to the next office on his list.

Proponents of the UN's climate change initiatives were Shon's responsibility, Langton and Mills were assigned to the deniers, but both sides were fed the same replacement data. You couldn't even call it misinformation because it was all completely accurate. It just wouldn't have been available to them for another lifetime or two. A few people would question the numbers, but their protests wouldn't get any traction.

Everything went smoothly in the next office, and the next, and all of the rest in the Secretariat Building. Shon passed through more blue-painted hallways with polished floors, down staircases crowded with people, and across the street to the Environment Program facilities.

The clear blue of the sky made him remember Raj's question about making a run for it—staying behind in the past. New York was a huge city. It would be easy to hide from the squads, wouldn't it?

The thought turned out to be a dangerous distraction.

As he was finishing his task in an inner office he heard, "Forgot my briefcase..." and the door opened. A young Asian man stared at him.

"Who are you?"

"IT department. Upgrading security software. Didn't they tell you?" Shon moved toward the door.

The man hesitated, then turned to someone behind him. "Janet, call IT. No. Call Security."

Shon shoved the man aside and ran past the secretary into the main hallway, which was mercifully empty. He quickly raised the Res-Ops tool and stood with his back to the wall, holding the disk in front of him. The Asian man rushed out the door and slid to a stop, looking in Shon's direction. He turned the other way, then made up his mind and ran past Shon to the stairwell. Fortunately, he didn't look back. There'd only been time for the field tool to project an image of the hallway in one direction.

As the echoing footsteps faded, Shon hurried down the corridor to deal with his last two tasks. When they were done his heart was still pounding, and he made up his mind not to take any chances. He went to the men's room, locked the door, took an item like a pack of chewing gum from his briefcase, and squeezed its clear gel contents into his hand. He massaged it thoroughly into his scalp and waited. Within a minute the first black curl came loose. He pulled the hair free in big wads and stuffed it into the waste bin, then washed the last few traces down the sink. The newly bald Shon Howard walked casually to the elevator and made his way to the street.

A block away he leaned against the wall of a building and drew in deep breaths. He'd told Raj he wasn't afraid of getting caught, but that was a lie. What if he couldn't be retrieved? What if he *had* to spend the rest of his life there, with no means of escape?

He wanted to be home, with his family.

The train pulled into Grand Central Station, wheels squealing. It was the color of unadorned steel and artlessly boxy like any other New York subway train. People started toward it, but saw the windows and doorways crammed with passengers. That persuaded nearly all of them to wait for the next train. A persistent one or two felt as if someone had pushed them back onto the platform. Shon put on a convincing act of squeezing aboard as the door's seal field allowed him through. There was plenty of room inside and he gratefully collapsed onto a seat.

He was surprised by a strange odor, and scuffling noises from the far end of the car. There were animals on board—two sleek mammals with tawny hides and long, awkward-looking limbs were lying anaesthetized in the aisle, guarded by human handlers in green camo apparel. Other people were gently stroking a pair of chubby creatures with long black-ringed tails and black masks on their faces.

It gave his heart a lift. That was what they were all working for, wasn't it? The preservation of life. Life from the time before poisoned air had ruined lungs, like the lungs of his poor Alya.

Some doctors boarded in a place where they were pursued by the faint thunder of explosions. They looked ragged and there were dark stains on their scrub suits.

Shon looked around for the soldier from the morning commute, but he wasn't on board. He could just be in another car, but what if the man had been killed? Retrieval squads would only come back for a body if the level of risk was acceptable. Did the soldier have a family waiting for him?

They passed into the Dead Zone and when the train came to a stop the men in the flowing white robes got aboard. They were dirty and utterly spent. One of them was injured and it looked like he'd been weeping, but not because of a broken arm. Something else.

"A school," the man said quietly. "We found a school buried under rubble and sand. It wasn't empty."

Shon nodded and swallowed, picturing eloquent little bones.

"You work climate change, right?" the man asked. "Never give up, OK? Maybe things like that don't have to happen."

Shon nodded, feeling inadequate. But his division was making a difference. The Dead Zone was being pushed back—its influence ended just a little earlier with each mission. Thanks to the Department of Restorative Operations he was able to live under an open sky his parents had never known.

Time was a big flowing river; you could scoop a bucketful of water from the middle and empty it onto the bank, and the effect on the river was imperceptible. It took many thousands of buckets before the flow was altered in any significant way. That was why it wasn't possible to fix everything all at once, why Shon and his compatriots had to go back day after day to make small changes and then return to their own time for new orders. The first restoration attempts had been blind rolls of the dice, but now that there were precision temporal monitors placed throughout the past three centuries in hundreds of spatial locations, each alteration of the timeline could be thoroughly tracked and analyzed and new plans made. It was a war campaign—a battle against their own ancestors, in a sense—but the tide was slowly turning. They had to believe that.

You didn't feel very important, hauling one bucket at a time, but the people of Res-Ops kept at it. Not just with climate, but disease, pollution, calamities fiscal and social. Repairing the world, moment by fluid moment.

Once they were uptime of the Dead Zone the train's decontamination field hummed. Shon looked down the car at the animals. They'd still have to be quarantined for months, just as Alya remained in quarantine, though not for much longer. It would be such a thrill to watch her play with other kids in person, as much as her injured lungs would permit. Some of the others were healthier and eventually might help repopulate the countryside, making up for the fragile birth rate.

The past had so many orphans.

Maybe it was his imagination, but as he stepped off the train the air seemed fresher than it had that morning. A promising patch of blue sky passed overhead.

Jill greeted him at the door of their home. She smiled a little uncertainly at his bald head, then softly said, "She breathed on her own for nearly an hour today. *Without the mask.*"

Hope surged through him like oxygen.

Alya looked shyly out from behind the sofa. Shon squatted in front of her.

"It's OK, Sweetheart. Daddy's hair will grow back. I brought you some presents." He gave her a few postcards of the UN, and waited to see how she would react to pictures of a time so near to her own.

She didn't pay them much attention. She was more interested in what he held in his other hand.

"What's that?"

"It's a doll. The first President to have skin like ours. Remember?" He reached out to caress her dark curls. "He had two beautiful daughters, just like you."

She pulled the mask from her face, showing off, and took the doll from his hand.

Shon's eyes filled. The doctors had said she would never breathe on her own. Never. He was witnessing a miracle.

No, he and his team had *made* a miracle.

He let the tears spill and suddenly found he looked forward to the next day, and the day after that.

Because there were more miracles waiting.

\#   \#   \#

LOCKDOWN

FINNEY FELT THE LEFT SIDE of his body go numb.

Jesus. Jesus, *no.* He wasn't really going to snatch the woman's purse. He'd only reached for it out of habit, that's all.

Too late—punishment had already kicked in. A warning, anyway. His cortical monitor had detected the thought coupled with a related action, and the proscribed combination had triggered a response. Partial-paralysis. He didn't even know how long it would last. He'd been so glad to get away from those goddamn prison walls that he'd never read the manual they'd given him as he left.

He could walk, but just barely, dragging his left foot. That attracted attention. Better to duck into a hole-in-the-wall café and grab a coffee until the numbness went away. Even paying the bill was an embarrassment—his wallet was in his left pocket. His contortions made the frizzy-haired woman at the cash register stretch her trowelled-on eye makeup to the limit, as if she thought Finney was about to expose himself.

There went the last of his money. It wasn't like anyone would give a con a job, especially while he was still doing time.

God, he was hungry. His bitch of a mother couldn't have given him a meal before having her latest boyfriend throw him out? No good trying to find his father. Finney couldn't even remember the asshole's face.

Was it like the one scowling back from the window? Sunken eyes, three days growth of beard, black moth-eaten woolen cap to hide the monitor jack.

Not a face anybody wanted to hire. Or love.

Now the thing in his head wouldn't even let him swipe a few bucks for food. Wouldn't even let him *think* about doing it. He should have chosen jail. At least he would've been fed.

The brick around the window looked nice and hard. If he beat his head against it just the right way, could he disable the monitor without killing himself? Nah, it must've been tried before. He remembered the surgeon saying cortical restraints were tough 'cause they were simple: a few electrodes and an EEG gizmo, some bits to measure blood flow and skin conductivity, a GPS tracker. Oh, yeah, and a cattle prod. All tucked away right inside the old skull.

The burned coffee was as bitter as his mood.

Odie had talked him into the robbery, and the money hadn't even lasted a week—just long enough for them to get caught. Then Odie got off with only a year in minimum security 'cause nobody would swear they'd seen his gun, only Finney's. Goddamn gun hadn't even had any bullets in it. Finney was a thief, not a killer.

That bastard shrink, Schneider, was just as much to blame, though. He was the one who'd recommended the cortical monitor instead of jail time. Made it sound like one of those cartoons: a little angel on Finney's shoulder wagging a finger at him if he thought about getting into trouble. Sure, an angel that could slap him down with a seizure like a miniature stroke. Partial paralysis as a warning for the wrong thoughts. Actually *commit* a crime and the body would go into full lockdown while the GPS in the monitor brought the cops running.

His stomach lurched, as if the foul coffee had worn out its welcome and was about to be tossed. He leaned over his folded hands and took deep breaths.

Folded hands...that meant his arm had moved. He tested it out—he could wiggle his fingers. Toes, too. The paralysis had only lasted a half-hour or so. Not so bad.

Now what? He was still starving.

Then he noticed that he was alone—the frizzy-haired bitch must have gone into the back for a minute. The cash register was right there, unguarded. His stomach gave a feral growl.

He scarcely realized what he'd done until he was out the door in the grey afternoon light. He turned right to avoid the windows, forced himself to stay at a walk until the next corner.

He didn't make it that far. Mid-step, his body froze solid, leaving him just enough control to hit the sidewalk with his shoulder instead of his face. He rolled onto his back within inches of the street, his right ear hanging over the curb. A passing car swerved and sprayed grit, but he could barely blink to protect his eyes.

When he opened them again he saw the waitress run out of the café, turn to see him and step closer, as if toward a slug that needed to be squashed. After a few attempts she reached into his jacket pocket and snatched the money he'd taken from the till. Then she just scurried back to her post in obvious relief. To call the cops? His digital conscience would already have done that.

He was screwed.

Nothing to do but swallow the acid taste of helplessness and wait for the sound of jackboots.

The first kick took him by surprise. His eyes snapped open in time to see the sneering face of a man who kept on walking. Someone went through his pockets—he caught a glimpse of his wallet disappearing into a jacket as sneakered feet jogged away. Another kick, from a fat kid. A third, from a grimacing old lady who swung her umbrella point precariously close to his balls. After that, he lost count. Then the spitting started.

Across his nose. At the corner of his mouth.

A rotten tomato splatted beside his head and filled his ear with rancid juice.

The people walking by knew what they were seeing: a sweet opportunity for revenge for every time they'd been victimized.

His body collected bruises while his clothes gathered trash. After an hour, someone stuffed paper up his nose and held his mouth shut to watch his face bulge in terror before letting go and scuffling away. After two hours a burst of cruel laughter told him he'd pissed himself. His eyes brimmed: hot tears mixed with cold spittle.

Something changed then. Something snapped.

A bus coming down the street gave him a sudden conviction. If he could only move enough to shift his weight farther over the curb.

With a howl of rage and effort he clenched his abdominal muscles. His purpling face and bared teeth scared his tormentors back a few steps.

His body lurched. Tipped. Started to roll.

The bus loomed like a specter, its grill a welcoming grin.

Then a booted foot slammed onto his chest and destroyed his bid for freedom. The boot was attached to a goddamn cop.

\#

The prison doctor said the monitor couldn't be removed, only switched off. Finney nodded, paying more attention to the starch and sour smell of his fresh coveralls, faint whiffs of bacon and onions, old metal, dust, concrete, and antiseptic. He took a deep, deep breath. It was different this time. He was different.

They wouldn't take him to his cell until they'd put him through one last indignity: a session with Schneider, the shrink. The bastard wanted to know why his precious cortical monitor hadn't been enough to keep Finney on the straight path. Pisshead had probably never missed a meal in his life.

The shrink's office was on the eighth floor of a high-rise—it even had a balcony like a luxury condo. A hot redhead gave a twitch of her sweet little ass as she told her boss she was leaving for the day. Maybe they were getting together for some extra consultation later. Finney was left alone with Schneider, with the guard just outside in the waiting room. After all, Finney wasn't dangerous. Not the Finney he'd known.

Finney flopped onto the couch and amused himself by making up convoluted answers to Schneider's ludicrous questions.

Then Schneider's voice stopped mid-sentence. Finney lifted his head and saw the man sitting at his desk, not moving.

Frozen. Paralyzed.

Finney rolled to his feet and hurried to Schneider's shoulder for a look at the computer screen. It was filled with kiddie porn. The guy was a goddamn pedophile!

With a cortical implant of his own.

Revolted, Finney worked his mouth to gather some spit, then thought, *wait.*

This could be fun.

#

The guard didn't seem to notice Finney's smile as they entered the elevator for the ride back down. Finney couldn't help it, picturing Schneider balanced on the railing of his eighth-floor balcony, only kept from falling by the cord caught in the sliding glass door.

The cops would be there any minute, maybe in the next elevator, responding to Schneider's porn violation. They'd look for the shrink on the balcony. They'd open the door.

Meantime, it was off to prison, but that was OK. He had a score to settle with Odie.

#   #   #

A TASTE OF TIME

THE TINKLE OF THE DOORBELL announced a customer.

That was unusual—there weren't many customers anymore. Gabby had owned the Shop & Smile dépanneur for thirty-five years, and in the early days the hand-painted brass bell on its curled bracket had rung like a wind chime on a March day. But no more. Most of the people on the concession road shopped at the new Price-Well in town now--even the ones who smiled to her face and wished her a good day before they sped past.

It took an effort to rise from the old chair in the backroom, but she tried to hurry. The bell-heralded arrivals might be some of those young smart-alecs who stole her candy.

Not this time. It was Marjorie Simm from the farm next door. And she had a little girl with her--eight or nine, with dark hair and a short sun dress covered in a print of odd-shaped orange blotches. No. Maybe a cartoon character? There was a single word that looked foreign.

"Hello, Gabby," Marjorie said. "This is Amanda. Amanda, this is Miss Dufour. She owns the store."

The girl gave a polite curtsy and said, "It's nice to meet you," making Gabby smile in surprise. Not many children were taught such manners anymore.

"Amanda's come to visit us for the summer," Marjorie said. "Her mother—remember our daughter Sandra? She lives in Michigan now."

Gabby nodded. She used to hear a lot about that daughter, especially when Sandra went off to university. That was before Marjorie got the job at the library in town. Since then she'd been too busy to drop by for gossip. Her husband, Edgar, had to handle all of the chores on their small farm himself, dawn to dusk. How did they expect to look after a child for the summer?

"Amanda's looking forward to roaming around the farm, but I've told her she mustn't go anywhere else on her own. Except maybe here, if we send her to pick up a few things."

So that was it, thought Gabby. They expected her to be a part-time babysitter. She ought to say something to quell that notion *tout de suite.*

The girl spoke first. "Gramma says you know lots about the farm property. And the town that used to be there. Gramma says it's covered with *blueberries.*" She said the word the way she'd speak a magic spell, her smile revealing small teeth that were just a little crooked, but sugar-white.

"Blueberries. Yes, there are blueberries," Gabby huffed. "You can hardly walk without stepping on the things."

"Don't you like blueberries?"

"Everybody likes blueberries." Her grandmother patted her shoulder. "But anyway, we just dropped in to pick up some flour and brown sugar and butter."

"Blueberry muffins, I bet. You'll need baking powder too," Gabby said. "It should be fresh."

"You're right. I haven't baked in a few months. Better give me some, please."

Gabby made up the order and accepted the money. The child was fascinated by the whole process. "Everybody loves blueberries," she repeated, as she and her grandmother waved goodbye and made the bell ring again.

But that wasn't true—Gabby didn't love blueberries. Hadn't since she was a girl herself about Amanda's age. Her father had hurt his back and couldn't work. They had no money. So the family spent the month of July picking blueberries, and ate them for months afterward, with very little else to break the monotony.

Blueberry muffins, of course, but also pancakes and porridge. Fritters and frying-pan bread. Buckle and grunt. Chutney. Cobbler. Even blueberry soup and blueberry shrub made with vinegar and watered down for drinking.

That was long before the days of itinerant vendors selling berries from the backs of pickup trucks along the highway.

Blueberries tasted like poverty to Gabrielle.

She dusted a few shelves while she was up, and made sure the mousetrap was fully hidden behind some cans of celery soup that nobody ever touched. Then she hobbled back to her magazine, surrendering once more to wastrel Time.

#

The next day was Sunday, a day for the Simms to be home with Amanda. The little girl didn't visit the dépanneur Monday or Tuesday either. It wasn't until Wednesday morning that she appeared, wanting more muffin cups and shortening.

"Amanda. Do people call you Mandy?"

"At home, and at school. Gramma and Grampa don't. Gramma had a cousin named Mandy, but they don't talk about her."

Gabby nodded knowingly. Then the silence became awkward. She didn't talk to children very much anymore. "So...what have you been doing with yourself? At the farm."

"Exploring. And eating blueberries." The bright crescent smile was all the more winning because it wasn't perfect. Soon her parents would take her to an orthodontist and some of her childhood would be sacrificed. "There are so many blueberries. Everywhere. Just like you said, Mrs. Dufour."

"It's Miss. And you can call me Miss Gabby. But you be sure not to eat any other berries there. The other kinds could make you sick."

"Gramma told me. There's a big bush with juicy red berries. Near the bottom of the hill. I won't eat them."

Gabby remembered. A great pin cherry tree had stood in the churchyard. The tree burned to the ground in the fire that took the town, but other trees had grown in its place. "There used to be a church right there," she said.

"I know. Beside the post office, and the li...livery stable."

Gabby snapped around. How could...?

Oh, but there were probably some remains of the foundations still left, overgrown by weeds. Maybe the Simms had tried to plough there and were stopped by the blocks.

It had been a fine church, the steeple stretching skyward as if competing with the hilltop to be closer to God—a sore point with the pastors who came and went every few years.

"The hill *would* have been a good place for the church," Mandy observed.

"Yes. Yes, it would." But the hill had belonged to the Laclé family for generations, and young Armand Laclé...well, he'd had very special plans for that hilltop, once he could finish his studies as an architect.

Plans he'd meant for Gabby to share.

She coughed and dusted invisible flour from her skirt as she hoisted herself to her feet. It took a few moments to find the muffin cups. Then she fetched the shortening, took the money, and sent the girl on her way.

#

When the tinkling call of the bell beckoned her from the back room on Friday, Gabby stopped cold in the doorway.

It was the girl again, a red scarf at her neck, tied in just the way old Mrs. Landry had worn her scarves, and no-one else Gabby could ever remember: the knot pulled to the left side, and the ends spread apart with the upper one pinned to the top of her shoulder. Silly, some thought. *Distinctive*, Mrs. Landry had insisted.

"Where did you get a scarf like that?" Gabby asked, without even saying hello.

"Gramma helped me with it," the girl announced proudly, pivoting from side to side, cross-eyed from trying to look at the scarf for herself. "I thought it looked...distinctive." She smiled as if pleased with the grownup word. Gabby found herself reaching toward the countertop for support.

"And what do you want this time? Sugar? More muffin cups?"

"No, thank you. I just wanted to show you my scarf."

"I suppose you're going to wear it blueberry picking. You'll catch it on the bushes, you know."

"I'll be careful. I found an old one like this under a bush yesterday. But Gramma said it was too faded, so she gave me hers."

"There could be bears out there." Though Gabby knew the old town site didn't have enough ground cover for the bears' liking. "Maybe you shouldn't eat so many blueberries."

"But they're *so* good. I like the light blue ones best. As if they're painted with blue Jell-O powder. Those are sweet. The others—the ones that are almost black—they're kind of pasty. If you use them for jam you need more sugar. They're better for chutney." She nodded her head wisely. "You get to know blueberries. The little crunchy ones. The fat juicy ones. Some with just a few berries in a clump. Others in clusters, like grapes. Sweet in the sunshine, fatter in the shade. But the tangy ones are good, too—maybe they wish they were oranges or lemons. A few bushes grow next to pine trees, and you can taste that in the berries."

"My, you've become quite the expert." Old Mrs. Landry had sounded just like that sometimes, too, showing off with the things she knew about food. Though she had been the best cook in town.

The child took the words at face value, and beamed, running her hands down her shorts to smooth them. Gabby felt ashamed. She reached for the jar of toffees behind the counter, took a couple, and held them out.

"Here. Just for a change from berries. And be careful around the farm. Those old buildings could have root cellars. You might fall in."

"I know where they are. I won't fall." Mandy turned with another smile, and the bell tinkled overhead as she went out. Gabby looked up at it for the first time in years, and was surprised by its whiteness, and the blueberry motif she'd painted on it by hand. She'd forgotten about that.

#

The girl didn't come again for nearly a week. Maybe Marjorie wasn't pleased that Gabby had given the child candy. No, that was silly. It was only because the weather was so fine. A sun-dappled day offered better things to do than hang around an old woman in a lonely store. Like picking berries. It was good picking weather. She hoped Mandy wouldn't get into any trouble with snakes or wasps. Perhaps Gabby should look for her—to make sure she was all right.

Just then the door bell chimed, and sunshine poured in.

"*Bonjour, Mademoiselle Gabby. Crème glacée, s'il vous plait. Et.... Ah, oui. Du sucre, du pain, et du lait. Merci.*"

"*Bien sûr!* Your French is very good, Mandy." She stepped toward the ice cream freezer. She knew the Simms weren't French, but then all the children learned it in school these days, she supposed. With such a good accent, though. That was surprising.

"*French,* Miss Gabby?"

"Yes, it's very good. Well done."

"I don't know what you mean."

"What you just said. About the ice cream and everything. *Très bien.*"

The puzzlement in the child's eyes was genuine. Gabby felt a knot of fear in her stomach. Was her mind playing tricks on her? Had she only imagined it and translated the English words in her head?

#

The next Thursday was wet. Mandy sat in a chair near the front window of the dépanneur with a small pad of paper on her lap, sketching in pencil. Old stock—not worth charging for. It kept the child occupied while Gabby worked. There was a ledger to update and new stock to order, even with so few customers.

When her back became too sore to bend over the counter anymore, she yielded to her curiosity and hobbled toward the front of the store. As she looked over the child's shoulder, her hand flew to her mouth.

It was a sketch of a familiar house. So familiar. And so *good*. Where could a child of nine have learned to draw so well? She knew that house: long, grey boards with swirled grain and dark knots, a portico too fancy for a frame bungalow, a telltale of peeling paint on the crosspiece.

Gustave Houle's house.

Gustave Houle, who was a painter twice. For money, he would paint homes, whitewash fences, stain barns. But for his own pleasure, he made canvases of the landscape, the simple buildings, and the simple people of Manqueville. He helped Armand learn how to draw for his architecture courses.

God in Heaven. The child was recreating Gustave's house, with Gustave's own skill!

How was it possible?

"Where did you see that house, Mandy?"

"In my head. I thought it was pretty. I was eating some blueberries down by the creek, where it slows down and gets a bit marshy. It's a nice place. Lots of flowers."

There would be, yes. Gustave had also been a devoted gardener. Some of the seeds must have lived to try again, the hardiest ones that didn't require care. The daffodils and day lilies maybe. And the hostas—they'd spread like weeds, if the deer didn't get them.

"Eating blueberries. Always the berries," Gabby mused. The low bushes were at home throughout the rocky expanses of northern Ontario. But they had a special fondness for burned-out clearings, where forest fires left behind acidic soil and shade-free spaces. They'd laid siege to Manqueville and then consummated their victory in its ashes.

The doorbell ringing broke into her thoughts. It was Marjorie come to fetch her granddaughter for dinner.

"Thank you so much for looking after her, Gabby. I hope she hasn't been any trouble."

"Oh, no. Not at all. She's a very nice girl. And talented. Look at the sketch she made."

Mandy proudly displayed her work. Marjorie looked at it and gave Gabby a conspiratorial smile. "Yes, it's very good. And it was nice of Miss Dufour to help you with it."

"I didn't...." But Marjorie had turned away to pick up a few things including Hamburger Helper, Gabby noticed. Home cooking was disappearing, even here in the north country. People had other priorities. She hobbled to the cash register.

"Amanda's French is very good, too," she said tentatively.

"French?"

"She learns it in school, does she?"

"No, Gabby. Amanda lives in the *States*. They don't teach French in the schools there. It's too bad, really."

Too bad? Was she talking about the lack of a second language? Or an old friend who might be starting to slip a little and imagine things? The look on Marjorie's face was hard to read.

#

When Mandy came again, Gabby barely acknowledged her. She turned away when the child looked about to speak, and made extra noise restacking cans of soup that needed no such attention. The sweet young smile was an unwanted reminder of her own age, and the fear that she was seeing and hearing things she might have only imagined.

People already talked behind her back when she went into the new town for nails or newspapers or notions. Or just to see a fresh face or two. *Old maid* was one of the kinder names they used when they thought she didn't hear. Now, thanks to Mandy and her stories, it might be even worse. No longer simply irrelevant, had Gabby become an object of ridicule? A joke to pass back and forth while strolling the aisles of frozen entrees and packaged desserts?

It wasn't fair! All because of a bored little busybody and her damned blueberries!

Mandy turned back toward the door, disappointment like a brand on her face.

Gabby's bitterness rose like a smoke that parched her throat and stung her eyes. She cleared her throat.

"Wait, child. Come. Sit with me." There was a stool behind the counter—the girl mounted it with a little help. Gabby dragged her chair from the back room. They sat together, not sure where to look.

"Tell me about the fire, please," Mandy said.

Gabby's eyebrows lifted. Did she really want to do that? What should she reveal? Especially to a child.

Manqueville had been a thriving town then, small but robust. Mostly lumberjacks and mill workers, and their families. The fire had sprung on them out of the night, sweeping in from the bush on a sudden change of wind, so there'd been no forerunner of smoke, no warning. Just hungry flames that found a feast of wood far drier than the forest, and wanted it all.

Most of the victims had died in their beds. Or behind parlour windows, staring at the flames that entrapped them until they were overcome by smoke, if they were lucky. Women and children—the husbands were away at lumber camps. Like Papa. Gabby and her mother had been lucky because Soyer's Pond, behind the house, was just wide enough, just deep enough. The flames arced over their heads though the dark sky as they hunched in the water up to their noses, submerging frequently to keep their hair wet.

Armand wasn't a lumberman, but he wasn't killed in his home, either. One of the survivors had seen him pull his mother out of the house and run into the night, but their bodies were never found. Like so many others, they became part of the ash and rubble. The fire was so hot it consumed everything.

That he was dead, Gabby had no doubt. Otherwise he would have come for her.

She shook her head slowly, aware of the child watching.

"It was bad, very bad. A lot of people died. And a lot of dreams. Let it go at that."

They were memories she hadn't wanted to relive. They tasted like dust.

Like blueberries.

#

Day after day Gabby expected to hear the bell at the door and see Mandy's picket fence smile again, but she didn't come. Gabby thought of an excuse to drive into the new town and dropped in to the library, where Marjorie worked. The girl wasn't there, and Marjorie looked surprised to see Gabby. Or maybe it wasn't surprise but awkwardness—her smile wasn't quite comfortable on her face. She looked away and said that Amanda hadn't been to the dépanneur because she hadn't been feeling well—probably too many berries.

Gabby thanked her, and left. Who could blame anyone for wanting to keep an impressionable little girl away from a lonely old woman who might be going senile?

Maybe it was true. It wasn't sensible to believe that things like knowledge, or language, or talent could be ingested like sugar and salt.

#

Gabby felt the summer slip away. The blueberry plants would soon be barren once more, their profusion of tiny pointed leaves turning rusty at the edges. Good riddance. Maybe that was the real message: that it was time for Gabby to be going too. Perhaps she should sell the store and move south. Somewhere. Anywhere. As she'd wanted so desperately to do all those years ago after the fire, but hadn't. Was it simply life's inertia that had held her back? Or because, by then, going anywhere at all had seemed so very pointless?

Then suddenly Mandy was back. With a jingle like a fairy's laugh, she appeared, as if she'd never been away.

"Gramma said I shouldn't come here and bother you so much. You're busy. But I don't think you're busy all the time. Are you?"

"No, child. I'm not busy at all. How have you been? How are the blueberries?"

"Not so many anymore. You have to look for them. But I ate a lot this morning from some bushes at the corner of the farm. Near the tallest part of the forest. There are some very old trees there."

"Yes, very old."

"I was thinking what a wonderful place it would have been for a library and town hall. With a beautiful clock tower. Grand and tall, with a clock face you could see from anywhere in town. And especially from a house on top of the hill. On a fancy porch with carved posts and a wrought iron railing, you'd look across a sea of rooftops under a starry sky, and catch a glimpse of the clock face in the moonlight just as the bell chimed twelve." Her brown eyes shone with the vision.

Gabby gasped.

The child sounded just like Armand with his lofty dreams.

Armand on the evening before the fire, holding her in his arms on the porch of his mother's house and talking, talking with the fervour of the true believer. Just before Gabby had finally confessed that she didn't *want* to stay there in a house on the hill or anywhere else in Manqueville. That she felt trapped in such a small town. Hated it and begged for God to free her. Begged to God.

Gabby sagged from the weight of years—all those years of a life that might have been. Such a waste. Her heart felt shrivelled like fallen fruit. The fire had been both release and punishment, offering a cruel freedom she wasn't worthy to accept. So she had stayed to serve her sentence, hoping to turn her back on the past while surrounded by it. Unwilling to see that the world had moved on.

The fire had not been her fault. She owed its ashes no more of her life. From those ashes had sprung new growth: the cycle of life as it should be, caring nothing for one old woman's imagined sins.

Old breath coursed from her lungs in a sigh and she looked at the child in wonderment.

"Amanda," she said. "Could you take me to those bushes you ate from this morning? I...I have a craving."

"Sure."

The girl held out her hand and Gabby took it gratefully.

The tinkling bell fell silent as the door closed behind them.

#   #   #

TARTARUS RISING

I T'S STILL HARD TO ACCEPT how quickly the Trogs took control of our planet. It wasn't just that no-one had known an advanced species lived only meters beneath our feet. Some people, even now, say that's impossible, and insist they must have come from space. It really makes no difference. What sealed our fate was that no-one believed we were under attack even weeks after it had begun.

Gamers were the first to use the name "Trogs". The word *troglodyte* refers to ancient cave men. But to say the Trogs lived in caves was like saying the Queen has a nice house. They inhabited vast caverns under the earth's surface—whole subterranean worlds. And we never knew until the disasters in New York and Tokyo.

There have been stories about dwellers underground for centuries. Just read the online ravings of the conspiracy theorists: tales of hairy creatures who attack amateur spelunkers, lumberjack types who visit trapped miners, or even more often, mysterious old men in robes with some connection to outer space aliens in

UFO's—the worst kind of lurid crap and no evidence worth a damn.

Trogs don't look the way any of those stories describe them. But they are killers.

They killed thousands when the Citigroup Center in New York collapsed into a hole in the ground on June 14th. Then the Mori Tower in Tokyo the next morning. The week that followed tore the soul out of the business world: the Sears Tower in Chicago, the US Bank Tower in L.A., the Gherkin in London, England, and the Hochhaus Treptower in Berlin, Germany. They toppled like dominos until the news media couldn't keep up. Not just some of the planet's most famous buildings, but the vital organs of the capitalist world. Wall Street, central London, the Nihonbashi district...all sank beneath the surface amid clouds of dust and rubble, the very crust of the earth taken out from under them before anyone suspected a thing. We knew nothing about the Trogs, but they knew all about us.

The world economy was gutted in a matter of weeks. Workers refused to go to work. Even then there was not one credible suggestion that the disasters were anything but natural. We knew of no technology that could explain it, so it was left unexplained.

#

I'm just a hardware store manager and volunteer fireman. My friend Damon Langdon is a real estate agent, an excuse to spend all his time with his iPhone, running searches on the 'net. At least until the internet collapsed after too many major nodes were destroyed.

"Shit, Craig," he said to me. "Maybe these conspiracy nutbars aren't so far off. What natural phenomenon would target only key financial centers?"

"God has a sense of justice after all? Doesn't the Bible say it'll be easier for a camel to pass through the eye of a needle than for a rich man to get into Heaven?" Damon's a good friend. He doesn't laugh when I'm not funny.

"It doesn't say He's going to send all the people who work for the rich men on a shortcut to Hell, too." He waved his iPhone at me. "There are supposed to be lots of legends among native American tribes about ancestors who lived underground."

"And what? Now they've developed technology that can make cubic miles of rock and dirt disappear?"

Even I can hit on the truth by accident.

#

There's a nightmare I remember from my childhood. I'd fallen asleep on the living room sofa after some forbidden late night TV. I woke up in the darkness and there was a face at the window, a face with lemur eyes, no eyebrows or lashes, and a head like a cartoon speech bubble. It vanished instantly and I ran to the bathroom to throw up. I always blamed the vision on cold pepperoni pizza and a few swallows of pilfered rum.

I've never had rum since.

As the globe fell defenceless under the worst recession it had ever known, the Trogs began Phase Two. They didn't even need weapons to get rid of us. We'd provided everything required.

The memory of that Fourth of July weekend is like a brand on my brain. As a volunteer firefighter I knew that New Jersey had more than a hundred industrial sites that handled toxic chemicals. The state was like a bomb waiting for a fuse. So when I got the call at 3:25 Sunday morning, the words 'chemical fire' were all I really remembered. Damon and I were rookies on the crew, so we were ordered to stay behind and keep trying to contact the heavy sleepers who hadn't answered their phones. The rest of the guys were asked to give assistance all the way north in Kearny.

The name of the chemical plant filled my gut with ice. A major fire there would trigger a full evacuation. Millions of people. I was sure it couldn't be done.

We never found out. Just after 6:30 am the firefighters lost the battle and the plant blew. No-one knows exactly why, because only a handful of people within a dozen square miles survived: smoke-eaters who had their breathing masks on and enough spare oxygen tanks to get clear of the deadly cloud.

Chlorine gas.

A variable wind allowed it to spread far and wide, especially to the northeast over Jersey City and finally New York. Most people were still in bed with their windows open to the night air. They had no warning. In their millions, they awoke coughing, and rasped a last few breaths as they felt the gas destroy their lungs.

I don't think the guys from our crew died that way. From what I could piece together later, they were diverted to the east when a big refinery in Port Reading began to come apart. The shifting ground snapped joints throughout the complex, releasing a real witch's brew of phenol, xylene, naphthalene, ethylene glycol and more. Sprays of butyl alcohol and propylene misted the air. The first spark was easily enough.

All of it went up—more than a dozen giant tanks in a hellish cascade of destruction. Eight companies of firemen were wiped out within minutes. The ferocious flames spread quickly along the waterfront to a shipping terminal for petroleum products, and then another refinery next to it. It became a true firestorm of World War II proportions, and the poisonous cauldron churned and bubbled over northeast New Jersey for more than a day. There was nothing to stop it.

Hundreds of thousands tried to escape to the west and south in their cars. The Turnpike, the Garden State Parkway, Interstate 1, and Highway 287 became clogged by caskets on wheels, filled with the dead and the dying.

#

I didn't learn any of the details until days later. None of us did, thanks to power blackouts that became more and more frequent.

When first light arrived Damon and I went outside and looked to the east.

The palette of the sky was extraordinary, the clouds painted with rose and amber and purple. I couldn't pull my eyes away as I backed toward my pickup truck.

Maybe I sensed it was the dawn of a new era.

"Where are you going?" Damon asked me.

"The hardware store." Not to get it ready for opening. It suddenly represented survival.

"Damon," I said. "You might want to go to your apartment and get stuff to last you a few days, then meet me at the farm. I think something really bad has happened."

Old Man Griffin, who owned the hardware store, was old-fashioned and the store was closed for the Sunday and holiday Monday. I filled my pickup with everything I could think of, from propane to bottled water and purification tablets to an eight-gallon gas generator and extra gasoline cans. With the electricity out, I swiped my credit card on one of the old-style imprinters lying in the back of a drawer, and tucked the receipt under the register. Maybe someday the debt would be paid.

A few gas stations and stores had begun to use generators and I made trip after trip for fuel and food. Part of me felt selfish as hell for not making like Chicken Little and trying to warn everyone, but I was sure they'd think I was one of those rabid survivalists, taking advantage of a tragedy to make converts. Old-family New Englanders have no tolerance for that kind of bad taste.

Some of the properties in our part of New Jersey are recognized historical buildings on famous old estates, but the place my grandmother left to me was a lot more modest: a few acres that hadn't been farmed in years, and a house with a small barn and a well. I'd considered selling once or twice when I was feeling lonely. Especially after Patricia left. She'd thought life outside the big city would be refreshing, but found it stifling instead. Now, with all Hell breaking loose, the place was a godsend.

That night the wind changed and the toxic cloud swept south along the Turnpike. It was only the rain after midnight that saved my neighbourhood. The power went out again, for good. When I drove into Franklin Park around noon on Monday the place looked like a ghost town. Those who could leave had done so— the rest were sick in their homes, I suppose. I didn't stay to find out. The sky was black and haemorrhaging rain.

The still bodies of birds dotted the side of the road under the telephone wires like God's tears.

Damon had been up most of the night, surfing the internet and listening to distant radio stations.

"It's way worse than we thought," he said, sitting at my kitchen table clutching a battery-and-crank shortwave radio I'd once bought, his eyes glassy. Catastrophes were happening all over. Philadelphia, D.C., Detroit...the rest of the world, too. "It's a nightmare," he breathed. "It's Armageddon."

"I can't believe that."

"Is that why your barn is packed with food?"

"I think we're in for some hard times, but I don't believe in the end of the world."

Even so, I knew we couldn't count on help anytime soon. Police and firefighters everywhere were the first to be killed. Most of the soldiers who weren't overseas were stationed on bases close to the very cities that had been hit. If any survived, they'd have their hands full protecting members of the government, not Joe Citizen in backroad New Jersey.

I shuffled to the cupboard, trying to keep my voice calm. "The toxic gases must've come within a few miles of here last night. I saw...things. We should be all right, though. The rain should wash the air clean."

I swear Damon's brown skin went pale, and he hurried to the bathroom. He didn't need me to explain it to him. If he'd stayed in his apartment near Somerset he would've been dead.

I made some more coffee.

#

The Trogs didn't start coming to the surface in large numbers until weeks later. Buildings continued to collapse. Subway and vehicular tunnels everywhere were flooded. There were reports of strange, silent men traveling through the shadows of city streets at night. A systematic disabling of power and communications systems. People disappearing. Then a TV crew recorded swarms of beings pouring up out of a giant pit where a building had once stood.

A few newscasters tried calling them "Morlocks" from H.G. Wells' "The Time Machine" but that was quickly stopped. The Morlocks were cannibals who came to the surface to feed: an image guaranteed to cause panic. Instead the pockets of the internet still functioning began to bristle with the name "Trogs" as forums and blogs spread rehashes of the UFO yarns, and fables about lost Atlantis and Lemuria.

"More like Hades...Tartarus...the Greek Underworld," Damon said in a lifeless voice. "Where the mighty but wicked were banished for defying the gods."

I began to worry about his state of mind.

I'm sure the Trogs stayed safely underground for those first weeks because they knew decomposing bodies were as much of a threat as poisonous chemicals. The weather stayed hot and the rainstorms were frequent, a good combination for cleansing the ground. But I wouldn't have taken a drink from the D & R Canal on a bet. Thousands did, I guess. One of the only times I got brave enough to drive through the subdivisions west and north of us, the reek made me close my windows, even in the sweltering heat. I stopped the car in front of one house when I noticed a child lying on the lawn. Then I saw the cloud of flies.

From what I can tell, thousands of people escaped west. Stragglers died. A few at my own hands, God forgive me.

One morning I opened my door to find my neighbour Miranda standing there, looking pale and shaky. She was a looker, with long hair on the reddish side of blond and a body she kept in good shape by jogging past my house every morning at 6:40. A widow, courtesy of Afghanistan, she'd always been cool to me, waving if I waved first and little more. I felt self-conscious about my smelly clothes and scraggly beard, but she didn't look her best right then either.

Sitting at my kitchen table she told us about the men who'd come to her place the night before.

"They wanted food, water...anything. I didn't open the door. I stood at the window with a rifle and told them my husband and brothers were watching from the upper floors. I don't think they believed me, but I guess they weren't hungry enough to take the chance, and they left. I spent all night going from window to window in case they came back." She was trying hard not to show fear, but her eyes glistened.

Miranda's house has lots of big windows, and the trees aren't far away. Plenty of cover for someone with a weapon and an empty belly.

My place is surrounded by a big field of stubbly grass with just a couple of oaks near one corner of the house, and some well-spaced apple trees near the road.

"Do you want to stay here?" I asked.

"I might bring you trouble."

"You could also bring us protection. Did Jeff have a lot of guns? Can we get them?"

She nodded a little too vigorously.

We made a few trips to Miranda's place. If we were being watched there was nothing we could do about it. As a soldier, Jeff had been trained to think about worst-case scenarios and he'd had a large supply of ammunition.

We needed it.

The raiders came after dark. Miranda saw their lights come along the road from the south and stop near my driveway: first one, then a second, then a third. We watched from behind drawn curtains, but nothing happened for forty-five minutes. Then we were startled to see flashing lights appear around a curve of the road to the north. I felt a rush of elation—the thugs would probably be scared away by the police. The pulsing flares of red and blue resolved into a black and white cruiser that turned into my driveway. The vehicles at the road didn't move.

A uniformed man stepped out of the police car and came toward the house. As he walked he was obviously counting windows and doors and scanning the ground for hazards. He finally climbed onto the front step and his hand hesitated at the doorbell before he remembered the power outage and knocked instead.

"Who is it, and what can I do for you?" I said through the door.

"It's Sergeant Peterson. Can I come in?"

I looked at Damon. He shook his head.

"I'd like to see some identification Sergeant."

The figure dug a hand into his pants pocket and I had a bad moment expecting him to pull out a gun. Instead he waved something at the door with a piece of metal attached that caught the barest gleam of reflected headlight. Damon was still shaking his head and knifing his hand horizontally.

"Sorry, Sergeant. I'm not prepared to let anyone into my house right now. I'm sure you understand."

"Just want to know you're safe, son. How many of you are in there anyway? Is the lady from next door in there?"

The alarm bells in my head kicked into double-time.

"I'm perfectly safe. Thanks for coming to check. If I have any trouble I'll call the police station."

He didn't move away from the door. After a long pause he said, "Look, son, we know you've got food in there—more than enough for just the three or four of you. The county has ordered me to collect surplus food and water to be distributed to people who don't have any. I hope you're not thinking of being selfish and giving us a hard time."

I couldn't think of anything to say. He leaned closer and raised his voice.

"You might want to change your mind about cooperating with us son. I'm going to have to call my headquarters and report this." He returned quickly to his car and backed it down the driveway until it was even with the line of trees. Then he dimmed the headlights.

Keeping my head below window height I scrambled over to Damon.

"I've helped a lot of the Franklin Township force buy and sell their homes," he said. "I met a Sergeant Peterson once, and he was a lot taller than this guy."

"You think he's lying?"

"Cops on duty were probably killed when the cloud came this way, and a lot of the others lived east of here. I'd bet these guys stole the cruiser and uniform..."

The crack of a gunshot made us dive for the floor as the small window beside the front door shattered, right where I'd been standing seconds earlier.

"*Shit!* So much for the law." I double-checked my gun and sent Miranda to the attic windows. Her semiautomatic would be most useful from a height if the raiders started coming through the grass. Damon scrambled toward the back of the house, but he'd never fired a gun. I would have given a lot for a couple of days of practice and some night scopes.

Our attackers probably expected us to start blazing away at shadows. Instead we waited, hoping we'd see dark shapes against the straw-coloured grass before they got too close to the house. My night vision had improved without the halo of city lights bathing the night-time horizon. In time I could see bulges along the dark trunks of some of the apple trees. When a bright flash came from one of them, I sighted my rifle and pulled the trigger. Miranda fired at almost the same instant—the bark of her gun echoed down the stairs. A flare of light erupted about twenty feet away from the first: an automatic weapon spraying bullets upward toward the attic. I prayed that Miranda was using the old oak dresser up there for cover. The raider let loose another stream of fire, and then I had him.

Someone closer to the driveway failed to learn from his partner's mistake and poured bullets into the front window beside me. As I felt glass pepper my face I was conscious of Miranda squeezing off three rounds. They found their mark.

The next hour was a waiting game. A single shot would occasionally flash from the trees, splintering the front window or the door. My eyes began to feel the strain, but I couldn't rest them. The raiders would have to make a move before it started to get light.

Just as I'd decided to check on Miranda, I heard the thunder of Damon's shotgun, and the crash of glass. I ducked low and sprinted from door frame to door frame until I could see into the kitchen at the back of the house.

"Jesus Christ," he said. "Jesus Christ, he was just outside the door!"

I could make out his silhouette slumped against the wall, and shuffled over to him. Then I popped my head quickly over the sill of the door window and back down. There was a large shape on the ground.

"I think I blew his head off," Damon said in a strangled voice.

The chatter of rapid gunfire came from the attic. I yelled, "Reload!" and ran toward the front. At least three shapes were coming swiftly across the grass, illuminated by muzzle flashes. I slid into a solid position on the window frame and emptied my lungs, struggling to keep my hands from shaking. My first target fell victim to Miranda's gun. I took aim again and squeezed...worked the bolt...aimed, squeezed. Took a man out. Tipped back to reload.

When I rolled flat again I could see the final man was less than twenty feet away, pointing his automatic toward my window. Right at me. A sharp crack reverberated down the stairwell, and the man went down. He didn't move. None of them did.

After a minute I slumped into a sitting position and let the shakes come.

It was probably three o'clock when I decided to make the rounds. Damon jumped when I called to him, and I thought I heard a sniff. Miranda was still at her post in the attic bedroom. As I slid to the floor beside her, she cleared her throat softly and asked, "Do you think we killed them all?"

"I don't know, but you were great."

Her breath caught a little, and then she thrust her face into my shoulder. I could feel her body shaking.

"God, Craig. This is a nightmare."

"We can hold out until morning. If any of them are left, they'll retreat by then. After that, we'll have to decide whether we dare to stay here."

I was looking over the expanse of grass toward the trees and the road. Miranda raised her head.

"The trees...the shadows.... Do you notice anything?" I asked. The dark of the road appeared even blacker than before, but to my weary eyes it seemed to ripple.

Suddenly we saw muzzle flash again. Rapid automatic fire. But it wasn't aimed at the house. There were two guns about forty feet apart and each of them sent three or four long bursts toward the north and northwest. Then they stopped.

We took turns keeping watch the rest of the night but didn't hear another sound.

\#

It was a couple of hours after sunrise before we dared to venture outside. We watched the shadows shrink and made sure there was no-one hiding in them. There was no-one at all, not even the one Damon had shot through the back door.

"I swear I got him," he said, looking ill. "You saw, Craig. Look!"

The burnt grass was stained with blood—a lot of it. But no body.

We carefully searched the front and found more blood and shell casings. The vehicles were all in the same places as the night before, but they were empty. Could a survivor have dragged the bodies away? No, they would certainly have used one of the pickup trucks.

We combed the property like a platoon on patrol. There was nothing more to be found. Finally we sat together on the front stoop.

"We'll have to get rid of the vehicles, especially the police cruiser," Damon said. "Otherwise, if they have friends who come looking for them...."

I agreed. Keys were in the ignition switches, as if for a quick getaway. Miranda stayed behind and used a rake to gather shell casings and disguise the blotches of dark red.

\#

It was on the last return trip in my own truck that we spotted the Trog.

There was a ditch with a culvert just across the road from my place. I pulled into the mouth of the driveway and we jogged across the blacktop with guns ready. Pale bare legs stuck out of the culvert with some kind of enclosed sandals on the feet. As we stepped down we could make out the rest of the body, the limbs awkwardly splayed, the head covered with dried blood. I jabbed my rifle barrel hard into the abdomen a couple of times, then bent over to check for a pulse.

"It's alive."

"My God," Damon rasped. "What do you want to do?"

I wanted to kill it. I wanted to raise my gun and pour out revenge on the thing that had brought such fear and misery into my world.

"Let's take it to the hayloft."

The hay was decades old, mildewed and musty. I'd taken a set of handcuffs before abandoning the police car, and we cuffed the Trog to a sturdy chain attached to an overhead beam. That would allow it to move around a little, if it woke up.

"Did you find one of the bodies?" Miranda's voice called up from the door of the barn.

"No. Something else."

She gasped as her head appeared above the loft edge. "Is that one of *them*?"

I went to get some water, a rag, and a first aid kit, then wiped the blood off its face none too gently, half-hoping to provoke a reaction. It lay still, a scrawny body with pale skin like a fish belly, wrapped in a long tunic of some dark grey material. There were differences from the average human: the ears were a fair bit larger, the skull round and hairless. The eyebrows and eyelashes were mere vestiges. I pushed back an eyelid. Oversized pupils were surrounded by a thin iris of a light salmon shade.

Was it possible creatures like this had come from somewhere else to make this planet their home, but couldn't stand the intensity of the sunlight? I didn't believe it, but I tasted bile in my throat and a sour memory of rum.

There was an ugly gash across the thing's forehead, unusually straight.

"Looks like it was grazed by a bullet." There were no other wounds that I could find. Miranda put a gauze bandage over the cut.

"What do we call it?" asked Damon. "A Trog?"

"Caliban," Miranda said with an odd smile. I didn't get it.

Damon did. "Not funny," he replied. "Shakespeare was writing about a primitive man. I have a feeling these people aren't primitive. Besides..." He looked at us. "In *The Tempest* Caliban tried to rape Miranda."

#

The Trog woke up during my watch that afternoon. I noticed a change in its breathing and waited to see what it would do. Finally I said, "I know you're awake. I have water for you."

It didn't move for at least thirty seconds, then slowly opened those huge eyes and glared at me. It tested its shackles and gave a brief glance at the cuffs and chain. I held out a plastic pail with some water in it and mimed the act of drinking, then carefully placed the bucket within its reach. It didn't show any interest in anything but me.

You can look into a dog's eyes and sense a curiosity and eagerness to understand. With a chimpanzee or a gorilla, you know you're reading an intelligence of near-human level. The Trog showed another order of perception entirely. The pink of its irises within a nearly colourless face was unsettling, reminding me of highly-bred Siamese cats. As our eyes battled, I was childishly pleased to see it blink first, reacting to a sudden brightening of the sunlight from a break in the clouds.

I touched my hand to my forehead. The Trog caught my meaning and gently investigated the bandage on its head with its fingers, but made no effort to pull it off. The only evidence of pain was some rapid blinking once, when it prodded too hard. Again I pointed at the pail of water, but the salmon eyes never left me.

"I am…" I waved my arm to take in the whole of my body. "*Human*. You are…?

There was no response.

For the next half-hour I tried variations on the "Me Tarzan, You Jane" routine, and scraps of inter-species greetings I could remember from science fiction stories. Finally I just laughed at myself and said, "Take me to your leader."

"How do you know he has one?" Miranda asked as she climbed up to the loft.

"I don't even know if it has a name. Or if it can talk at all. The radio reports say these things keep pretty quiet. This one's not giving me anything."

She cautiously lifted the pail and held it out to the Trog.

"Don't bother. Won't even acknowledge it."

The Trog reached for the pail and took a long drink.

Miranda laughed. "You just need the right approach. Maybe I remind him of his mother."

"If it's anything like a human male, those aren't the thoughts it gets from looking at you." Especially in her tight cut-off shorts. "I've tried getting it to talk. It's not interested."

"Probably can't understand you. Written language might be a better bet. There are lots of examples of ancient peoples who lived in caves and used some kind of pictograph system." She saw the look on my face and smiled. "I studied archaeology and anthropology in school, but dropped out when I got pregnant. We lost the baby, but I couldn't bring myself to go back. Anyway, I still remember a few things. I don't suppose you have a blackboard and chalk?"

"My grandmother was a schoolteacher before she married. Maybe in the attic storage room. Be careful. Keep your distance and keep your hand on your gun."

"Yes, Dad."

Miranda used the blackboard to make simplified drawings of human beings, trees, and buildings, and said the English word for each of them. She even drew a man near a cave and tried to ask the Trog the name for its race. It never made a sound, but at least it paid attention to the lesson. After a couple of hours Damon and I brought some paper plates with food on them.

"We thought root vegetables would be the best bet," Damon said. "If it eats meat, I don't want to know what kind."

We left it alone with the food and had a conference outside the barn door.

"Are we going to have to watch it twenty-four-hours a day?" Damon asked.

"I hope not." Miranda's exhaustion was plain. "The handcuffs are solid. There aren't any tools nearby to help him escape, and he's still too weak to do it if there were. I think he's hurting a lot worse than he's letting on."

I just nodded. I couldn't imagine trying to stay awake much longer, and our efforts to do so might look like weakness in the Trog's eyes. Leaving it unguarded would either show confidence or compassion. Hopefully not stupidity.

I'd offered Miranda my main floor bedroom when she'd first come to us, but she'd refused it in favour of the small attic room, claiming she'd be more comfortable higher off the ground. Damon used the bedroom at the back that I'd converted into a workroom.

Late into the night I heard a creak from the old stairs, and moments later there was a silhouette in my doorway.

"I'm.... This isn't a come-on," Miranda said. "I just don't want to be alone."

"I understand." I shifted toward the window and pulled the covers back for her. She whispered, "Thank you" as she slid into the queen-sized bed, then said nothing more. It was strange and familiar at the same time, having a woman in my bed again. I couldn't help but be aroused, yet the simple feeling of comfort was so much stronger. I lay awake for a time, just to hear her breathe.

#

Something woke me in the darkness. I listened for a few minutes, then rolled lightly out of the bed to squat at the window. The sky was overcast again, and it took a while to make out the trees by the road. Then my skin began to crawl.

"Miranda," I whispered loudly, gently touching her arm. She snapped awake. "Come here and take a gun." I always kept two beside the bed, loaded and ready.

"Raiders again?" she asked, pulling back her long hair.

"I don't think so."

The longer I watched the better I could see shapes passing slowly over the grass. A lot of them.

"Trogs," I said.

"My God. They're looking for him!"

"Shit. We should have left it in the ditch. But I thought we could find out what they want."

I had a child's impulse to turn the porch light on, to scare them away. But these weren't foxes or raccoons, or even sneak thieves. What if they really were capturing humans as they went? If we were lucky, they might think the house was abandoned.

I cursed myself for leaving the truck in the driveway instead of hiding it in the barn.

The barn.

What if our captured Trog heard its companions and cried out to them?

I didn't say anything to Miranda, but I offered one of the few prayers of my life.

The passing Trogs made no sound themselves. They'd surprised some heavily-armed men in this same spot the night before, and had taken casualties. If they were searching for the Trog in our barn, they left disappointed a couple of hours later, probably unsure where it had fallen from their ranks. I sent Miranda back to bed, but stayed at the window. I wasn't ready to sleep. I began to think about my sister and her husband and kids in Wyoming. Some other relatives in Arizona. And I wondered where Patricia was, and if she were still alive.

#

A few days later Miranda came to the breakfast table after a visit to the barn.

"I think he's dying," she said. "Caliban's dying."

"Why do you say that?" Damon and I hadn't spent much time with the Trog. We'd been busy trying to cobble together a manual pump system for the well water.

"He's getting weaker," she answered. "He can barely lift himself to get clean." I'd hung a large metal watering can over the loft with a rope attached, for a makeshift shower. The Trog used it often.

"If its head wound is infected, we could try giving it antibiotics," Damon suggested. "But we don't know anything about its body chemistry."

"There's no sign of infection. He's just sick."

"Maybe it had internal injuries," I said. "Or maybe it caught a disease from us and has no immunity." I was thinking of 'War of the Worlds' when the helpless humans were saved from invading Martians by earth germs.

Why should we care if this Trog lived or died anyway? My plan to interrogate it for strategic information seemed far-fetched in the cold light of day.

Light of day?

I sat up straight, thinking hard, but didn't say anything to the others while I pushed the scraps of my breakfast around the plate. It didn't work. I was stalling, and the reason shamed me.

I was jealous of Miranda and the Trog.

"There's something we could try," I said quietly.

First we had to clear enough space in the cellar and choose a solid pipe to anchor the handcuffs. Then Damon and I had to carry the Trog most of the way. Miranda was right: it was terribly weak. I saw its eyes watching me as we brought it indoors. They looked more puzzled than anything else.

By the next morning we could already see a big change, and the Trog's health improved steadily after that. Maybe it hadn't been the excess of light. Maybe a subterranean creature just needs to be close to the earth.

#

Beneath one of the small cellar windows, Miranda set up her blackboard, and continued her lessons. Two days later she told us she was making progress.

"I think they do have a pictograph language," she said. "I tried what I could remember of very early cuneiform, before it was simplified and stylized. Pretty much stick figures and symbols," she explained to our blank faces. "But that didn't work out. I've had better luck with some basic hieroglyphs. I think he's beginning to understand some of my words, too, although he never makes a sound himself."

After four more days the Trog picked up a piece of chalk and drew some symbols Miranda could recognize.

She was elated—on a real high. That night she rolled over in the bed and we made love for the first time. I just hoped I wasn't a surrogate for someone else.

#

The news on the radio kept getting worse. The Trogs were everywhere. There were stories that they were spreading killer diseases, creating terrible epidemics. Damon pointed out that the lack of fresh water, sewage treatment, and proper burial of the dead could account for most of that. Some people suggested we should deliberately weaken the Earth's ozone layer, the way we'd once done by accident. The Trogs wouldn't be able to stand the extra ultraviolet radiation, they reasoned. Thankfully, the idea didn't get any traction. The Trogs avoided daylight—we would only have hurt ourselves and devastated our food crops.

Countries were becoming destabilized, their people desperate.

Then we heard the most frightening news of all: a splinter group in Pakistan had tried to stop the Trogs by exploding a nuclear warhead in a major city.

#

We had a near tragedy of our own on the last day of July.

We'd all gathered in the cellar after dinner so Miranda could show us some of the writing she'd exchanged with the Trog. It reminded me of the decorations you see on walls in Hollywood movies about ancient Egypt: some obvious human figures, the shape of an eye, a jagged horizontal line that might be rippling water.

"It looks like a kid's sketchbook," Damon said.

"Or like your notepad when you're doodling beside the radio," Miranda teased. "Except his skill level is higher."

Damon opened his eyes wide in mock offence and reached out his hands as if to strangle her.

The Trog was on him in an instant, slamming him against a shelf and sending a cascade of jars crashing to the floor. Damon struggled for breath with the creature's long fingers around his throat.

I tackled the Trog hard, and we rolled across shards of shattered glass. It clawed at me, but I got an arm free and started pummelling its face, pinning it with all my weight.

"*Stop!*" Miranda screamed. She had a rifle aimed at us, and her hands were shaking badly. I rolled off the Trog and leapt to Damon's side.

"He's unconscious, but he's still breathing. What the hell was that all about?"

"He thought Damon was attacking me."

"For Christ's sake. It could've killed him!"

"I know. I know...." She gave me the rifle and began a pantomime in front of the Trog. She pointed to Damon and me and pulled her hands to her heart. Then she went into a series of gestures that must have been meant to show Damon had only been joking, though humour is nearly impossible to translate that way.

Suddenly my brain came out of its fog.

"Look at its wrists."

No handcuffs. They were still attached to the chain. I gave the gun back to Miranda and went to retrieve the cuffs. I tucked them into my belt and slowly lifted one of the Trog's hands. There was something strange about its wrist and thumb joints I'd never noticed before.

As I started to point it out to Miranda, the ground began to shake. She fell against the stair frame, and more jars came crashing down.

An *earthquake* in New Jersey!

"Get upstairs!" I yelled to her. "I'll get Damon." I ran to my friend and squatted down to lift him in a fireman's carry, but a heavy tool cabinet toppled onto us and pinned his legs. I scrambled to my feet and reached forward, but the Trog beat me to it, lifting the cabinet enough for me to drag Damon free. Then it grabbed his legs and together we carried him up the stairs and through the house to his bed. By then the quake had stopped.

I leaned my hands on my knees to catch my breath. There was fear on the face of the Trog that I knew must be mirrored in my own features. Miranda stood in the workroom doorway, her eyes saying, *What do we do now?*

What indeed.

I beckoned her over to me, and looked at Caliban. Holding his gaze I deliberately pulled Miranda close into my body, and she returned the hug, nuzzling my neck. The Trog lowered his eyes, and then his head.

Not in subservience or surrender, but in...apology? When he looked up again I held out the handcuffs.

And put them in my pocket.

He dipped his body slightly, like the beginning of a bow, and walked toward the basement stairs.

#

"You did *what?*" Damon sputtered.

"What was the point in keeping him handcuffed? He's double-jointed or something. He can get out of them."

"Then something else. The chain..."

"You're missing the point, Damon," I said. "He could have slipped the handcuffs any time he wanted to. He could have killed us in our sleep, or just escaped, but he didn't. He only attacked you because he thought you were going to hurt Miranda."

"And now suddenly 'it' has become a 'he'?" Damon accused.

I hadn't even noticed the difference in my speech, in my attitude. But it was there.

"Yes," I said finally. "Look, I understand how you feel. I almost killed him myself. I'm glad I didn't. If there's any chance at all of us being able to live in peace with the Trogs...then I'd rather be on that side." To be honest, I felt like I was living out a movie cliché right then, but a man can't make a life out of endless killing. Can he?

"Well I'm sure as hell locking my frigging door," Damon said.

#

For all of my well-meaning words, I didn't sleep much that night. I was listening.

The next morning at breakfast I looked up to see Caliban standing at the cellar door. I made a beckoning motion to him and pulled the empty fourth chair out from the table. I didn't know if Trogs used chairs, but he could certainly see how we used them. Miranda made a point of giving him some samples of our food to try. He ignored utensils but ate everything, even the bacon we'd thawed as a treat, though he seemed indifferent to the piece of toast. There was a lot of tension around the table that first time, but in the days to follow it would become astonishingly routine.

Earthquakes came every two or three days from then on, and they grew stronger. I think Caliban could sense them coming. He still preferred to sleep in the cellar (on an old down mattress—not straw anymore) but when the quakes came he would be found aboveground, often stretched out on the living room sofa. Even so, they left him agitated. Not from fear of injury. It was something else. He was more urgent in his efforts to communicate with Miranda, clearly frustrated when she didn't catch his meaning.

Then one afternoon she came up from the cellar carrying the blackboard.

"I think he's trying to tell us to go to the mountains."

"Mountains?" Damon echoed. "Wouldn't they be even more dangerous in an earthquake? Rock falls and landslides?"

"We've got the things we need to survive right here," I added. "We'd have to leave most of it behind if we moved."

"I know that, but he's very insistent. We agreed on a symbol for danger, and he keeps drawing it. And mountains. And Trogs. He also drew this." She pointed to a lower corner of the slate. It showed a Trog at one end of a large cave that was perfectly regular in shape. The Trog looked to be operating something. *Machinery?*

Could it be the Trogs' excavating device? There'd been wild stories on the radio about them being able to vaporize or transmute large quantities of rock, using energy tapped from the mantle below the Earth's crust. We didn't know if these were pure speculations, or if someone had actually found evidence.

"We'd have to be crazy to move," Damon argued. "Like Craig said, we've got tools and food that should last us at least through the winter. We won't be able to carry all of that. And so far the Trogs have left us alone here. Who knows what will happen if they catch us out in the open?"

I had to agree. Our survival depended on us staying put.

#

That night the Trogs came again. I awoke to a low vibration that wasn't an earthquake. It was from a parade of heavy vehicles along the road, and what looked like thousands of Trogs on the move. The sky was brightly lit by a half-moon, the kind of night Trogs don't like. Caliban stood near the front door and I could see him looking from me to the window and back again. Yet he made no attempt to leave, to rejoin his people, in spite of whatever was causing his fear.

At one point I was shocked to see figures passing by in pants and shirts—human clothing. Were they prisoners? Slaves? Or just Trogs wearing stolen clothes?

With the morning came another earthquake, the worst yet, and Caliban was more upset than I'd ever seen him. We were stunned when he prostrated himself in front of us, then stood and went to the blackboard. He wasn't acknowledging us as masters; he was begging us to believe his message. He pointed to the symbol for danger. Then a pair of legs that signified walking. Then the mountains. Danger—walking—mountains. Again and again.

Finally I held up a hand to stop him, and looked at my friends.

"I think we should go."

\#

We retrieved one of the raiders' pickup trucks and filled both vehicles with as many supplies as they could carry. Then we closed the house up as best we could, in case we ever returned. I climbed into my truck with Caliban beside me, and led the way toward US 22 and I-78, with Miranda and Damon following behind.

The highways were straight out of an apocalyptic movie. Thousands of abandoned vehicles sat eerily still, filling the lanes. Even the shoulder of the road became impassable after a time. We had to take smaller roads and hope the Trogs still shunned the bright sun.

We broke into an isolated motel for the night, hiding the trucks behind it, then moved on at first light. It was nearly dusk again when we started to climb into the Poconos.

We had stopped to stretch our legs at the crest of a long rise, when Caliban jogged up to me and began pulling at my shirt. I looked along his pointing arm. Down the mountainside, along the road we'd just traveled, a dark mass was moving.

Trogs.

I called to the others and raced back to the trucks, but before I could climb in, Caliban yanked fiercely at my shirt again. He beckoned to Damon and Miranda, then squatted on the dirt shoulder of the road with a stick in his hand. He drew a large circle, and another slightly smaller one inside it, like the cross-section of an orange showing the peel. Then he drew two more consecutively smaller circles within the others. I'd seen a diagram like it in geography class. Not the cross-section of an orange, but of the *Earth*.

He quickly followed with a rough sketch of the Trog in the cave with the digging device, followed by a danger symbol, and then finally a series of curved lines from the inside of the Earth out through the crust.

"Oh my God." Miranda took a step back with a look of horror on her face. Then I got it, and felt my heart miss a beat.

We stood there in disbelief staring at a picture of doom in the dry dust.

Finally Caliban waved to get our attention. He pointed at us, and the road toward the west. Then he pointed at himself, and the road downhill, toward the Trogs. I nodded. I didn't see how one person could delay a whole army, but he was going to try to at least give us a head start. He stepped up to me, placed his hand on my chest and then his own chest. He did the same with Miranda and even Damon. Miranda impulsively gave him a hug. Then he was gone, running down the road.

This time Miranda climbed into the cab with me, and we poured on the gas, racing toward the setting sun.

For so long we've been afraid that the human race would destroy the planet with a nuclear war or a giant particle collider accident. Instead it was the Trogs. With their advanced technology penetrating the Mohorovicic Discontinuity into the mantle below to tap its power, they'd destabilized the Earth's crust. Soon flood basalt eruptions—slow but relentless flows of magma—would burst forth all over the globe, coating the landscape and decimating all life.

We—humans and Trogs—could find safety from the magma in the mountains somewhere, if we could learn to stop killing each other. But the geology and the climate would be our enemy for centuries to come.

I watched the sun settle onto the tops of the trees.

It was going to be a very long night.

\#   \#   \#

MARATHON OF THE DEVIL

THE SANDSTORM HIT on the third day of the marathon. Eli was well ahead of the pack—he could have stopped and found shelter. Instead he kept running, confident that he knew the course. After all, he'd helped select it. Except he didn't know every little crack and gully, which was why a bad step while blinded by grit dropped him three meters onto a rock. He was lucky to suffer nothing worse than a few scratches. He should have checked his gear after the impact—mistake number two. The wall he'd fallen over was too high to climb, but the crack appeared to curve toward the west, the way he wanted to go.

Which was how he got lost.

#

"You don't have to go into space to be somebody," his father had said. Eli knew the words were only out of concern for his safety. It was a familiar refrain: if it hadn't been for the discovery of the

Einstein-Rosen Junction just sunward of the Kuiper Belt, humankind wouldn't have been blundering through other solar systems before it was ready. Engineering that hadn't realized any major advances since the 21st Century wasn't good enough.

But the argument hadn't kept Father on Earth when the system known as Gliese 581 beckoned, quickly renamed Sola by its colonists.

It didn't keep Eli on Angel, either. He'd trained as a meteorologist to report for the colony's Vid feeds, but Angel, Sola's fourth planet, had weather only a vacation planner could love. Consistent. Boring. Before career stupor could claim him, he made plans to re-train. Then he learned about the Diablo consortium.

At that point, they were really only looking for grunt labour for their exploration of the third planet. The priorities were to find water or indigenous life. Either would make Diablo valuable. Otherwise Earth was pushing hard to use the planet as a thermonuclear testing ground and waste dump—they'd already messed up Mars that way and needed another lifeless landscape for their experiments. Eli's qualifications gave him an edge for the consortium's expedition. He knew how to operate spectroscopes, nephelometers, solarimeters and the like. In a pinch he could give assistance to Dr. Howarth, the expedition's hydro-specialist, that the other grunts couldn't offer. He looked forward to the mental challenge. It was only a coincidence that Dr. Andrea Howarth turned out to be one of the most beautiful women he'd ever seen. When he finally met her, they did little more than exchange names because she was lined up for one of the innumerable Vid-news interviews she offered like royal audiences.

It didn't bother him that the crew quickly translated his surname Marone into "moron", like so many schoolmates had done before them. But the fitness facilities on the *Diablo Venture* were atrocious. When muscles could be kept in shape by electro-stim, why would anyone want to work up a sweat? So the exercise wheel had been overlooked when the ship's cooling system was installed, and by the time Eli finished his daily one-hour run the compartment felt like a sauna.

Compared to that, conditions on Diablo's surface were at least dry. Eli volunteered for surface duty the other crew didn't want, and found he enjoyed it.

That was what had made him think he could win the Marathon.

#

He admitted that he was lost the next morning, after the crevice had regurgitated him onto a flat plain and a lull in the storm showed him that the course markings for the marathon had vanished. Buried by new sand. Or he'd wandered so far that he couldn't see them from the top of a high dune. Either way, it was justification for calling the *Venture* to get a fix on his position. That was allowed by the rules. Unfortunately it was denied by the laws of electronics: you couldn't call orbit with a broken radio. He glared at the blank display screen. His sunsuit had an emergency locator built into it, but without radio contact the *Venture* crew would assume he had a real emergency. That meant sending down a landing craft—a big expense just to bail out one crewman the rest already called *moron*.

He couldn't be far off track—he'd only travelled a half-hour or so before the intensity of the storm had forced him to stop and hide. And just a few months earlier he'd overflown the course three times with Governor Juarez. He should be able to spot familiar landmarks, limited as they were. Unless the sandstorm had changed those, too. He wiped his goggles and looked at the man-sized boulder he'd hidden behind. On the windward side it had swollen into a humped creature of prehistory with a long, curving tail.

Epsilon base was nearly due west from his position, but Diablo's magnetic field was subject to a lot of local interference, and navigating by compass over a distance of a hundred kilometres he could easily miss a fifty-meter tower flanked by hills and dunes.

The locator tempted him again.

No. He could survive another day or two, even without the water cached at the waypoints. If he didn't find the course by then, it would make little difference where the lander had to pick him up.

He took the best directional reading he could, wrapped the mask of the sunsuit over his lower face, and began to walk.

#

If not for the governor, Eli wouldn't have considered the marathon. Juarez was a running fanatic—had competed in the brutal *Marathon des Sables* four times back on Earth, in Morocco. When he was assigned to govern Angel, he opined that the planet was too friendly. There weren't enough physical challenges to test a man's mettle. He had a vision that the Sola system could flourish through the development of niche tourism, and was fiercely opposed to the nuclear pollution of one of its worlds. When he learned that a human could survive in the polar regions of the sand-swept third planet nearly unaided, he was rapturous. He quickly conceived of the *Maratón de Diablo*, right in his new backyard.

Once Juarez had settled on the Beta and Epsilon drilling stations as the end points, he needed to find a route that would stretch the 170 kilometres between the rigs into something closer to the 250-kilometre course he wanted. Somehow he found out that Eli was a runner. Refusing to help the governor wasn't an option.

Then Eli had become a convert, almost as enthusiastic about the project as his temporary boss, and together they surveyed the wasteland until they both needed treatment for mild sand blindness. They found a route Juarez thought was perfect, and he became determined that he and Eli would challenge it together, along with the toughest men and women the colony of Angel could offer. The governor even announced a transportation subsidy to lure competitors, because passage between the two planets was not cheap. The response was modest, but Juarez was undeterred.

The only thing that could stop him was cancer.

#

Sunlight was like a living thing on Diablo. Sola was a red dwarf star, but it was still luminous and it was *close*, only eleven million kilometres away, burning like a great eye in the greenish sky. Eli could swear that its rays bent around corners, crept into cracks, and spread like oil. Andrea Howarth had told him that if it weren't for the planet's high albedo from all the brilliant white sand, the surface would have been a scorching miasma of unbreathable gases. Which was exactly how he experienced it at first. He pictured the cilia in his lungs crisping like hair over a candle flame. But he got used to the heat.

Or so he'd thought.

More than four days in a furnace had begun to suck his cells dry, and his desiccated bronchial tubes protested with a relentless urge to cough. His sunsuit was company issue—not as good as some of the other competitors could afford to buy. But it was advertised as being able to capture sixty-eight percent of the moisture he exhaled, which was re-used to moisten inhaled air, or stored in small bladders within the lining as drinking water for emergencies. Eli had tried that once. A whole day's hard work had produced a few mouthfuls, and it had tasted terrible.

The mylar skin of the suit was almost perfectly reflective; the loose fit and porous inner lining were meant to allow evaporation. But where sweat could get out, superheated ground air could get in. It was a trade-off: he wasn't directly grilled by Sola's radiation but felt like a filet in a convection oven. The thermo gauge on his left sleeve was as hypnotic as a rattlesnake.

Fifty-two Celsius degrees. Without the suit, the proteins in his brain would have been like egg whites in a frying pan. Even with it, his body needed every one of its cooling systems in high gear: the blood vessels under his skin were fully dilated and his heart pumped hot blood into them as quickly as they could take it; millions of sweat glands opened and closed in sequence, trying to cover him with a salty slick in just the right volume to evaporate efficiently without falling in wasteful drops. He'd used up the last of his drinking water. A sweat requirement of five litres or more per day meant that, before nightfall, his body would be using osmosis to draw water out of the less important organs to dilute his thickening bloodstream. The sunsuit preserved some perspiration, but cooling was considered more important, so most of the vaporized sweat escaped and drifted away. He imagined an ever-so-thin cloud surrounding him, and wondered if Howarth could detect his trail.

A spell of dizziness made him stop. A bad sign. His body fluids were probably down by nearly ten percent. He looked back the way he'd come. Each of the drilling rigs had one or two surface vehicles, so it was conceivable that one might be sent out from Beta after a crewman in trouble. But there wouldn't be much point. Smaller sandstorms had whipped up every six or seven hours after the big one. Just often enough to remove any sign of his passage.

He triggered the emergency locator patch with an angry slap, then realized that there was no way to tell if it was working.

#

"What's all this gear set up to look for? Mineral deposits?"

Howarth gave him a look as if he'd made a bad smell. It couldn't make her ugly, but it did make her even more intimidating. He excused her irritability because she was under a lot of pressure to find something that would keep Earth off their backs, and time was running out.

"No. We've already done mineral surveys. We need to find water. It's too expensive to bring from Angel. We can process oxygen out of ore, but it requires huge amounts of energy, and hydrogen is harder to come by on Diablo. Far better if we can find a good supply of liquid water or concentrated vapour."

"It's a desert planet."

"That doesn't mean there's no water. Just no rain. There could be deep groundwater somewhere. If Diablo once had seas there could be layers of metamorphic rock hundreds of kilometres below the surface, releasing its water because of heat and pressure. Magma would carry it closer to the surface."

"Diablo has volcanoes?"

"Surprisingly not. But there could still be pockets of magma with water dissolved in it. We drill down, release the pressure, and the water bubbles out like the foam on your favourite beer."

"A beer that's been shaken. Creating our own volcano doesn't sound all that safe."

"Are you here to help me, Marone? Or just annoy me?"

"Sorry."

"And when you're trying to look contrite, don't stare at my breasts."

Eli flapped his jaw, but couldn't think of a response.

"Anyway, a comet impact could have left deposits, too. *How* it got here doesn't concern me. What

I want to know is where it is." She gave his hand a light swat and calibrated the LIDAR herself.

"So you've found some?"

"We've found water vapour. What we have to do is track where it's coming from. Trace it back to the source."

"By infrared."

"In part, but with the winds so variable on Diablo, the vapour shows up as a swath or a smudge, rather than a plume. Not so helpful for pinpointing its source. Which is why you and your friends keep going down to the surface to collect air samples for me."

"They're no friends of mine. And that sounds like an awful lot of hit and miss."

Her blue eyes rolled toward the compartment ceiling, drawing his gaze to the smooth skin of her neck. "I thought you were a meteorologist. Didn't you ever do isotope tracing?"

"Water isotopes? Oh. I see what you mean." Evaporation caused water to lose some of its heavier isotopes, like the molecules with ^{18}O and ^{17}O, a depletion that increased over time. So isotope concentrations could reveal a lot about the vapour's travels. Chemical comparison could even place the body of water it came from. At least, that was the way it worked on a watery world like Earth or Angel. "But I've never heard of it being done with anything but liquid water."

"You work with what you've got." Howarth scowled. "We make educated guesses, take samples, and look for matches."

"Any likely targets?"

"Not a goddamn thing." She sighed. "There are water isotopes all over the place, in concentrations much higher than they should be—five or ten times higher—but almost no mixing. For Diablo, water of ^{16}O and ^{2}H seems to be the standard. Then each site has one additional isotope and almost no trace of any others."

"You'd expect more?"

"Of course. We've taken samples from a dozen sites in six different zones of the planet. The isotope mixture reflects the original water source plus the cycle the water molecules have been through: the number of evaporations and condensations, and what form the condensate took. Distance travelled...through what kind of conditions. It doesn't make sense that every place we sample has two main forms of the molecule and almost no others. And there's no rhyme or reason to how they're placed, either. If there's any pattern at all, it's more than I can see." She wasn't a woman who could be complacent about failure.

A sudden thought struck him. "Are you looking for water just for our use? Or because where there's water there might be indigenous life?"

Howarth actually looked sheepish. "It doesn't hurt to keep an open mind. And open eyes. There is life on Diablo—tiny stuff. As for anything more complex...well, there have been rumours."

"You mean somebody's seen something."

"No. But items have mysteriously moved from one place to another at camp sites. Or even gone missing. Always containers of water or water-based liquid." She looked into his eyes, as if daring him to laugh. "Maybe it's nothing. That's not my field. My priority is figuring out where those water isotopes are coming from."

Eli was suddenly hopeful. His looks and personality didn't impress her, but maybe he'd learned what would.

"It's possible you'll spot something I've missed, when you're down there," she said, turning away. "But that doesn't mean I'll sleep with you."

#

It was the sixth day. He sucked at the storage bladders of his suit every few hours. The scant drops they provided did little more than tease his thirst. The suit wasn't designed to collect urine, so he used an empty water bottle for that. His gear included a filter/purifier for liquid water that no-one had ever expected to use on Diablo—good enough to remove urea and other impurities, he figured. But it still took a major effort of will to sip at the liquid produced. Squeamishness was something he couldn't afford. He was in a survival situation now. If his locator had been functioning, the *Venture* would have sent someone for him. So he had to assume the race had continued after the sandstorms, and no-one had realized he wasn't on the course. Either that or they'd flown over while he was unconscious—hidden in shade, or dug into a deep hole to shelter from the bitter night. He didn't want to think about that.

Stomach cramps had begun the evening before: water was stolen from the gut by the bloodstream to rebalance its salt content. Muscle pains would be next. He was rapidly losing strength. And he'd begun to hallucinate. Not about water—not yet. But some of the whitest patches of the dunes seemed to change positions while he wasn't looking. That couldn't be good.

#

"Promise you'll run the race without me," Juarez had rasped over the video link from his deathbed.

"It's all organized and ready to go, sir. The competitors are *en route*. They've raised lots of money, too. Don't worry, the race will go ahead."

"No, I mean *you*, Eli. Run it for me. Win it for me."

"But sir, I really should...."

"To hell with your work. It can wait a few days. That'll give Howarth a chance to catch up on her interview requests. Must be tough working with a scientist who looks like a Vid star, hmmm? Have you had a chance to do some personal *probe* sampling with that one yet?"

"Governor Juarez...."

The dying man laughed, and it turned into a horrible cough. "That's another reason you have to run the race, Eli. To make people sit up and notice you. You're too good at fading into the background. You deserve better than that."

There'd been no response Eli could make, except a promise he dreaded. But he made it, and he kept it, never expecting it would lead him to follow the governor to the grave.

#

The precious drops of water from his suit storage were sweet now. Almost no salt left in his sweat. That process would have begun in the first few days of the race, along with some other adaptations to the heat that were probably keeping him alive. He was more grateful than ever for his persistent workout routine, and even the sweltering conditions of *Venture*'s exercise wheel. He'd read about some of the physiological changes in runners' bodies. More efficient muscles burned less energy and so produced less heat. Heat shock proteins kept body cells from losing the folded shape they needed to function. And altered enzymes slowed chemical processes that otherwise began to run amok with higher body temperatures. Experienced distance runners could still function with core temperatures that would make non-runners collapse at death's door.

In spite of all that, his brain was beginning to lose its grip on reality. The most dazzling patches of sand had begun to move, even as he watched. He lost his balance and fell to his knees, and white patches seemed to scurry away.

No. They *did* scurry. He slammed the ground with his hand, and a half dozen white shapes jittered a meter farther away.

They were alive.

He stayed still and waited to see if any would creep closer, then struggled to his feet, nearly passing out. But he saw them move. Goddamn right, he did.

There was complex life on Diablo.

Stunned, he watched the white shapes form a circle around him. His best estimate put them at 25 to 30 centimetres across, nearly round but a little elongated toward one end. The trailing end, he thought, as he watched them move. An image flashed into his mind: a flounder from Earth's oceans—that's what the things reminded him of—a flat disk of a fish, hugging the dirt, invisible unless it chose not to be. He still couldn't be sure where a creature ended and the sand began—their camouflage was that perfect. Did that mean there were predators, too? Or was it just a natural occurrence that didn't signify anything? Maybe Diablo life didn't see the way humans did. Those questions and hundreds more would be up to the xenologists to answer. Eli's prime concern was survival. If anything, his find gave him even more incentive to live. He'd return to civilization as the discoverer of a whole new species. Earth would have to leave Diablo alone.

One of them sparkled. And another. And soon a third. He watched closely for five or ten minutes. It looked like the flounders' skin was covered with dots that changed their reflectivity, creating fluctuating patterns.

At will? That would mean it was for a purpose.

Like talking. Communication by visual pattern wasn't unusual, even among Earth life.

Were they trying to talk to *him?*

He turned his head and saw that the line of flounders was no longer a circle. The ones behind him were much closer. Those in front had moved farther away. And they all seemed to be pointing in the same direction, the direction his body was facing. What could that mean?

They moved again, the rear ones nearly touching his heels, the forward ones gliding a few centimetres ahead. His brain had made the right interpretation: they were not only moving forward, but trying to move *him* forward, too. He experimented by taking two steps. The lead flounders slid ahead, the others closed in behind. He tried it again with the same result. Then he began a careful walk, and tried to gauge how fast he could go without treading on the ones in front. He needn't have worried—they could move at least as quickly as his diminished strength would propel him. The curved line ahead of him became more pointed.

He thought of saying something, but the obvious cliché made him giggle. Who knew if they even had leaders? And what was the point of making him move at all? Could they somehow have deduced his plight, and be taking him to safety?

Was he being led?

Or herded?

#

"You're crazy to be a part of this stupid race. Besides, I've run out of samples. What am I supposed to do while you're tramping across a desert trying to kill yourself?"

Eli refrained from mentioning Governor Juarez's suggestion about Howarth's interview schedule. Instead he said, "Maybe there's another force at work that changes the isotope content in water vapour on Diablo. Some chemical reaction to the high level of solar radiation? Or the different spectrum of a red dwarf? Or...I don't know, higher gravity. Diablo's a lot larger than Earth. Maybe isotope depletion doesn't happen the same way here. You could check out things like that."

The cold look she gave him was no more than he expected. What caught his interest was her condemnation of the marathon. Was she really so irritated about the delay? Or could he dare to hope there was more to it than that?

As he left the lab and bounced along the corridor, he shook his head. He wasn't even in the heat of the desert and already he was having delusions.

#

Delusions. That's what these silent white pixies were. Will o' the wisps—sun devils, from his eyes playing tricks on him.

Yes, that was the right name for them: sun devils. The inhabitants of a planet called Diablo, running their own marathon as they urged him on. But not for much longer. He'd already fallen four times. Or was it more? The last time he only got back to his feet after he felt scaly flutterings against his skin, where the mask had slipped away from his face. There was a slight rise ahead. He'd go as far as the top of the rise, and see what he could see. If there was nothing more than the same featureless desert....

But as he neared the crest he noticed a band of brighter white just a short way off. With a few more steps he began to comprehend what he was seeing: a shallow hollow in the sand—dish-shaped, about fifty or sixty metres across.

Full of sun devils.

He stepped to the highest ground, and the carpet of white shapes began a barrage of flashes that would rival the photographers at an Earth video premiere.

Something struck him about the nearest ones. They weren't all the same size. In fact, very few were as large as the ones that had brought him. Most were only about half as wide.

Children? Could this be a colony?

The burning of his skin didn't stop a chill from welling up inside him.

He remembered what Andrea Howarth had said about missing containers of water. Of course. Water would be the most precious commodity on the planet. Any source of water would be ravenously desired. Especially for the children.

Even a source like him.

He took a step back and felt something slither from under his heel. Then others began bumping at his feet and ankles. Urging him forward.

Not bloody likely.

The sand ahead changed colour beneath a slick of white that oozed forward. They were coming for him. Could they overwhelm him if he stood his ground? Climb his suit? Catch him if he tried to run?

He needed a distraction. He tugged his water bottle from his pocket. There was only a centimetre of liquid at the bottom, but maybe that would be enough.

He popped it open and lobbed it a few meters into the pack.

As expected, the devils near the bottle swarmed it. But the leading edge of the tide barely reacted. They kept approaching. They'd only be diverted by something bigger—more irresistible.

His suit. There wasn't enough water in its reservoirs for him to drink, but the lining might still be semi-saturated.

With a rasping whimper he peeled it off and tossed it onto the encroaching line. He took a stumbling hop to his left, and began to run across the open desert, naked except for his boots, fuelled only by cannibalized body cells and a heavy dose of adrenaline. Terror carried him a long way.

The roar in the air was very close before he consciously heard it. His shambling jog slowed to a halt and he looked around, up and down. There was a large patch of white on the sand, only twenty meters behind him. But that wasn't where the noise was coming from. He turned again, and saw the thing drifting into his field of vision from above.

A lander. Settling down onto the desert about ten meters away.

He stood numbly trying to swallow, as the clouds of sand subsided and the door began to rise. There was a shape in the doorway. Human. Female.

Howarth.

And Eli was naked.

"My, my, Marone," she said, looking him over. "You'll try anything to get my attention, won't you?"

#

Blowing sand had crippled the lander sent for the marathon competitors and they'd had to share cramped quarters with the operators of the Beta drilling rig for five days. Though Eli was quickly discovered to be missing, the *Venture's* other lander was overdue for one of the periodic strip-downs the planet's harsh conditions dictated. The pilots were permitted only one flyover, so they'd made it at night, when Eli's body temperature would stand out from the cold sand.

"I was in a hole," he said quietly.

"You certainly were."

As he'd already guessed, Beta's tractor had been sent out, but soon had no trail to follow. There'd been no need for high-powered optics on the *Venture*. And thermal imagery had been stymied because his sunsuit did too good a job reflecting the sunlight. Just like all that white sand.

"But that bare ass of yours lit up my instruments like a solar flare. Except in reverse," Howarth cackled. He tried to enjoy her smile, but he didn't dare copy it for fear his dried-out skin would split.

He avoided mirrors for weeks afterward—he looked more like a mummy than a man. But the doctor said he'd recover without any organ damage. And, yes, he'd go down on record as the man who'd made first contact with the natives of Sola three, known as Diablo.

He told everyone about the light show on the sun devils' backs, and how he was sure it was a form of communication. Whether by intuition or something more, he thought he knew another secret about them, too.

"Your pockets of water isotopes?" he said to Howarth. "It's the devils—they make them."

"*What?*"

"Sure. Most creatures that form social groups have ways to tell members of the group from non-members. That's their way. They use manipulated water molecules. Not quite like pheromones, though some of the functions might be the same."

She was sceptical, but it turned out to be easy to confirm. Devils were readily bribed with water, though they almost never flashed any messages when they knew humans were present. Eli said they were snobs. If you didn't give off the right isotope, you just weren't worth talking to.

"Why did they talk to you down there?" Howarth asked a few days later.

"They didn't." Eli could finally smile. "They were talking amongst themselves. Planning. Because I didn't smell right, they decided I couldn't be sentient, so I wouldn't understand what they were talking about."

She gave a rueful nod, but there was a new air of respect to it. Then a bleep signalled a radio call, and she answered it.

"*Who?* Net-News? An interview? Sure, I guess. *Oh.* Oh, of course." Eli thought he saw a look of annoyance pass over her face. But then she gave a shrug and looked at him with a genuine smile. She held out the radio microphone.

"It's for you."

\#   \#   \#

BODY OF OPINION

AT FIRST, IT WAS A GREAT BODY—I was glad to have it.

My girlfriend Evvy liked it, too. When I surprised her with it the first night, her wide eyes told me she thought I'd be a lot more fun in bed now. More muscle than my original body, among other things. She looked me up and down. Especially down.

Then when she raised her eyes again, they were a lot greener than I remembered. In fact, it wasn't Evvy's face at all. It was some foxy stranger with a nicer body and Hollywood hair.

I must have jumped in surprise because I heard Evvy's voice coming from the fox's mouth. "Whatsa matter with you?"

WTF, could she have had transplants, too? And kept it a surprise?

No. No way Evvy could afford that on a hair tech's salary. Mine had cost every penny I had, including my inheritance. And if I'd got it the legal way, through a licensed Replacium, it would have cost more than I could ever earn in a lifetime driving cab.

While I was thinking about that, her face and body turned back into Evvy's again.

I figured it was a hallucination. A side-effect of the anti-rejection drugs I was taking. Something like that. Scared the crap out of me. Even now, after days of mind-numbingly dull reading, the most I've got is a half-assed theory about what's happened to me.

I guess I had it coming. I knew some of the stuff at Hack's Discount Emporium was probably stolen—what did I care? I didn't go there expecting to find transplant parts. I was just looking for another TV. Then I saw Hack showing off this complete vat-grown replacement body and...well, a guy can do stupid things when he's just been told he has cancer.

There's Hack saying it's got certification papers from the farm and everything. I wanted to believe him. So did the other customer, in a wheelchair, asking his questions with a synth-voice from his neuro-link. They agreed on a price. I offered a thousand more. Not much, but enough. Hack said, "Sorry, kid" and drew up the transfer file for me. I watched the wheelchair roll away in slow motion. The guy couldn't even lift an arm to give me the finger.

I didn't look too hard at the papers. I mean, I skimmed over them—quality control bullshit about the parts vats and generic synth-DNA and the safety features to prevent deviant cell replication. Warranty stuff. Legal fine print I couldn't even read when I borrowed Evvy's eyeskins. If I had, I would have clued in that none of the farms makes a full-body unit that comes with the spinal cord and brainstem.

The operation was done in a real hospital, though. Hack knew a guy. Same anaesthetics, same anti-rejection shots, same nanites to clean up all the connections and seal the incisions without scarring. The only difference was the government never heard about it, which was why the clinic could charge twice the price. It was all I could afford, but what I couldn't afford was to be on a three-year waiting list. I paid cash.

The hard part was over. That's what I thought.

Soon after I started seeing another woman's face and body in Evvy's place, there were other clues that something wasn't kosher. Like my golf swing—suddenly my chronic slice was gone and I was hitting close to par. I was a little surprised when I climbed into my cab and tried to change gears with a stick-shift. But I was feeling like a kid again, that's all.

It wasn't all. It didn't explain the green-eyed hottie with Evvy's voice. Or that sometimes when I walked out to my cab I'd get a vision of a shiny black Caddy instead. Or the jolt of pain from my new knee that made me remember a ski hill with a bad bump and a big, hard tree. See, I don't ski. Never have, never wanted to.

Even a college dropout can see the writing on the wall if you ram his mug into the brickwork enough times.

Hack had lied. It wasn't a vat-grown body he'd sold me. It had to be black market—previously enjoyed. Hopefully a back-door deal from the morgue, and not a live donor who provided the chassis without his consent.

When I finally admitted all that to myself, I lost the lunch I'd just finished, moved downwind twenty feet, and sat on the curb for a long time, thinking. See, there wasn't anything I could do about it. My old body was worm food for weeks by then. And anyway, the new body was still good.

Except for those weird visions. They had me spooked. Waking up from one stomach-churning nightmare, I finally decided that my only chance of staying sane was to figure out where all that crap was coming from.

That's when I started reading. I hadn't hit the books so hard since I'd dropped out of med school. Evvy didn't get laid for weeks.

#

I still haven't got a real explanation. Only a few puzzles pieces that don't belong together, but might look like a whole picture if you squint hard enough. Odd bits of info from DNA experiments, studies of people with brain damage, and philosophers sitting around picking their noses.

The key thing, I figure, is that the brain doesn't see what the eyes see. It takes too much processing power to analyze every single detail our eyes take in and then reprocess it all over again every time the light changes or our eyes move. So the brain makes assumptions. It keeps templates in storage, and tries to match them to objects in view. Some might even be from racial memory—I don't know. Others are learned through repetition over a lifetime. If it's a lifetime of privilege, I guess every car starts to look like a Cadillac and all women with dark hair have green eyes and slim waists.

Basically I was seeing somebody else's memories of what the world looked like. Thing is, how could that happen without the other guy's brain? That's where all the memories are kept, right?

Maybe not.

I had to dig through some of my old med school websites to find out that memories are stored by capping the genes of neurons with methyl groups—something called DNA methylation. It's supposed to happen in the hippocampus and cerebral cortex—I never read about anybody suggesting the process happens with DNA in other parts of the body. But I figure I'm living proof. Maybe I'll write somebody a memo.

The kicker is that, after a couple of sexless weeks, the best explanation I could come up with still got me absolutely nowhere.

#

Evvy was shaking me. The sheets were soaked, and I was breathing like a cuckolded husband was on my tail.

"You had another nightmare," she said. "It's all right. Evvy's here."

She even looked like Evvy. Not the green-eyed woman. And not the faceless silhouette that had just been burned into my mind by the dream. A silhouette with something sharp in its hand. A memory of death.

"It's OK, baby. It's OK. Maybe you just need a little sugar." She took my hand and pressed it to her chest, but I pulled it away.

I wasn't about to tell Evvy that the body she was trying to seduce had once belonged to somebody else. I also couldn't tell her I was sometimes seeing another woman's face when I looked at her. And especially not that I was beginning to like it.

I had to find the other woman.

It wasn't that I'd fallen in love with her, or any crap like that, but think about it: whoever my body originally belonged to, he had money. Maybe there was still a way to get my hands on some of it. How else to find him but to track down the woman whose face was embedded into the very DNA of his cells?

Yeah, I know. One woman among the millions in New York City.

You've probably already realized what took me nearly a week to figure out: if the memories from my body could turn Evvy into this woman, what did I expect to happen when I looked at a dark-haired stranger on the street?

I saw her everywhere.

It was ludicrous, but I couldn't stop. As if it was an addiction my body had brought with it.

I did find her, though.

I turned away from the counter of a donut shop and there she was, trying to dodge out of the way of the coffee that spilled from my hand as I jumped in shock. She nearly made it too. I tried to tell her that a coffee stain probably wouldn't show on a brown skirt once it dried, but the look she gave me could've turned my coffee to vinegar. I followed her to the street and tried to get her talking.

"I'm sorry for your loss."

"What did you say?"

"Your loss. You had a death in the family recently, didn't you? Your husband? Sorry about your husband."

"I don't know what you're talking about. Please leave me alone."

"I was sure I saw you at the funeral. Was it your brother? Or a friend of the family?"

She stopped and turned on me. "Look. Nobody in my family has died recently." That was the truth—I could see it in her eyes. "Nobody I *know* has died recently." Not true. "So for God's sake go away and leave me alone." She stalked off and I followed her from as far back as I could manage. I didn't want her calling a cop.

From there, I had to do things the hard way, picking up fares in front of her office building.

Sara. Her name was Sara—it was the first thing I had to learn before I could ask my passengers about her. It was also the only thing most of them knew, except that she was a secretary at a law firm. Eventually I noticed that the ones in the most expensive suits were people who worked for the same firm as she did. One of them had to know the man in her life that had recently died.

Only there wasn't one.

She had a husband, but he was still kicking. No brothers. Bosses were mostly men, but also demonstrably alive. Hell, she didn't even get mail delivered to her door.

I'd found a needle in a haystack, only to learn there was no thread dangling from it.

About then I noticed I was walking with a limp. The muscles of my left leg weren't obeying my brain the way they ought to. I knew that couldn't be good.

\#

It took another weekend and plenty of the Boar's Head pub's finest draft to come up with another approach. I'd check Sara's company client list. Maybe one of them had been infatuated with her. Maybe she'd even offered extra services on the side.

A TV private eye would just charm one of the other secretaries and the file would be in his hand and a woman between his sheets before the next sponsor break. Apparently I don't have that much charisma. It was only a sudden inspiration that made me pick the mousiest girl in the office and hint that helping me out might get Sara into trouble. Worked like a charm. The woman didn't offer to sleep with me, but I was OK with that.

The identity of my body's original owner was one hell of a surprise.

Senator Fielding Campion. *A senator,* for God's sake. The Caddy must have been his limo—the stick shift I'd remembered would belong to a Mercedes or Beemer or Lexus, for when he wanted to drive himself and impress a woman. Like Sara.

The Mouse all but confirmed my guess. She'd seen the looks that had passed between Sara and the senator. And the tears when he'd died of a brain tumour.

The fact that he was a public figure made things easier to verify. The date of his death seemed right. A little money to a hacker acquaintance of mine got me into his hospital records. I found scars left by tendon surgery and an elbow repair from before they started using nanites for cosmetic purposes. Everything matched. It was his body I was wearing.

The knowledge didn't stop my flashbacks, but I hoped it would let me get some sleep. And it might have, if not for the rest of what I found out.

#

"It's another woman, isn't it?"

"*What?* What are you talking about?"

"Why you're never home. And you never have any money to spend on me. And why...why you never want me no more. That way."

"Jesus, Evvy. I'm not giving it to another woman."

"So how come you walk around like you been riding a horse all day?"

I laughed. I laughed so much it hurt. Especially when Evvy threw an ashtray at me. But what really hurt was knowing that she'd noticed what I was pretending not to. That my new legs, bought and paid for, were turning out to be a chump's bargain, becoming stiff and slow, turning my New York cabbie's hustle into a geriatric shuffle.

"Don't damage the merchandise," I said.

"What do I care?" she answered. "Seems to me you've got a hose that needs replacing."

#

Flashes of a room. Fancy—maybe an expensive hotel. Bodies circling each other—Campion and someone else, in conflict. Verbal sparring—no contact. Then a raised hand with something sharp in it. Poisonous. But moving away, having already done its worst. Moment of panic...heart racing, nerves tingling. A sudden desperate need to speak. Can't think of the words. Too late. Too late!

I snapped straight. Spilled coffee again, this time all over the table in front of me. I hadn't even been sleeping, just staring into space thinking about how Campion's funeral had been attended by thousands who were told the popular senator had passed away after a brave battle against a brain tumour. The tumour hadn't killed him. Campion had been murdered. I knew it in my gut that used to be his.

A lot of deep brain tumours still can't be cured outright, even with lots of money to spend. But nanites can do a lot, and Campion's tumour shouldn't have killed him for another year or more. Somebody else had done the job. So either the doctors had missed that, or the family had needed to keep it quiet.

Either scenario could mean money for me.

I mean, I had an obligation to find the son-of-a-bitch who'd killed my body, didn't I? Not for vengeance—that doesn't help anybody. A small financial arrangement would be best.

I just needed to figure out who the killer was, and then get some proof. For that I had to find a motive.

Campion was a Harvard grad. Two tours of duty in the Air Force: Iran and the second Korean conflict. Inherited the senate seat from his father, more or less. Made a name for himself, though. Progressive. Popular. Wife with a respectable pedigree—a son and a daughter who didn't get into more trouble at school than a good press secretary could cover up. Lots of talk that he was already being groomed by his party for a potential shot at the White House in ten or fifteen years.

Then there were some sour notes. He took a sudden conservative stance when some key fertility legislation came up, and his women constituents hadn't liked that. He began to waffle on health care technology and reform. There were even rumours that he delivered political favours to some high rollers in return for services rendered.

Something had begun to knock the white knight off his charger. The brain tumour? They sure as hell can change a man's personality, but he'd shown no other signs of that. It was another puzzle. I was getting goddamn tired of them.

#

Green eyes and long, dark lashes. Shoulder-length jet hair with a TV commercial sheen. A fresh face that belonged in *Good Housekeeping*, and a figure straight out of *Playboy*. Sara. The girl of my schizophrenia.

When I tried to picture her, I couldn't. She only came unbidden—a flagrant tease of the mind from a perverse body. Not that I cared. I thought of her because something told me she was a key link in the mystery I was trying to unravel. That's all. But sometimes when I thought of her I'd suddenly find myself back at Campion's death scene, reliving his final moment of helplessness. One time it was even stranger: as he was dying I kept picturing a number, over and over. It was important. A code of some kind, maybe. But for what?

Then I dropped a fare off on Broadway and stopped for a coffee. As I came back to the street I had a compulsion to turn around and look at this big, fancy-ass bank. The building faded and all I could see was the code in numbers of fire. I stood there, stunned, until an old woman ran her shopping cart into the back of my knees and my traitor legs collapsed. Spilled my coffee, of course, but at least now I knew: the number was for online banking.

The next trick was to figure out what name Campion had used with it. I tried all of his official titles, his family members, even his pets. Then I remembered he had two middle names: Justin and Traynor. I typed in *Justin Traynor* and got to a login page. It asked for a password—I entered the number—and I was *in*: Campion's secret bank account. All four million dollars worth. Swear to God. I'd never seen so many zeroes. It was a simple thing to move some of them to my own bank.

And that's when I knew something was really wrong with me. Because I started thinking about Sara again, and somehow I knew—I *knew* that he'd set that money aside for her. It was what he'd been thinking about so hard as he died.

There was only one thing I could do.

Spend it. But judiciously. For one thing, I was going to need it for medical treatment. My legs were worse than ever and my left arm had begun to play tricks on me too. For another, I needed a new place to live. Evvy'd kicked me out after our last fight. Too bad I couldn't tell her about the money—I'd like to have seen her face.

As for Sara, she looked to be doing all right on a legal secretary's salary and all. What she didn't know wouldn't hurt her. That's what I told myself.

#

It didn't take a genius to figure out that money isn't a lot of use if your body is headed for the trash heap. I dug deeper into Campion's medical history. Maybe the guy'd had Parkinson's disease or ALS or something that hadn't shown symptoms while he was alive, but was playing hell with his body now. Maybe I could get a black market treatment. Without an official transplant registration number, a legitimate doctor wouldn't treat me.

There wasn't any disease like that in his file, though. His tumour had been in a part of the brain called the *anterior cingulate gyrus*, an area that handles judgment and evaluative processes. I couldn't see how that would give his limbs progressive paralysis, especially since they were no longer connected to the original head.

No sign of a motive for his murder, either. Or maybe too many—doesn't every politician gather enemies like a dog gathers fleas?

Then one web page made me sit up and take notice. Campion had given a press conference to announce new legislation he planned to introduce. It would have set a limit on the amount of transplanted body tissue a person could have at any given time: forty-nine percent of their body mass. Sounded pretty arbitrary to me, but he claimed to have evidence that excessive transplantation could have serious consequences.

No shit. I was proof of that. Except Campion hadn't been talking about grave-jobs. He meant even vat-grown transplants could be dangerous if they made up the majority of the recipient's body. That wouldn't have been welcome news. Not only did it make the whole body-farming industry look bad, it also pissed on the hopes of a lot of people whose bodies were beginning to fail them. Rich, powerful people.

I followed the story, skipping ahead through the months, and found what I expected to find. Three weeks before his death Campion withdrew the legislation. The research it was based on had been discredited, he said.

Somebody had got to him. He went into seclusion—wouldn't appear in public or meet with anyone. Soon after that, he was dead.

There had to be a connection—I could feel it in our bones, his and mine. Except withdrawing the legislation should have satisfied the people who were fighting it. They wouldn't have needed to kill him.

Unless he'd planned a double-cross.

Only someone close to him would have known that.

It was time to talk to Sara.

#

While my cab was stuck in traffic, my mind hit cruising speed.

What if I did get proof that Campion had been murdered? What if I knew beyond a doubt that it was connected to the transplant legislation—that his original evidence was the real deal, and millions of people might be at risk? What was I going to do? Go to the media?

Stand in front of TV cameras and claim I knew all this because I was wearing the dead senator's body?

Even if people believed me, I was screwed. It would be like putting a target on my own back. Not to mention that the cops would try to connect me to the murder. At the very least I'd received stolen goods—something you can't exactly deny when you're wearing the evidence.

Why should I care about the public good anyway? Were this dead guy's cells turning me into some soft-spined *liberal*? I didn't want any part of that.

But, see, that was just the trouble. I had every part. Which part was in charge?

Did I own a replacement body? Or had Campion found himself a new head?

#

I was still thinking about that when Sara walked out of the building.

The first thing she saw was the fancy new leg braces I'd bought with her dead lover's money. I don't think she recognized my face.

"I need to speak to you," I said. "About Senator Campion."

I'd never really seen anybody stop as if they'd hit a brick wall, but she did. Her face drained of color, too.

"I don't know what you're talking about." She tried to hurry away.

"That's because I haven't started yet. Wait up! Or would you rather I just yell what I know?"

That stopped her again. I suggested we go for a coffee—from the look of her face I couldn't be sure any food would stay down. We found our way to the back of a dim restaurant.

"Before I say anything more, I want you to know I'm not a cop or anything like that. I don't work for the Campion family and their friends. Or enemies. I'm not interested in your love affair, either."

"Then what do you want?"

"I'll explain my connection later. First of all..." I sat down too heavily, my legs giving out. "Did you know the senator was murdered?"

She looked horrified. "No, he wasn't."

"He was—I'll tell you how I know in a minute. I think it was political, probably connected to his legislation about transplants. What do you know about that?"

"He withdrew it. What do you care, Mr...?"

"My name's not important. I care because...I've had a transplant myself. What was the danger that got Campion worked up about them? About excessive transplantation."

She shook her head. "I don't know the science. It was something about the nervous system connections. Brain load, I think. Too many new connections could become overwhelming beyond a certain threshold. Then the communication with the muscles and organs would begin to break down. He told me it would be fatal if the brain had to choose among priorities and dropped a connection to one of the vital organs."

I nodded. It explained a lot.

"Then what made him change his mind and withdraw the bill?"

She didn't give an answer. Just a good view of her shiny black hair.

"I need to know," I said. "It could lead me to his killer."

Her head snapped up. "You don't understand. It was his brain tumour."

"No, it wasn't. Someone poisoned him."

"I mean, it was his tumour that made him change his mind about the bill. He didn't want to. The tumour was in a part of the brain called the anterior...something."

"The anterior cingulate gyrus."

"Yes. It...it affected his will. His inhibitions, too." She gave a wan smile at some memory. "But the worst part was that it made him susceptible to suggestion."

The fog in my mind began to clear.

"And somebody found out about that. His party cronies? Maybe even the leaders?"

She nodded, and her green eyes filmed with tears.

"They exploited it. He tried to resist them, but he couldn't. Not forever. They'd keep at him about something, and gradually he'd agree. Then, afterward, he'd know what he'd done and hate himself." She looked straight into my eyes. Defiant. "They were turning him into a puppet. He couldn't live with that."

The final pieces clicked into place.

I hung my head and shook it like a punch-drunk boxer. Finally I managed a low croak.

"It was you. In the hotel room. You took the needle away from him."

"Yes." The word was a weak sob. "But it was too late. A huge overdose. He was in Hell...the guilt, the helplessness, and the pain of the headaches." Her heart tried to wrench itself through her throat. "*I loved him so much.*"

"Overdose. That explains why the organs and tissues were still usable."

"What?"

"Never mind."

There were other questions I could have asked. Instead I threw some bills on the table to pay for the coffee, and hauled myself to my feet.

"Wait," she said. "You have to tell me. What has any of this got to do with you? Why did you track me down?"

"I've got his body," I rasped. "A transplant. Someone has one sick sense of humour."

#

So now I'm in a wheelchair. It's state-of-the-art—Campion's money can buy the best. My synth voice sounds a lot like me, and I can steer the chair with my thoughts. Arm movements are a problem, though I can still do a few things with my right arm, thanks to mechanical motion enhancers. Unfortunately, my brain's connections to the neuro-link are failing too. No-one knows why.

I'm still trying to track down Campion's research source. Whoever it was seems to have gone into hiding, but I'll keep looking. Documents and files can be destroyed, but traces nearly always remain somewhere. Kind of like memories. If I get enough proof I'll send it to the media outlets and see what happens.

I saw Sara again, too. I went back to Hack's discount place, hoping against hope that he might have another body for sale. He pretended not to know me, and denied any involvement with body parts. But Sara was there. She'd quit her job and left her husband—I'd known that much, had kept track of her. And obviously she'd hit hard times if she had to shop at Hack's.

I set my wheelchair to make a printout while I rolled over to her. She recognized me, and if she tried to hide her dismay, the effort was a total failure.

"You're dishonouring his memory, you know that?" I said.

"What do you mean?"

"Destroying your life. He wouldn't have wanted that. In fact, I'd bet part of the reason he killed himself was to protect you. To keep your secret, before someone could get it out of him."

The green eyes filled with a mixture of horror and shame.

"You owe it to him to live. Be happy. Do your part to make the world a better place." It was cheesy, but probably true. I think by now I have a pretty good idea how Campion thought.

She tried to find something to say, but couldn't. Instead she leaned down and gave me an impulsive hug before she hurried away. That was when I slipped the printout into her pocket. One of the last movements this arm will ever make, I'm afraid. Nothing to be done about that. Especially not with the amount of money I kept for myself.

She'll make better use of all those millions, and Campion wanted her to have it.

I know what you're thinking: Campion's body has won.

You may be right. But if I've been stupid...well, I'll have a long time to think about that, sitting in this chair.

#   #   #

DEMOCRACY

 JAYNE SLAMMED THE WALL with the palm of her hand.

How could Foster do this to her? After she'd pulled off that interview last month with the Pakistani Prime Minister, just before the assassination attempt. And her series from within the Myanmar protest movement. There was buzz about the Pulitzer for that one. She wanted the Nicaraguan rebel assignment, to document the rebirth of the FDN after 30 years. Or at least the more subtle warfare of Washington politics. Instead...

"It's an island in the Indian Ocean."

"Davis...?"

"*Devis Varta*. Population of about a million and a half," Foster said. "The home of perfect democracy, they claim. They don't have any elected representatives. Every household has a computer and a 'net connection—every important issue of government is decided by a vote of all eligible citizens."

"You're kidding."

"They tell me it's the way democracy began, back in the ancient Greek city states." The editor's bushy grey eyebrows pushed another two tiers of wrinkles into his hairline. "Surprised you didn't know that."

"Give me a break, Ed. They were tribes. They could vote with a show of hands. How could anybody do that in the 21st Century? Why would they want to?"

"Maybe so they won't have a pack of ex-lawyers with their sticky hands in a citizen's pockets all the time. What matters, Connor, is that I'm telling you to look into it."

Jayne's response had been mid-way between a snarl and a whine. Colleagues called it her courtroom voice, after it had enabled her to squeeze the juice of considerable alimony from the dried rind that was her marriage.

"Seriously, Ed, can't you just get the information you need online? Something like that—there are bound to be a dozen Wikipedia entries. Not to mention the forums of the electoral reform geeks."

"They all say the same thing." He waved a dismissive arm, wafting a stale tang of old cigarette smoke from the pinstriped sleeve. "Because it all comes from the same source: the government of Devis Varta. Of course they say it works. It's kept them in power for seven years. A Prime Minister and twelve cabinet ministers to lead the government departments that were deemed absolutely necessary. They're paid staff, not politicians. There's no legislature. No Senate. No veto. No bullshit. That's what they say."

"They said 'No bullshit'?"

"I want you to find out what the average Joe says." He leaned the chair back. "Marjorie is already taking care of your bookings. Have a nice flight. Oh, and these are genteel people. Wear a dress."

Not on your life, she thought, remembering the dismissal. She slammed the wall again, then heard the glass door as it opened behind her.

"I'm pretty sure that's as bright as the light gets," Marjorie offered dryly, nodding at Jayne's raised hand. "Here's your flight and hotel information."

Jayne had barely shaken off the jet lag from her southeast Asia assignment only two weeks earlier. She had to admit a fondness for that part of the world, though, and her dark complexion served her well there. According to family lore, the Connors originally came from Sri Lanka or some place close to it. Faint childhood memories included a dottie great-grandmother who insisted people treat her like royalty. Didn't every family have one of those?

She popped some passionflower extract on the flight, washed down by chamomile tea she'd brought from home, and then a couple of melatonin capsules during the stopover in Colombo from a secret pouch sewn into her purse. After checking into the hotel on Devis Varta she slept for nearly twenty-four hours.

The room was brightly sunlit when she awoke. There were English instructions on a card by the phone, and she ordered a light breakfast from room service. While she was finishing her coffee there was a gentle knock at the door. A young man stood there in dun-coloured slacks and a loose white cotton shirt that draped nearly to his knees. He offered her an envelope. The note inside told her that the Minister of Governmental Affairs, Anshuman Rajamahendran, would be expecting her at eleven o'clock. The young man would lead her to him.

That gave her almost an hour to shower and dress. The messenger waited patiently in the hallway.

Outside the protection of the hotel's air conditioning, the syrupy atmosphere clung in her nostrils. It was thick like a New York summer smog, but perfumed with floral esters instead of hydrocarbons. The street was lined with palms. Traffic islands sprouted bright clusters of frangipani, and flowerboxes overflowed with orchids. The narrow alleyways and broader thoroughfares were scrupulously clean, confettied only with delicate flower petals instead of the candy bar wrappers of American cities.

There could be worse assignments, she mused.

By the time they reached the Palace of Government, the heat and humidity had drawn kindred moisture from her skin into beads above her lip and eyebrows. Her young companion proffered a handkerchief. She shook her head. She was Jayne

Connor, battle-hardened reporter for Worldnews Magazine. She wasn't afraid to sweat.

She paused a moment to look up at the colossal structure, its weathered masonry reminiscent of English colleges she'd seen, yet its lines unmistakably eastern. There were no minarets, but the higher points of the building evoked them in a boxlike fashion. The delicate parapets spoke of decoration rather than function, and the stonework was a lighter shade than that favored in Europe.

They navigated a maze of long corridors and stopped in an anteroom where Jayne stood admiring a wall of barely-opaque glass. A tall figure with a handsome profile was just visible through it.

She decided to pluck the handkerchief from her escort's hand and daub the wetness from her face after all.

Minister Rajamahendran had the looks of a movie star and the poise of a prince. Immaculately coiffed silver hair was a perfect contrast to his dark skin. His baritone greeting slid smoothly into warm bass tones as he took her hand in a firm grip.

"Ms. Connor, of course. It is gratifying for such a small country as ours to have the interest of such a prestigious publication as Worldnews."

"A small country perhaps, sir, but with big ideas when it comes to government, I'm told."

"No, surely, a small idea for a small government. That is the point." He raised an arm and they moved into the hallway. The messenger had vanished. Rajamahendran made small talk and offered a few tidbits about the rooms they passed—appetizers before the main course: the central computing floor of the Division of Democratic Administration. Its well-sealed doors held back thoroughly-conditioned air, easily ten Celsius degrees cooler than outside, and dry. Jayne knew it was for the benefit of the machinery, not for the comfort of the twenty or so data-entry clerks. Most of them wore light shawls over their shoulders.

"Only a handful of these people are required to actually tabulate the votes," the minister explained. "Most of them work to provide the necessary information to the voting public. When there is an issue to be decided by a vote, they transcribe the official releases from the pertinent government department, and ensure that every significant detail is made available through further documentation and relevant web links both inside and outside the country."

"And the opposing side?" Jayne asked.

"Certainly there are many differing opinions about most issues, and we do our best to present a balanced overview. But in addition, our citizens are encouraged to offer their views using online forums hosted by our government web page. There is no censorship of these forums, I assure you. In fact, occasionally the government actively seeks out representatives of opposing viewpoints and assists them to present their arguments in debates provided by video link."

"Providing all of this information to every voting citizen on every issue of government...webcasts, document archives, even advertising the issues themselves each time a vote comes up...that's got to be expensive. Not to mention the cost of providing each family with a computer."

"Not as expensive as dozens of elected representatives and their office staff, believe me." Rajamahendran showed perfect teeth in a practiced smile. "And you might find it fitting that much of the cost is paid from real estate holdings and other investments once owned by the royal family, when we had such a thing.

"As for advertising, there is no need. When the citizenry is asked to vote, each family's tablet computer produces a special alert tone, and a notification is displayed on their screen until they deactivate it. Another page gives a brief outline of the issue, with pertinent web links, and a more detailed package is sent to them by e-mail. A reminder notification pops up once a day until the date of the vote. Then the actual voting window lasts for exactly 24 hours."

"What about voting fraud?"

"A combination of identity questions, passwords, and fingerprint-scanning software has proven to be adequate," the minister replied. "Of course, if there are special interests involved—high value business contracts, for example—our department watches for suspicious voting trends and irregularities. That happened a time or two in the beginning—not anymore."

Jayne smiled. Could this obviously well-educated man really be so naïve?

"How many times is the average person expected to vote on affairs of state?"

"They are expected to vote *every* time." The minister's own smile was tighter this time. "Statistically, our machines show that ninety-three per cent of the eligible population votes on any given issue. The remaining seven per cent can be explained by sickness, or by people who are temporarily out of the country, or away from home in a handful of un-serviced settings such as fishing boats or logging encampments. If you are asking how often issues are put to a public vote...there are certain criteria written into our constitution. You are welcome to read it. I would estimate that it averages out to once or twice a week. Sometimes more, for instance during our annual budget process. At such times there are often multiple issues to be decided on the same day, but they are usually related."

He gave a modest nod. "To you this may perhaps seem an onerous responsibility, yet how many choices are people in your western society called upon to make every day for the most mundane of reasons? From daily wardrobe choices out of room-length closets, to the *grande* low-fat-milk mocha frappuccino with extra foam while commuting to work, or the perfect evening's television viewing from among one hundred and eight channels?" He lowered his eyelids. "Our people are spared such demands. Surely spending a modest amount of time shaping one's country's destiny is not too much to ask."

Jayne refused to acknowledge the implied rebuke. Instead she looked around the room, noting that all of the clerks appeared to be busy at their screens and keyboards. None of them ever looked at her.

"I appreciate hearing the official government position," she said. "But my editor sent me here to get a sense of how the system really works in practice. I'd like to speak to people in the streets, and in their homes, to learn how it affects their day-to-day lives."

"Certainly," he said, the hesitation barely noticeable. "I will arrange for a translator to accompany you. I will also see to it that you have a government-issue tablet computer delivered to your hotel room, with a guest identity set up to allow you access to all of the resources available to our voters. You will see," he added confidently. "Our system is indeed democracy in it's truest form."

Ten minutes later, once again in the anteroom of the minister's office, Rajamahendran returned with a younger man in tow.

"May I introduce Chander Cook, a very capable translator, fluent in all of our country's dialects, as well as English."

The young man gave a courteous bob, then, lowering his eyes, he suddenly blushed. Jayne realized that the visit to the cold computer floor had made her nipples stiffen. She had an impulse to cross her arms, but resisted it. This could be useful.

"Cook?" she asked.

"It is said," the minister replied, "that the famous explorer left his...reputation behind in many parts of the world."

The streets were more crowded near the middle of the day, and the humid air bore less floral essence and more animal musk. That section of the capital city featured wide boulevards lined with modern shops. Jayne thought a less cosmopolitan part of town would provide a better sample of opinions. She decided to ask her translator for suggestions, and had to turn around to find him.

"Please don't walk behind me." She laughed. "I come from a society where everyone is equal."

"Oh, everyone is equal here also, Miss," the young man replied. "We simply expect each person to know his place."

"Well please make your place beside me. I can't talk to you back there. And don't be shy. I have trouble hearing you over the street noise." She waited while he grudgingly moved forward. "Have you been a translator for long?"

"Two days."

"*What?* I thought the minister said..."

"Two days for this assignment, that is to say. Since they found out you were coming. I am normally a student of languages at our university. I hope to study in England someday. At Oxford."

"Good for you. Is your family well off? I mean wealthy?"

"Oh, indeed no." He blushed again. "But there is a trust fund, provided by a...friend of the family. It will help when I turn twenty-one."

"Can I ask your family about the voting system?"

"No," he answered a little too quickly. "My family is...not at home. They are visiting. Friends."

"Then take me to a less fancy part of town. Is there a market for produce—fruits and vegetables? Maybe we can talk to some shopkeepers."

He nodded energetically, and led the way.

After twenty minutes, the shops had given way to stalls and she stopped in front of one that displayed baskets and trays of fruits and vegetables. She recognized giant green breadfruit off to one side, mangoes, pineapples, and guava, and realized she was hungry. There were several different varieties of banana, but her mouth was too dry for that. Instead she chose a purple passionfruit and Chander helped her pay for it. She offered to buy one for him, but he declined.

"I've come to Devis Varta to speak to people about your government system," she said to the woman collecting the money. Chander translated. The old woman nodded her head. "Do you like it?" Jayne asked.

A nod. "Do you vote regularly?" Another nod. The woman reached for a bunch of sour bananas and held them out inquisitively.

"No, thank you." Jayne shook her head. "I'm not interested in more fruit. I'd just like to know if you and your family vote whenever your government asks you to." She waited while Chander spoke.

The stall owner leaned forward past the thatched overhang to look up at the sky, then shrugged and chattered a few words.

"She, uh...very much believes in democracy," Chander translated. "And votes as regularly as...rain." He gave a sheepish smile, and a quick glance of his own at the blue sky overhead.

Jayne looked from Chander to the old woman and back again. The woman reached for a small coconut and held it out. Jayne shook her head and edged away, then turned toward the next stall while the fruit woman brandished a pineapple, sword-like, at her back, and jabbered some more words that Chander did not translate.

The conversation with a basket weaver wasn't very different. They stopped to talk to a street sweeper, who offered half-hearted shrugs and a vacuous expression. A cab driver gave stock responses, but with many more words, and then expected a tip for his time.

They stopped for lunch at a small café that claimed to cater to foreigners, but none of the staff or customers spoke English, and none had anything illuminating to say about the democratic process. Most were reluctant to talk, and after she had questioned a half-dozen people the owner complained that she was driving his patrons away. Frustrated, she arranged to meet Chander again later in the afternoon, and returned to her hotel.

Her government tablet was waiting for her. She found the interface intuitive and the speed of the 'net connection impressive. The government website was everything the Minister of Governmental Affairs had promised. The next vote, due in four days, concerned an expansion of customs and security facilities in the island's three main commercial harbours. But she found an archive of past voting issues sortable by date, topic, and other parameters. There were reams of documents and web-links available on every subject, and the final vote tally on each question was readily displayed. It was easy to compare voting trends in table or graph format. As Rajamahendran had said, voter participation was very high. Results varied widely, but there appeared to be few issues contentious enough to produce a close vote. What would be done in the unlikely event of a tie? She should ask.

Her ex-husband, Michael, would have been fascinated by this system.

They'd met while she was a hungry Washington reporter digging for facts, and he was a party insider trying to build the next dynasty. They'd been very useful to each other, a great team, until the partnership had become a marriage. He was a public policy analyst; statistics and graphs were not only his stock in trade, but also the love of his life—a fact Jayne had discovered too late in a cold bed that couldn't compete with a warm computer. She'd reacted by taking assignments all over the world, and soon the marriage was over. Michael had never meant to hurt her. There had simply come a time when neither of them wanted to continue sharing their possessions with a stranger.

She pushed away from the desk, annoyed. If she couldn't find anything wrong with this damn system of government there was no story. But there had to be something—some dirty secret. That's what governments were built on.

Unless...what if it really did work, and could be scalable for any size of population? No more two-faced politicians, mud-slinging campaigns, backroom deals, corruption scandals.

A global utopia.

No! That was optimism at its most simple-minded. Syrupy pie-in-the-sky fantasy.

The responses of the people she'd interviewed nettled her. They were too much alike. Her reporter's nose smelled a rat.

Of course, they were all citizens of the capital city, the center of government, such as it was. People rarely rock their own boat.

When she met Chander later they mapped out a tentative route for the next day to get a more varied sample of the island's populace. Then Jayne did some half-hearted window shopping, ordered dinner from room service, and went to bed early.

#

In the morning they hired a cab for the whole day and set out for a small fishing village on the south coast. Jayne reasoned that it was at the opposite end of the island, and ought to be at the opposite end of the social and political spectrum from the sophisticated capital.

The cab ride was an ordeal of sticky heat, exhaust fumes and human sweat, accompanied by ominous mechanical clatters, squeals, and bone-rattling thumps plus a few heart-stopping close calls with hairpin turns, other vehicles, and livestock. Everything that a foreign correspondent learned to expect. Some of the time she was able to ignore the road and enjoy the tropical scenery, though the majority of it was dense bush.

Chander was clearly not so used to vehicular travel. He disappeared for a few minutes when they arrived at the village, and returned to his duties looking pale.

The coastal hamlet was far removed from the capital in flavour as well as geography. The picturesque thatched-roof fishing huts and brightly-coloured banners of laundry flanking them were as welcoming as the rank odour of the previous day's catch was disagreeable. As a reporter, Jayne had endured the stench of death mixed with diesel and cordite. She could handle the smell of day-old snapper entrails.

But her optimism quickly cooled as she began to survey the locals. The responses she collected in these dirt streets were almost no different from those she'd heard in the paved avenues of the day before. Yes, the people voted regularly. No, they didn't find it too demanding or monotonous. Yet she mentally confirmed an earlier impression: rather than being the proud heralds of a new democratic age, the islanders were reluctant to talk about their unique system of government. Their body language didn't match the words Chander conveyed to her, which turned her disappointment into a simmering suspicion.

It was time for a change of strategy.

They bought some fruit and bread and asked the cab driver to take them to a tourist beach a short drive away.

Floating on the warm sea, rocked by gentle swells, her mind was freed. It came back well-salted and ready for battle.

As she stood beneath the fresh water shower, she caught Chander eyeing her hungrily. She let her hips sway as she strolled through the soft sand, and arched her back just a little as she stopped near him, toweling her hair.

"Something occurred to me, Chander," she said casually. "How can I know you're giving me an accurate translation of what these people are telling me? What if you're just making it up as you go along?"

"Why would I do that?" he stammered.

"Perhaps because the government told you what to tell me. And especially what not to tell. Otherwise, I have to conclude that your people are all brainwashed into memorizing the official party line. They all say exactly the same thing."

His eyes burrowed into the sand like a crab in the shadow of a plover. "They all say the same thing because they all agree."

"I've been a reporter all my working life. That many people never agree on anything." She lifted his chin to make him look at her. "Are you ready to start over again, and tell me what people are really saying? Their actual words?"

He pulled free. "The people said what they said," he insisted.

"That's too bad," she purred. "Because I was going to tell Minister Rajamahendran how well we've been getting along." Her voice dropped. "Until you tried to grab my breasts."

His face couldn't decide whether to blush or to blanche, so it did one after the other.

"*No!* No I did not!"

"That's the way I remember it."

"No! You can't! Please. You can't tell them that. Please Miss Jayne. I am begging you."

"Well maybe if I could be sure you were giving me the straight goods when you did your *translating* from now on. How about it?"

His expression was so pathetic she might have felt pity, if she hadn't purged herself of that weakness long ago.

In the end he simply nodded. She said, "Good" and led him down the beach.

At first the new answers she got were the same as the old: of course the people voted each time they were asked; the system was wonderful; the country had prospered since the arrival of true democracy. But then she questioned them about the coming vote on harbour security. Eyes widened a fraction, and there was an extra second before the responses came: certainly they would vote—they always voted. She asked how they intended to vote, but she misrepresented the choices offered on the ballot. Not one person caught her in the lie. She asked about the recent budget bill and grossly exaggerated a few numbers. Throat muscles worked, and verbal answers were replaced by half-hearted nods.

By the end of each new interview, her prey lay vanquished at her feet, each confessing to a dereliction of his or her democratic duty. They pleaded with her to pardon their unworthiness. Certainly their neighbours voted regularly, and the system wouldn't collapse from their own occasional neglect. In fact, they'd discovered that the government got along very well without them—maybe even better. After all, they were poorly-educated, and pressed for time. It was better to leave important decisions to those who understood the issues.

The litany of excuses reminded Jayne of all the man-on-the-street interviews she'd heard so many times in her own country during election season.

As she and Chander returned to the capital city late in the afternoon, she was surprised to find that the glow of vindication she'd expected was tainted by disappointment. Was she really sorry to learn that the 'perfect democracy' was a fraud? Wasn't that what her jaundiced journalist's psyche had been hoping for?

The golden veneer of sunlight on the whitewashed walls had lost its luster.

She climbed out of the cab at her hotel and turned to Chander.

"Your Minister Rajamahendran will have some explaining to do tomorrow."

The young man's eyes grew wide. "*No, Miss Jayne. Please. You can't tell him about this. About today.   Please.*"

"I'm not going to get you into trouble, don't worry. You co-operated today and a deal is a deal."

"No. I don't mean that." He reached for her hand, then thought better of it. "I mean...what the people said. You can't tell that to the Minister."

"What are you talking about? He and his government are perpetrating a fraud. They're telling the world you've got this wonderful, shining example of the new democracy, and it's a joke. A scam."

"No, no..." He looked utterly miserable. "I am sure the Minister does not know this."

Jayne laughed. "How gullible can you be? Of course he knows it. They're lying to you and your people. And to the rest of the world. That's what governments do."

Chander went to his knees on the seat of the cab, begging her to change her mind. His head swung from side to side as if wracked by horrible indecision. She waited, speechless, until he finally rose up, his face covered with a sheen of sweat.

"Please wait for me tonight," he said. "I will take you to someone. Someone who will convince you."

She didn't know what to say. Could her life be in danger? Could this meek young man be plotting to lead her into a trap, where she'd be silenced?

She looked into his eyes and couldn't believe it.

"All right," she said.

#

In the warm dusk she waited on the balcony of her hotel room, enjoying the aerobatics of the swallows and swifts as they wheeled through the sky chasing their evening meals. When she could no longer see them, she looked over the rooftops, noting how few lights sparkled in the darkness compared to cities at home. Then a pair of headlights swung up the street and a cab stopped in front of the hotel. She went down to meet it.

Chander said little. His fear sweat was only slightly masked by some cheap cologne obviously for her benefit. Jayne looked out the window, trying to identify where they went.

"There's the Palace of Government, off to the right," she said. "Aren't these all parts of the palatial estate?" The street was bounded on that side by a long, continuous wall with thick foliage behind it. She expected guard posts, but didn't see any. The cabbie surprised her by pulling over to the curb.

Chander walked toward a small copse of trees that grew close to the wall. After a moment of fear, she steeled herself to follow.

In the shadows stood a cleverly concealed entrance to a short tunnel. Chander offered his arm to lead her down several steps to a cobbled floor she could feel but not see. They walked a little farther, climbed an equal number of steps, and branches brushed her face and shoulder. The moon had begun to rise, and as she stepped out into its light she could make out a modest tropical garden with a small, rough building at the far end. The fresh night air on the street was replaced by something that made her nose wrinkle. Rotting vegetation, maybe.

"Is this part of the palace grounds?" she asked, automatically whispering.

"Yes," her companion replied. "But no-one comes here. Don't worry."

His naïve assumption that those words would be reassuring rather than intimidating removed the last of her suspicions.

They moved quietly forward and he gave four light taps on the door of the hut, then three more, then two. She heard a voice, presumably inviting them to enter. The opening of the door released a waft of sweetly-scented air.

Inside was a medium-sized room with another small door at the other end of it. The room beyond that was in darkness, but the main space was lit by a series of candles spaced evenly around the walls. Near the center of the far wall sat a desk with several shapes on it, but the lone occupant of the hut was not behind the desk. He was sitting in the lotus position on the floor in front of it. Smoke rose from stands at the corners of the desk, stirred by a very slow fan suspended from the ceiling.

Chander cleared his throat. "Miss Jayne Connor, this is my uncle, Devarsi Shanmukhan."

She looked at the wizened face and gave a slight bow. "How do you do?" she asked, and waited for Chander to translate.

"I am doing very well, thank you," the man replied.

"Oh. You speak...." She bit her tongue to stop the rookie outburst.

"Yes, when I get the opportunity. Which is not often, except when my nephew wants to practice." He gave a wink. "I spent some years at Oxford, actually. In England."

"I see."

"I was the servant of a wealthy Englishwoman named Lady Blair of Cadbury, and when she decided to return to England later in life, she took me with her. She was eccentric, and believed an unworthy soul such as myself still deserved an education, may God Bless her. Then when she died, she left me some money, which I used to return here to my homeland. Though I fear I have not made use of her investment in the way she would have expected." He gave a charming smile. With his balding head, he reminded her of the Dalai Lama.

"What...what are you doing here?"

"Has Chander not told you?"

The young man was silent.

"Ah. Well, my nephew tells me that you have some questions about our system of government."

"A few," Jayne said wryly. "Like why your government pretends that every major policy matter is decided by all of the people, when in fact it appears that *no-one* votes."

The old man nodded, smiling sadly. "This is because the government does not know."

Jayne's mouth dropped open.

"What are you talking about? I saw a room full of computers dedicated to preparing information for the voters and tabulating vote results. Yet none of the average citizens I talked to *ever* votes."

"They did, once. The government still thinks they do."

He gestured toward the floor. Jayne hesitated, then folded herself into a comfortable lotus posture. Chander sat awkwardly.

"When I returned home those many years ago," Shanmukhan began, "I hoped to exercise my new-found knowledge of statistics and political science, and applied to work for the government. Sadly, the low station of my birth was still a barrier here—I am of our society's lowest caste, Ms. Connor. And so I could find no better position than that of a janitor." He bowed his head slightly. "Still, it gave me access to nearly all of the palatial quarters and offices, and I was able to befriend many of those who did important work. Quite a few of them learned of my background and occasionally even sought my advice. Eventually I made my peace with that.

"There came a time when the government hired a Canadian software engineer to create a program that would facilitate a more representative democracy. They truly had the best of intentions—I believe they still do—and young David Thomson delivered just what they wanted. With a staff of five other programmers, he fashioned a voting process almost exactly as we find it today, and developed the support system by which information is delivered to the citizenry. Once the procedure was tested, launched, and proven, his task was accomplished, and Thomson and three of his staff prepared to return to Canada. Sadly, they were killed in a plane crash en route." A shadow passed over his face. "The two remaining programmers were capable enough to fine tune the software, and keep the process running smoothly. In fact, the program was such a remarkable achievement that their efforts were needed less and less. Eventually one of them retired and the other died of an illness, but with a room full of data-entry clerks, no-one in the government noticed that there were no actual programmers left."

"Unbelievable," Jayne murmured. "No, I take that back. It sounds just like the bureaucracies I'm used to."

"Indeed."

"And your connection?"

"I had befriended Thomson. We liked to play chess together. He was pleased to show me his creation and exactly how it worked. With his encouragement I developed some skills as a programmer myself and, on a whim, he set up a dedicated computer link for me, here in my janitor's hut. My station wasn't originally authorized to let me run the program, only to be an interested spectator. But such digital barricades can be overcome, given time. Especially with the assistance of the last member of the programming team left here on Devis Varta.

"When he learned of his fatal illness, he revealed to me a terrible secret: *the great democracy was failing.* Not because of any computer problem, but because the people had lost their zeal for their newfound power. The novelty had worn off, and it had turned into a chore instead of a gift. In greater and greater numbers they were simply neglecting to vote.

"It was a disaster, not only for the credibility of the government, but for the bright hope of true democracy itself. If this man revealed what he knew, a dream would die, perhaps forever. He was also naïve enough to hope that voter participation would simply stabilize at a new, albeit lower level. And so he created a method to extrapolate a representative result from a lower total number of votes, and adjust the totals themselves for the sake of appearances. I believe you would call it '*fudging the numbers*'. In his last days he taught me how. And told no-one else.

"Regrettably, his hopes died with him, and now actual voting is almost non-existent. Even the government ministers skip their turns more often than not."

"Good God!" Jayne blew a breath through tightly drawn lips. "But then, how are decisions made?"

He gave an impish grin and pointed toward the computer on the desk nearby.

"*You?*" she sputtered. "You decide all of the 'votes' yourself?"

He inclined his head to one side and gave a little shrug.

"This is inconceivable!" Jayne slapped her knees and looked from Chander to his uncle. The young man was too embarrassed to meet her gaze, but the elder smiled, unperturbed. "But then that makes you the head of the government. Like a dictator. 'Power corrupts. Absolute power corrupts absolutely,'" she quoted.

"An axiom I embrace," Devarsi Shanmukhan nodded. "But you see, I don't really have that kind of power. I do not—I *cannot*—choose the questions that are asked, nor the options offered. I can only select my choice from the courses of action presented. The day-to-day running of the government is still in the hands of others, and it is from those daily needs that the issues and the voting questions arise. It would require a Machiavellian genius of the highest order to be able to manipulate future questions through the results of past votes alone. And a genius I am not. Perhaps you will say that I could become rich by investing and manipulating the markets through government policy. But again, my caste would make that very difficult and, in any case, I am too old to enjoy the ill-gotten gains.

"No, Ms. Connor." He leaned forward. "I honestly try to choose the path that is best for my country."

"But why prop up a failed system? Why not let the truth come out and force the government to go back to the drawing board?"

"Because the system should work, and I believe it *will* work someday," the man said simply. "Except the current generation is not ready for it. They are used to having others make their decisions for them. The young adults of the next generation are children of the Internet age, habituated to a myriad of choices as a matter of routine. It will be second nature to them. Providing the system survives."

For a moment she was too stunned to speak. The man radiated sincerity, a quality to which she was wholly unaccustomed. Her eyes roamed the room, looking for inspiration. They found the smoking pedestals and she waved at them.

"I suppose this is a mystical experience for you? Seeking the true path?"

"You mean the incense?" he asked. "Oh, no. The septic system of the palace is nearby, and on a still night I must cover the smell."

Was he mocking her?

"How do you make your decisions, then?" she persisted.

"I investigate as much as I can, and try to make the choice that will benefit the greatest number of people." He shrugged. "And then sometimes I flip a coin."

"*What?*"

"Random chance is a potent force in the workings of the universe, Ms. Connor. We can try to deny it, or we can embrace it."

He laughed at her shocked face.

"Don't toy with me, Mr. Shanmukhan," she snapped. "What you're doing is reprehensible."

"Is it?" He looked crestfallen. "I am truly sorry that you think so. I'm a simple man, and I have done what I thought was best in an unthinkable situation." He leaned close to her face and pierced her with his earnest eyes. "What would you do?"

She pulled back. "Oh, no. Don't try that on me. I've interviewed too many politicians to fall for it."

"I promise you, I sincerely would like to know. You see...." He looked at Chander apologetically. "I am old. Sick. I am *dying*, Chander. I have a few months left, but no more." The sudden wetness of his nephew's eyes reflected the guttering candlelight, and he reached out to take the young man's hand. "So you see, Ms. Connor, I have been urgently seeking a successor."

For long seconds she didn't get it. Then she straightened with a jolt.

"*Me?* You've got to be kidding!"

"My nephew is the spark of my life, and as true-hearted as anyone could wish for. But he doesn't yet have the maturity or experience for such a task. He will soon go to England to attend Oxford as his uncle did, with money from Lady Blair, which I have held in trust. I have great hopes for him. Perhaps even this high calling, if he wishes."

"But *me*," she breathed. "I can't do this. I'm just a journalist. I have no political training. And I haven't got any connection to Devis Varta. I probably couldn't even get permission to live here."

"In that you are mistaken. Our constitution provides for perpetual citizenship for members of the royal family."

"Of the.... You must be joking."

Even Chander gasped. "Those Connors! The royal line?"

His uncle gave another of his impish nods.

"Great-grandmother," Jayne breathed.

"Her husband, actually. A younger brother of the last king, but his elder left no heir."

She shook her head as if trying to reawaken to reality.

"Don't try to tell me that I should run this country by divine right. I don't buy into that bullshit."

"I would not. A case might be made for you, but certainly not for me, and I have been...intervening already. I merely wish to point out that you do indeed have a connection to Devis Varta, and automatic citizenship. And I have no doubt you will grow to love our country. Surely you must have felt its call. A near paradise on this Earth."

He read the truth of his words in her face, in spite of herself.

"As for your journalism experience, there can be few professions so thoroughly versed in the pitfalls of government. You might also be surprised to learn that I have read a great deal of your work. A very great deal."

His voice grew quieter. "It was I who planted the seed that resulted in your assignment here. Through several letters to your editor, under false names." The puckish smile was back. "Chander did not know of this—I only insisted that he report to me about your actions. They were much as I had expected. And hoped for. Did you know that, in Hindi, the name Jayne can mean 'Victorious'? An auspicious sign, I think."

He took her hands gently in his.

"I sense an idealism deep within you, Ms. Connor. It has only been masked with cynicism. Am I wrong?"

Jayne was overwhelmed with emotions she hadn't allowed herself to feel for many years. It had to be the incense making her dizzy.

She pulled her hands free and leapt to her feet, striding forcefully toward the door and the garden. Shanmukhan stopped his nephew from following.

She stumbled into the outside world and found herself breathless, her mind raw.

What an outlandish story! Impossible to believe and impossible to discredit. Her reporter's instincts knew the taste of fact from fiction as readily as sugar from salt. Here was hoary truth, both sublime and ridiculous, served up in lavish portions when a mere pill would be too much to swallow.

And then Shanmukhan's offer! Was she tempted by it? Seduced by the pheromones of power? She'd inhaled them at close range before, but had never had the means to claim the prize for her own. Here was the definitive test for all of those times when she had gleefully exposed the warts of politics and politicians, and sworn that she could do better.

She slumped against a tree and yearned for guidance. The space around her was split between golden light and dark shadows, odours sweet and sour, sounds of life but also utter peace. Was the land of her ancestors indeed calling to her? She'd always rejected the trappings of religion with her mind, and yet sought out the purity of a cosmic oneness with her heart, seeing no contradiction in this. She knelt on the moist earth and opened her soul to the night.

A dam burst, and memories flooded in: of her childhood, and her grandfather the senator, stung by an unjust political scandal and seeking comfort in his granddaughter's butterfly kisses. The fierce joy of victories on the high school debating team. A brilliant mentor at university, toasting her thesis with champagne. Her first big scoop at the Newport Daily News, followed by image after image from her career: scandals and scapegoats, hacks and hardheads and heroes. And then finally...Michael. Her ex-husband. The smartest man she'd ever known, except when it came to understanding her.

He'd never remarried. Last she'd heard he was between jobs, as his Democrats had fallen out of favour.

Her mouth slowly drew into a smile.

They'd once been a great team, until marriage got in the way. Could they be again? If anyone could reignite the country's interest in participatory democracy it would be Michael. And in the meantime, with Chander to help her understand the country of her heritage, at least until he left for university....

The door pushed softly open, and the two men looked up.

"Mr. Shanmukhan? Let's talk. But first...can we ditch the incense? We have a lot of hard-nosed planning to do."

"And the smell of the septic bed?"

Jayne smiled. "This is politics. What could be more appropriate?"

#   #   #

SAVIOUR

H E HAD SAVED THE PLANET, but his own life was forfeit.

It sounded like the plot of an ancient myth. Or maybe just a bad Hollywood movie.

He reached for his favourite teacup in the cupboard, surrounded by so many other dishes that were never used. It had been a gift from the wife of a favourite professor at MIT. Dresden china. He filled it with a dark brew and drank it clear. Something about the act of sipping the warm liquid calmed and centered him, and he needed that, but as he drew the cup to his lips a second time, he frowned. There was a crack from base to brim, near the handle. It had never been there before. The brief lift in his spirits proved equally fragile.

"I was drinking tea the day NASA came knocking on my door, all those years ago," he said to the reporter, filling a second cup and gesturing to a chair. What was the man's name? Gordon? Morden?

"Had you been expecting them?"

"Not really," Heissman replied. "Perhaps I should have—I was certainly an expert in the field, and familiar with the scenario they described. It was the brainchild of a former astronaut and some others. For a time they thought the asteroid *Apophis* would make a very near pass by the Earth in 2029 and then collide with the planet in 2036. But the original project was shelved after better measurements showed conclusively that *Apophis* would miss."

"You worked with him, didn't you? Uh...the astronaut."

"Yes, of course. A good man, very earnest. Courageous, to face that kind of ridicule in those days. The idea that human effort could deflect a killer asteroid had been turned into trashy fantasy by some Hollywood movies."

"I remember them."

"Yes, so it was hard to get anyone to take him seriously for a long time. 'Goliath' did the trick."

Goliath wasn't going to miss, the men in the expensive suits had told him when they came to his door. But they had a plan. If a defence mission could be brought on stream within seven years, that might just allow enough time for the deflection apparatus to succeed. Eleven years to nudge a four-kilometre-wide chunk of rock and rubble off its course and save humankind. It would work, they said, if Heissman would help them make it work, but they'd only have one shot. He remembered maple leaves falling slowly through the air behind them as they spoke, a harbinger of the coming winter.

He massaged his temples, as if to rub the memories away. The reporter leaned on the kitchen table waiting for more.

The media had once again hauled out all of the doomsday details, as they'd done every so often over the past eighteen years: the catastrophic effects of a cosmic body the size of Goliath striking the Earth at fifteen kilometres per second. Global winter. Mass starvation. The collapse of civilization. It was all prime fodder for the sensationalist press and TV networks.

And it was all true.

Project David had been born out of the shadow of death.

"It was a strange time," Heissman remembered. "Almost overnight the pariahs became the prophets, and they were ready. They hadn't given up. Plans...blueprints. Nearly all of the technology was already available, if you had the money. And they got the money. I've never seen anything like it."

"The future of the race was at stake," Borden said.

"The future of the race had been threatened in dozens of ways, and we'd done *nothing* about them," the astro-engineer replied with an edge of bitterness. He heard it, and steered the subject away. "As you know, it was agreed that the Russians and the European Space Agency would join forces to apply the Yarkovsky effect to Goliath."

"They painted half of it with reflective paint."

"Large areas of it, yes. The physics is sound: the painted areas absorbed much less heat from the sun, so the thermal energy of the dark regions created a slow braking effect through space. It wasn't necessary to destroy the asteroid, just alter its course enough to miss us. If done early enough, the change didn't need to be very big."

"But you knew it wouldn't be enough."

Heissman cocked his head. "No-one *knew*. In fact, we hoped it *would* be enough. We simply couldn't afford to wait to find out. So we Americans worked with the Japanese and Chinese to create the Titan Mass Driver: essentially a kind of electromagnetic catapult that could fling huge payloads of dirt from Goliath's surface at high velocity into space, and act like a crude rocket motor. Push the monster into a harmless orbit by brute force. But you know that. I've read your articles."

Borden nodded. "I was assigned to work on the money angle, originally. The costs were...*astronomical*." He allowed himself a slight smile. "You were justified, though. The Yarkovsky effect didn't work."

"The threat hadn't been identified early enough. Perhaps with another five years warning...."

The two men lapsed into silence for a moment. Then the newsman picked up his tablet and stylus again.

"You must have been inspired by the level of international cooperation. We saw a threat to the whole race, and we put our differences aside to battle it together."

Heissman's dark eyes bored into the other's to see if the comment indicated true naiveté, or a conscious mockery. He decided that the man was simply oblivious, like so many others of his profession. How was it possible that even those tasked with keeping the public informed could allow themselves to remain so ignorant?

He couldn't keep silent anymore.

"Nothing noble or inspiring about it," he snapped. "Desperation. Nothing more. We could see the Sword of Damocles when it presented itself as a mammoth chunk of rock hurtling toward us through space. Tell me why we couldn't see it in any of the dozens of other ways we had doomed this planet ourselves?"

The reporter was startled. "I don't know what you mean."

"I know you don't," the older man growled, mollified a little. He had no right to accuse. He'd been just as willing as everyone else to turn a blind eye to the way his species ravaged its world. Before the trip to Costa Rica.

#

He'd been on the way to yet another international meeting when his pilot had offered a low flyby over the Galapagos islands. They'd been ruggedly picturesque from the air, nothing more. It was the fishing vessel a few miles offshore that had caught his attention.

"What do they fish for here?" he asked the pilot. "I thought the whole area was protected."

"Sharks," the man replied. He pointed to a series of wide-spread buoys that Heissman hadn't noticed. The dotted line stretched to the horizon across the calm water.

"What are the buoys for?"

"That is their shark line. They bait hooks on long leaders hanging down, all along that line. Then come back to see what they've caught."

"*All* of those floats are attached to one line? That can't be, surely. I can't see the end of it."

The pilot nodded in reply. "Yeah, fifty miles...maybe a hundred. Lot of fish. Lot of sharks, but also many swordfish...sea turtles. Whatever will take the bait. Takes a long time to check all of the hooks. Many days. So lots die. Don't matter. Lots of fish in the sea." The man's attitude brought a chill to Heissman's stomach.

"What could they want with that many sharks?"

"Shark fin soup," the other answered. "Very big in China. Cost a lot, so very big prestige to serve it to guests. Don't taste like anything—only meant for showing off."

The engineer tried to grasp what the man was saying. "Are you telling me they catch the sharks and *only* use their fins?"

"Sure. Cut off the fins and throw the shark back in. Have a hard time swimming with no fins!" The man's laugh was like cold water in Heissman's face.

"*Alive?*" he breathed.

"Sure alive. Only good-for-nothing sharks. Don't matter."

He later learned that shark finning was illegal in Costa Rica and many other countries, but the market was so lucrative it was second only to the world drug trade, and controlled by organized crime. Governments paid lip service to the laws, but most often just looked the other way, thanks to well-placed 'political contributions'. Meanwhile the ocean's most important predator, a crucial link in the food chain, was being annihilated for the sake of middle class pretentiousness. A million sharks a year.

That was the beginning of his awakening. The next watershed moment had come near the end of a transatlantic flight, when the lower altitude of the plane had allowed him a glimpse of a giant trawler on the ocean surface below. He'd been astonished. It was like a floating city, dragging enormous nets behind it, all the way to the bottom, sweeping the ocean floor barren for many kilometres to port and to starboard. Leaving a watery desert in its wake. He'd been so strongly affected that he didn't remember landing or getting off the plane.

He did remember a news report from years earlier that had made headlines for a few days. An analysis of fish stocks data for several decades had boldly predicted that the oceans would be empty of harvestable fish before the year 2050. The world had ignored it, just as it had ignored all the evidence of land animals' extinctions. And climate change. And the poisoning of water with endless chemicals.

Years of such warnings had suddenly crystallized in his head into three stark conclusions:

The human species was quickly pushing all other Earth species into extinction.

The human species was now facing its own extinction.

And the human species was the only one that deserved it.

#

He looked up from the table. Borden's face wore an expression of horror that had nothing to do with images of mutilated sharks or ravaged seamounts.

He knows, thought Heissman.

"I...I just want to file our interview...so it makes the next update," the reporter prevaricated. He took a few steps backward toward the door, then turned and busied himself with the tablet for several minutes. The room filled with a heavy silence. Finally the man's arms lowered and his head turned a little over slumped shoulders.

"How did you do it?" he asked in a voice just above a whisper.

"A simple matter." Heissman sighed. "They'd left the final design to me. Why not? I was the expert. Easy enough to include a small number of electrical components that would suffer a gradual voltage drop under the stress of extreme temperatures. Then some key circuits too fragile to handle the fluctuations. Very hard to spot. And no reason to look."

"So the mass driver failed before it could produce enough thrust to change Goliath's course. Billions of people—the whole of civilization as we know it—doomed. Only a few months left to live. All of our suffering, knowing that the end is coming and there's nothing we can do about it. Your fault. Your doing."

"Many people will survive," Heissman said. "All over the world, in shelters and caves, with stored food and supplies. Presuming they don't decide to blow each other up with the remaining nuclear arsenal. But it will be many centuries before they can once again threaten all other life on the planet."

"But you've doomed thousands of other species along with us."

"Perhaps. Perhaps not. I believe they'll have a better chance than *we* gave them." He took a half-hearted sip of cold tea from the cracked cup. Then he looked calmly into the other man's stricken face. "What will you do when your editor returns your message?"

"Does it matter?" Borden asked.

"Not really." Heissman slowly shook his head. "The end will come a little sooner for me, than for the rest of you. In this country the penalty for Treason is still death."

#   #   #

NODE OF THOUGHT

HENDRICKS WAS A LONG WAY from home when he discovered that he was no longer alone.

Forty-seven deep-sleep cycles out of Triton Station—nearly four years. *Orphion* had been at ramjet speed for just over a year, but was still within the Oort Cloud. It was the first of the supply ships to Centauri Station since the original colonization decades earlier—he was more alone than any human before him, and liked it.

As usual, he spent his first waking day on routine checks, entering everything into his manual log. When the music started—a melancholy piece in a minor key—he found himself humming it before he realized it didn't belong.

VILMA, who asked you to play music?

"I responded to a command."

Command? A command from Earth would be nearly fifteen months old.

Identify the command source, he requested.

The answer took seconds to come. "I am unable to comply."

Shit, he thought.

"I am unable to comply."

Was that a joke? Had VILMA developed a sense of humour? He hoped not. Every one of *Orphion's* systems was under the control of its Virtual Intelligence Locus. VIL's weren't supposed to evolve. That lesson had been learned from the artificial intelligences of the *Clarke* and the *Le Guin* that went rogue on the first Centauri mission. Hendricks hadn't been born then. But he was a child on Mars when the mining colony in Belt Sector Four lobbed an asteroid toward the Earth. After that, AI's had been severely constrained.

A computer command without an ident was trouble.

He rolled off his bunk and reached for the cello strip on the wall ridge beside it. The ship had only stocked enough chewing gum for a year, so at eight months he'd started reusing it. On second thought, this problem deserved a fresh piece.

#

By the middle of the next day he was no closer to an answer. VILMA's systems had passed every diagnostic test. He asked her to appear—it was easier to have a discussion when he had someone to look at. The default avatar he'd chosen for her was a long-legged redhead with green eyes, wrapped in a form-fitting jumpsuit. Good to look at and not argumentative. The kind of woman that could help a man fend off the chill of space.

That was an uncharacteristic thought. The complications of sex were a trial he was glad to avoid on a long mission like this.

"I still can't track down the command to play that music," he said out loud, his voice a little rough. The VIL's Mental Actuation didn't require him to vocalize but he liked to keep his vocal chords exercised.

"Neither can I."

"Were there any anomalous readings on the ship's instruments at the time? Electromagnetic interference? Any transmissions received?"

"Instrument readings matched projections with no indication of interference. No directed transmissions have been received for one-hundred fifty-five days."

That would have been his anniversary congratulations message, a year after his launch from the refuelling station at Triton. VILMA also received news and general information transmissions as well as the occasional mail, but the ship wouldn't respond to a command embedded in one of those.

He shivered.

Ease up. The situation wasn't serious yet.

He asked VILMA for some ham-gel sandwiches, and as he pulled them from the food processor, he shivered again.

"VILMA, what's the current cabin temperature?

"The temperature is sixteen degrees Celsius."

What the hell? "Raise the cabin temperature to twenty degrees, please. And maintain that until my next deep-sleep cycle." He shouldn't have had to mention that. "There's no malfunction in life support, is there?"

"There are no malfunctions in any system. The temperature was lowered as commanded."

"Commanded? What was the source of that command?"

A pause. "I am unable to provide that answer."

This time the chill that ran through him had nothing to do with the air.

#

"You should go out with people. Real people. Make friends"

"How do you know I don't? You're never here."

For someone who had no other mothering skills, she'd still perfected *the look*. She turned it on full blast.

"What am I supposed to do, Baird? Give up my practice to stay home and babysit a fifteen year-old? People's lives depend on me." She sighed. "It's a phase, right? You're going through a phase. I was a teenager once."

Prehistory, Hendricks thought. For someone who knew her way around the brain with a laser scalpel better than the layout of her own home, she knew dick all about the workings of the mind. Especially her own son's.

"BH," he said. "My friends call me BH."

"You have no friends. You have avatars in VR games, and I'll bet they're all computer personalities. Why don't you get together with your classmates at the academy?"

"Why? So they can laugh at the kid in the float chair because he's too weak for Earth gravity? Poor little Mars rat?"

When he'd entered the space corps he'd expected to be surrounded by like minds. But they weren't like him at all. His Olympus City accent and manners inevitably marked him as a breed apart, and an inferior breed at that. Solitude was his salvation.

"Maybe one of the people I know has a son or a nephew," she said half-heartedly.

"One of the men you bring home? That ought to cover half the city."

In the real event he'd been about to say, *You could double your income if you charged them money*, but she had slapped him before the words had come out.

"All right, VILMA, that's enough of that crap for this week."

"Your psychological evaluation and calibration requires an additional four point five minutes."

He turned around to find that she was projecting the figure of a man. Tall, handsome, but more stooped than he should have been for the few traces of grey in his hair. The evidence of great pain, Hendricks knew.

"Baird, I need you to look after your mother for me."

It was what the man had always said before he left for endless months on a freight run, including the last, when cancer would take Baird Hendricks Sr. in the emptiness between Jupiter and Saturn.

"Enough, VILMA. Enough."

"Your mind does not provide much material on this subject for my simulations to use."

"It is what it is."

"Would you like another simulated interaction for relaxation purposes? Perhaps with the dancer avatar?" The default redhead in the jumpsuit reappeared, the closest approximation his memory could provide of an entertainer he'd known in Phobos City.

"No, thank you. I don't feel like company. Just tell me if I passed the evaluation."

"Your psychological status has not changed." Which wasn't a ringing endorsement, but it had been good enough for the company to hire him in the first place. After all, if Hendricks weren't a loner, he'd be out of a job. The economics of interstellar freight delivery didn't favour a larger crew unless they were going to stay on at Centaurus Station. VILMA was supposed to be all the company he needed. She had a repertoire of hundreds of characters—he could sing duets with Streisand, or play chess with Asimov. He never did, though. He liked to be alone. Given a choice between solitude and society, solitude was easier. He knew what to expect.

#

Right now he wouldn't have minded having another human around to ask for advice. Earth was too far away, and the frozen embryos in cargo compartments 255 to 280 weren't big on conversation.

VILMA's systems were thoroughly integrated. If there was a glitch, any attempt to fix it would involve terrible risk. There weren't any studies on selectively disabling a VIL—it was not to be done. If he screwed up, he might wipe a key element in the navigational sequence, shut down life support, or terminate the embryos he was transporting. Yet if he did nothing, a phantom command might produce the same disastrous results.

Maybe he couldn't ask for help from Earth, but he'd better tell them there was a problem. While he still could.

He'd just begun to compose a message when a movement at the edge of his vision made him jump.

It was a slim woman with long golden hair, sitting on air, holding her face in her hands. Hendricks could see the wall panels through her. His breath caught. Whoever she was, her body language spoke of despair, and there was a faint keening sound. The melancholy music from hours earlier began again.

He watched her for fifteen minutes, until she slowly faded away. He'd learned nothing about her, except that she was very sad and very beautiful.

He didn't believe in ghosts—the blond woman must have been projected by VILMA. But why?

She had no answer to that—could not even confirm that the vision had been her doing.

He spent the next five hours trying to refine the parameters of her diagnostic program. It found no malfunction. He ran it again.

A reflection in a nearby metal surface caught his eye. He turned to see a tall man in an old-style one-piece flight uniform. The man stood slightly bent, maybe looking into a display, one hand clenched into a fist held tightly against his ribs. After a moment of taut stillness, he slowly reached forward to take something into his palm, and gazed at whatever it was for a long time. The face stayed turned into the shadows, then the figure seemed to recede into the distance before vanishing completely.

Where had these images come from? And why were they so...spectral?

VILMA had no answers.

#

None of the phantom commands had been life-threatening so far, and the visions were simply that: nothing manifestly able to cause harm. Were they hallucinations? He isolated the med station from VILMA's main processor to eliminate the risk of contaminated data, and ran some tests on himself. Blood, hormones, neural functions all showed normal— no reason to expect delusions. The finger of blame still pointed at VILMA

No harm had been done, but how long could he afford to wait? His hands had developed a tendency to sweat and his neck muscles ached as he ran test after test. He called up VILMA's default parameters, focusing on the command interface. The Mental Actuation function was operating as designed, responding to Hendricks' brainwaves and his alone. There couldn't be any other sources of input anyway. The huge ship was nearly half a kilometer long from the intake at the bow to the trailing edges of the fusion motors' giant thrust nozzles, but it was all cargo and machinery space in near-vacuum. No room for stowaways and no air anywhere but the crew quarters. It took Hendricks no more than three minutes to search that, feeling like a complete idiot as he did. There were no bogeymen under his bed.

He'd just decided to resume his message holo to Earth when views of space began to appear in the middle of the cabin like inflating balloons. A small fair-haired boy in a plastiform jumper stood amid the projections, bouncing with excitement and stabbing the air like invisible buttons. He was childhood personified: insatiable curiosity provided with hands and feet to do its bidding.

The boy looked up with a start, and the joy on his face burst like a bubble. Caught with his hand in the proverbial cookie jar, the image dissolved into a dim afterglow.

No child had ever set foot on *Orphion*, not even during construction. How could it have become the vehicle of a child's thoughts?

#

Hendricks sat on his bunk and used dried kernels of chewing gum to mark off the possibilities:

One was that he'd gone off the deep end and hallucinated everything. It was a damn strong possibility, but if so, he was screwed. The second was that the ship's brain was suffering a major malfunction. Screwed again. But the third possibility was that VILMA really was responding to other thoughts than Hendricks' own.

VILMA detected thoughts as pattern changes in energy fields: Quantifiable...transmissible. But what if thoughts had a permanent presence no-one suspected? Maybe quantumly-entangled particles? Could they accumulate like dust drifting into cracks and crevices, shed like old skin cells and hair? Could they leech away, like molecules from the surface of metals into the vacuum of space, and float among the currents and eddies of the galactic wind? Buffeted by cosmic rays, prodded by photons. Pulled by gravity?

"VILMA, is there a gravitational source near the path of the ship?"

"There are no readings of significant gravity in this area of space."

That didn't prove anything. It might not be strong enough to affect *Orphion* itself.

The picture in his mind was fantastic, but compelling: a micro-black hole, teasing thoughts from the unwary inhabitants of passing craft, and winding them together like a ball of yarn. Loose threads might trail from the fringes, even breaking loose once in a long while to drift with the cosmic tides, perhaps to be captured....

By an electrostatic scoop tens of thousands of kilometres wide?

A node in space—a node of accumulated thoughts. And a passing ramscoop.

A true gathering of minds.

\#

As *Orphion* penetrated deeper into the node's zone of influence, Hendricks became convinced that whole minds hadn't been collected, only vestiges of them, like short loops of video and audio.

The woman always sat crying; the man fought his pain; the child played with switches. And there were soon others: a teenaged boy with an eye blackened from a fight, and a twenty-something man struggling to repair his malfunctioning EVA suit.

The images became more solid and Hendricks began to hear voices—scraps of words that he thought he understood. The woman with the golden hair had just learned of an unwanted pregnancy. The tall man's affliction would kill him before he could reach his destination.

Maybe these fragments endured because they were moments of great emotional power, raising them above the cosmic static. They must have been tagged with an underlying self-image, allowing him to see what the people looked like. He didn't know why he saw the same figures again and again. Perhaps he drew certain manifestations to himself, without meaning to.

They were not visual apparitions alone. Meals were delivered that he hadn't requested. Instrument readouts came and went. Even the ship's lighting was capricious. If the effect didn't soon subside, he'd have no choice but to alter VILMA's programming. Just thinking about it left him exhausted and dizzy from a fierce headache. It was damn hard to concentrate.

The cabin began to sway. His lungs complained.

"VILMA. Give me the readings on the cabin breathing mixture."

"14.2% oxygen, 74.5% nitrogen, 10.3% methane, 1% trace gases consisting of...."

Methane!

"Methane concentration increasing as requested."

How could...?

Yes, it was possible. *Orphion* used a gas synthesizer, not only for life support, but also to provide specialized gases to store certain cargoes. Easy to bind carbon molecules into CH_4.

It was displacing the oxygen. He'd suffocate.

He slid off the chair and sprawled across the floor, unable to catch himself.

Then he saw the spider.

It had a smooth cylindrical body like a fuel canister, with only six legs. The two lateral limbs were tipped with a pair of claw-like prongs and a thicker opposing prong, like a thumb. They waved and darted urgently through the air. There were no obvious eyes, but textured patches were spaced at intervals around the torso.

Hendricks dimly registered a polyphonic wailing in his ears, spanning several octaves at once.

An alarm? Or a *scream*?

"VILMA," he said. "Restore the breathing mixture to normal."

"Methane concentration increasing as requested."

No! Earth normal!

"Give me manual systems override," he wheezed.

A holo of a touchpad appeared beside him. He struggled to his knees, and fought to remember the sequence of commands. It had been so long. When it was done he collapsed onto the floor again.

He looked at the spider. Its movements became more frantic.

"VILMA...?"

"Methane concentration increasing as requested."

No. He must have missed a step!

He tried to rise but couldn't. He could only lie there and watch as the spider went into spasms. The seizure peaked, then slowed, and finally stopped. Its body slumped.

Then it was gone.

"Oxygen levels rising," VILMA announced.

Hot tears splashed to the floor.

#

He disabled VILMA's Mental Actuation and programmed her to respond to his voice or digital commands only. He didn't dare do more, and couldn't risk any less.

Lying in his bed with oxygen flushing his system, he thought about the spider. If what he'd seen was real, it was the first evidence of another sentient species in the galaxy. Methane breathers. And they had passed close to human space.

He thought he could decipher the tragic vignette. The creature's ship had been pierced by a micro-meteoroid and the atmosphere had begun to bleed out. The pilot had tried to increase the partial pressure of methane to compensate. But it hadn't worked. Hendricks' life had been saved by the spider's death.

Human interference with VILMA was bad enough. He'd never imagined the computer could respond to the workings of a wholly alien mind!

Wait. Of course, she couldn't. She was attuned to his own brainwaves *and no others*. Not even other humans. Which meant that the intruding thoughts were only detected by VILMA because they were somehow resonating in his own brain first!

If that was true, he should put himself back to sleep—break the connection. But for how long? How could he know when the danger had passed?

How old were these lingering scraps of cognition? Had the alien met its end centuries in the past? A year ago? Last week? What if thought energy wasn't shackled to the same continuum of space/time as the electromagnetic spectrum?

Had he been hearing voices from the future?

Maybe they weren't wisps of energy bound to a node in space, but the trailing mental debris of a fleet of ships, like the discarded offal in the wake of a sea-going vessel, or the cast-off tail of a comet. Would he someday catch up to the bodies from which such potent thoughts had escaped?

Would he someday meet the woman with golden hair?

His body could not survive deep-sleep for the duration of the voyage, and what if he was wrong? What if VILMA really was responding to commands other than his own?

He might never wake up.

#

Orphion descended into pandemonium.

VILMA no longer responded to the lost scraps of souls, but the faces and voices still besieged Hendricks. He closed his eyes and they were there, dancing on his eyelids. The blond woman wept and he felt the tears running down his own cheeks.

In a grim moment of insight he understood.

They were inside him.

He tried to distinguish his own memories from theirs and found that he couldn't. His hand rose to brush back long golden hair. He winced at the stabbing pain in his abdomen, then clutched at his shoulders and neck, trying to find the deadly leak in a spacesuit. He knew the first hot blush of love, the ache of hunger, thirst, regret...a powerful urge to urinate, his first wet dream.

Sorrow, desire, delight. Anger. Shame.

Fear.

The thoughts were not his. *The mind was no longer his.*

He was a leaf under a waterfall, his identity drowning.

"VILMA!" he blurted. "Collapse the ramscoop."

"I cannot comply with that command."

Of course not. She couldn't endanger the ship. Without the protection of the scoop it would be at the mercy of charged particles with the velocity to turn them into missiles. If the scoop stayed down for long, the fusion drive would run out of fuel and might never restart.

"Give me manual override."

The ship shuddered beneath him as the field collapsed, the cells of his spine resonating with the vibration. He began to shake like a dog shedding water, scattering memories, spilling sensations, casting out demons.

Then his body fell still and he knew no more.

#

When Hendricks awoke he gave a gasp, then held his breath.

Yes, he could hear the drive, though the ramscoop was still off.

Re-engage the ramscoop please, VILMA.

No response. Mental Actuation was still disabled.

"VILMA, re-deploy the ramscoop please."

"Acknowledged."

"How is the hull integrity? Have there been any collisions?"

"Hull integrity is near 100%. Do you require the number of particle collisions?"

"No."

What should he tell Earth? Ship's telemetry was transmitted automatically—they would know he had shut off the ramscoop. But VILMA's records would only show a series of commands given and obeyed. Part of him still wondered if all that he'd experienced had been the result of a malfunction: a cognitive misfire, electronic or human. The thought brought a stir of nausea.

"VILMA, were any gravitational anomalies detected while I was unconscious?"

"No nearby sources of gravity have been detected."

Maybe they'd passed the node.

Or maybe it had never existed at all.

He felt OK, but something was different. It took time for him to identify the feeling.

Loneliness.

He called up a view of space behind the ship. Whatever lay in *Orphion*'s wake, it was a secret he would keep to himself.

He left VILMA in voice-recognition mode. But he did make one change.

He asked her to maintain a continuous visual presence, occasionally switching at random among her repertoire of different personalities to engage him in conversation.

The rest of the time she looked like a beautiful woman with golden hair.

# # #

THE CLEANSING

KAYDEN ATTENDED HIS FIRST MEETING of the Council with a five-star hangover. It shamed him, but not as much as the memory of all the wasted food at his inauguration party. That made his stomach twist as he learned the Council's disastrous news.

The air of the Great Hall was humid and close, with the dusky odour of a wooden enclosure with windows discretely shut. The room was a comfortable size for the usual rank of twenty councillors, but never meant to hold the additional twelve heads of the Food Guilds plus their assistants. Kayden felt like an imposter occupying the seat so long held by his father, Leeum. Unprepared for his father's retirement, he was even more shocked to be chosen as the next clan leader, and his first reaction had been that it would entice women into his bed. He'd been so much younger just two short days ago.

Matriarch Gwinn called the meeting to order and her chief advisor, Hannis, nodded a head of dark silver curls as he stood for their attention.

"I ask Daffid of the Guild of Fruit Trees to speak to us first. There is no significance to this choice, and you may take that fact as very significant indeed."

Heads cocked in puzzlement as an elderly man with a luxuriant growth of dark hair and beard got to his feet.

"I approached Hannis a week ago," he said, "because we are facing a near total failure of the fruit crop this season. Almost every tree species under our supervision requires bees for pollination. Without pollination there is no fruit. This year, *there are no bees.*"

There were sharp intakes of breath around the table. Some of the other Guild representatives straightened suddenly in their seats.

"Do you have any explanation for this?" Gwinn asked.

"My specialists cannot agree. The unusually wet weather this season would keep insects from traveling far, and cause fungal outbreaks. A mutated varroa mite has also been discovered—a serious threat to bee colonies. But neither of those are severe enough to explain the losses we're seeing. This year's bees have simply died. Or were never born."

He sat down, while Hannis introduced the head of the Grain Crops Guild, a black barrel of a man named Otes.

"My news is just as bad," Otes said, looking dismayed to find that he wasn't alone in his troubles. "Barley, wheat, and the rest—all but wiped out."

"No bees?" asked a councillor named Soozen.

"Grains don't depend on bees. They pollinate by the wind. We figured it was all the rain, washing the nitrogen from the soil, but that'd still leave fertile patches where the water pooled. There are none."

A third representative told of unprecedented losses among the root crops and tubers that could not be accounted for by blight or a lack of sunshine.

"Is this what you meant by the non-significance of your choice?" Councillor Almar asked Hannis in a hoarse voice.

"Yes. It didn't matter who spoke first. The story is the same from them all. *Every crop we have has suffered a catastrophic failure.*"

The thick silence that fell was finally broken by Pedur, five years older than Kayden, a Council member for only a year. "I don't understand. I was always told these things couldn't happen. The Tech Legions assured us that the crops of Earth could not fail—that they had been secured against pests and diseases and droughts. Even against too much rain or heat."

Almar spoke again. "It has been more than two hundred years since The Departure. Perhaps the genetic solutions they engineered have deteriorated."

Mykle was the leader of the Corn Guild. "Some mutations are inevitable, and fatal variations can occur, but they could not effect every crop in just one generation. Or every species of bee. It's impossible."

"There may be a whole host of different threats at work," Hannis acknowledged. "If so, they have all struck at once. There are no records of anything like this in the archives of The Digital. I have asked our Treasurer, Semanta, to give us an estimate of the Valley's current food supplies in storage."

A grey-faced woman struggled to her feet.

"At our current usage, we have only two-weeks worth of most vegetables, and a month's supply of corn and other grains, thanks to last season's good harvest. If we stop feeding the livestock immediately, we might stretch that to two months, but it would require careful rationing. A subsistence diet only."

Matriarch Gwinn cleared her throat. "Each of the guilds must make a detailed estimate of the maximum crop yields we can expect. And *keep all of this to yourselves*, for guilds' sake. We'll meet again in four days."

"Is there...is there any chance of contacting the Tech Legions to ask for their help? Or even the

Uploads?" Soozen's clansfolk were herders of sheep and goats.

"As far as we can tell, the last representatives of technological humankind left the solar system eighty years ago. We don't know where they have gone," Hannis said. "As for the Uploads...they could not help us even if they were willing. They no longer experience the world we know—we might not even recognize them as human anymore. I'm afraid we're on our own."

#

Kayden watched the dark-haired woman step lithely from the Great Hall to the small field of clover between the building and the edge of the forest. She sank to the ground in the midst of the blossoms, and held her knees in her arms. Sunshine fell on her like false hope. Romana was her name—Hannis's assistant. He should leave her alone with her thoughts, but as he tried to walk quietly by, she looked up.

"Maybe the last clover we'll see," she said. "Waiting until death, for bees that never come."

"I wish I could do something to help."

"Like what? Emptying all of the jars of ale so we can store food in them?"

His shoulders slumped. "I'm not a drunk. It was an inauguration party. I had no idea what...what was coming."

"I know you, Kayden of the Hood clan. You have a clever mind more used to finding loopholes than solutions."

"Then I'll leave you alone," he said. "A cloak of righteousness like yours only has room for one."

She turned her head as if to reply, but he was already many meters away.

#

Four days later, Romana stood before the Council.

"The Digital has no record of crop failures coinciding in the way we're now seeing," she began. "There have been many instances of individual crop losses throughout human history. But since The Departure, most have been deliberate."

Throats rasped with indrawn breath.

"It's a phenomenon known as *die-out*, and it was genetically introduced into all of our domesticated plants and animals, as far as I can tell. The purpose was to maintain genetic purity. In earlier times this was accomplished by physical methods, known as *rouging*. The DNA of all species can spontaneously change, because of sexual reproduction, cosmic radiation, and other factors. Over time this causes genetic drift, with the risk of significant and permanent changes that alter the characteristics of the plant or animal. The gen-techs of two centuries ago decided to use their recombinant DNA technology to fight genetic drift by building safeguards into the genomes of each species." She looked around to see if they were following her. No-one was napping.

"Minor changes are tolerated on the assumption that they're probably temporary. But when the genome strays too far from the desired template, a *failsafe coding* comes into effect, and the next generation dies out, without reproducing. Or most of it, anyway. The original calculations assumed that such mutations would not affect the majority of individuals in just one generation, so the best solution would be to allow a die-off down to a carefully-estimated number just above the *minimum viable population*, usually between five to ten percent. It also appears the gen-techs arranged for die-outs to happen on a regular basis even without severe mutations, as a periodic...cleansing. With each species on a different cycle, of course."

"The gen-techs thought that a five percent survival rate was enough to guarantee the regeneration of a species?" Almar's face was nearly crimson.

"Since they believed they'd successfully nullified any significant threats to the plant and animal species we need...yes, they thought it was enough."

"Except they didn't stick around to find out." A heavy fist made the oak table boom.

"It's hard to believe anyone would deliberately engineer crops to fail," said Robbun, the representative of the Cook clan. "But that still doesn't explain how all of the crops, and even the bees, would *die-out* at the same time."

"You're right," answered Romana. "It may be that some solar or climate event caused a sudden large mutation in the genomes, and triggered the failsafes. Or it may be simply a matter of the odds. Given enough time, even a large number of cyclical events can eventually coincide. And it's our bad luck to see it happen."

#

False smiles and over-hearty handshakes were exchanged as scouts were sent into the surrounding countryside over the next few days in the hope of finding an enclave that had been spared from the die-out. It was a faint hope—only the most remote reaches of the planet would have crops unaltered by gen-tech. Most edible wild plants also suffered from the loss of bees, and though many berry crops were pollinated by other insects, they weren't enough to provide more than a small supplement to the stored food.

The heads of the Livestock and Poultry Guilds shouted him down when Pedur suggested their animals might have to be used for meat. It had been generations since humanity had slaughtered animals for food, and the thought sickened them. He gracelessly pointed out that the animals would die of starvation anyway.

Gwinn deferred that decision, but sent her son Wain and a party of twenty strong young men toward the sea coast in the east. The Coasters isolated themselves from the other people of the continent, but perhaps they would permit the gathering of water plants, shrimp, or clams, if Wain and his men found they could stomach that.

In the meantime, Kayden was assigned with Semanta to coordinate food supplies. They had to move quickly. As soon as the word got out about the coming disaster, hoarding would begin, and even the non-violence of three centuries might come to an end under the threat of starvation. Kayden persuaded the Guilds to announce a competition to honour citizens who proved themselves the best stewards of the harvest.

People proudly proclaimed the extent of their remaining food stores from the previous season. Then Semanta's men impounded the declared stockpiles.

Though the plan worked, the congratulations of his fellow Councillors sounded forced, and Romana shunned Kayden entirely. He gave her up as a fallow field not worth the ploughing.

He rarely saw her in any case—she and Hannis spent their days in consultation with Gwinn. On the fourth day he found out why.

"The coming famine is a battle we cannot win," the Matriarch told the Council. Kayden had never seen her look so old. "There is a chance that the supplies we have, stretched to their limit, could enable a small number of citizens to survive. It would have to be few enough to then subsist on a portion of the *next* harvest that would still leave enough plants for regeneration. Most of us will die. *Must* die."

"The minimum viable population of humanity itself," Romana breathed.

"Perhaps," Gwinn said. "My heart desperately hopes that this was not what the gen-tech engineers intended, but the end result is the same. And though we cannot control what happens beyond our borders, the likelihood is that all the peoples of the Earth are facing the same terrible choice."

Her head had begun to sink like the westering sun, but she found the strength to raise it again.

"We must save the children. And since they cannot care for themselves, a very few adults also, carefully selected. These must be of the most fertile child-bearing age, because the survival of our race will require many more children as soon as they can be fed. The upper limit I have chosen is somewhat arbitrary: twenty-five years of age."

The room exploded into sound. Kayden's heart froze at the sound of his death sentence.

Yohan, councilman of the outlying clan of Jonus, threw a goblet of water against the wall. "You mean no-one over twenty-five will be given food? Our children will have to watch us starve?" The logs of the wall behind him shed fat drops.

"They will watch nothing." Gwinn's calm voice penetrated the clamour. "Everyone over twenty-five, and even most of the adults younger than that, will *leave the Valley.*"

Shafts of sunlight through the hall's small windows held dust motes suspended in the suddenly stilled air.

"It is the only way." Gwinn spoke in a voice so soft it could barely leave her lips. "There is an ancient tradition among some tribes of humanity that elders should voluntarily leave the community when they become a burden to it."

"To die in the wilderness," Pedur said. Gwinn's eyes turned to him, but she said nothing. Further protests did not come. Silence was the more honourable response.

"The caretakers for the children will be chosen by noon tomorrow. The rest of us will leave the day after. We cannot wait any longer and still give the young a chance to survive."

#

Kayden sat on a hillock, facing the distant sunset. Its vibrant reds and golds brought no warmth—he knew they only heralded the coming of the darkness. Gwinn's summons found him there.

"You are twenty-seven, Councillor? " the Matriarch asked. He only nodded. "Yet you must stay behind. The survivors must have a leader, and there is no-one younger to whom I would entrust this responsibility."

"You can't mean that," he said, his eyes wide. "I have no experience as a leader, and certainly not the wisdom to safeguard the future of our race."

"No-one has that. But you have always led. People follow you naturally—you have a gift. It was no accident that you were chosen head of your clan. Leeum planned for it for years."

The revelation shocked him.

"Please. I don't want such a responsibility. I'd rather take my chance in the wilderness."

"Good. A leader who did not understand the full weight of such a charge would not be worthy to bear it." In spite of everything, she managed a smile. "The other reason I've chosen you is that your thoughts and actions aren't bound by convention. I think our survivors will need that trait before the dawn finally comes."

Kayden looked for a place to sit, but didn't trust his knees to let him down gently. His habitual cockiness had drained into the floor.

What the survivors truly needed was the wisdom of Gwinn or Hannis, but it had already been announced that the executive couple would lead the exiles.

"You will need help," Gwinn said. "Romana of the Brown clan will assist you. She has the knowledge to reap the reduced harvests without destroying the organisms' chance of survival."

"Romana and I...don't get along."

"Then I suggest you learn."

#

The parting could have been a noble time. Instead, rubble littered the streets, and the thin smoke of protest fires soiled the air. Voices trumpeted their refusal, wailing children clung to trembling knees, long-time neighbours clashed like butting rams over scraps of shrivelled lettuce they would have tossed to the goats only days before. A crowd of those who refused exile gathered on the lawn before the Great Hall, with bravado bolstered by their numbers. But when an envoy of the Council went to speak to them and barely escaped, the sight of her bloodied face was a shock that wilted the raised arms of defiance into fluttering confusion, and the would-be rebels drifted meekly away.

Gwinn, Hannis, and other elders spent a precious two days persuading and pleading, threatening and begging. The hold-outs finally went along rather than face utter disgrace. Perhaps some believed it was only a kind of trial and they would be permitted to return. They took no food and almost no tools—mainly knives from the community's kitchens.

The loss of Kayden's parents seemed to steal the solid earth from beneath his feet. The sight of their struggling shapes fading into the distance made his eyes burn, but to turn away was to face the responsibility he now bore. He wasn't ready for that—would never be.

Yet he was given no time to brood. Soon after sunrise the next morning, the first of their scouts returned, a ragged shell in the shape of a man, young eyes hollowed from seeing too much. Famine loomed everywhere, he reported. No-one was willing to share.

"Most have begun to slaughter their animals for meat. Some..." He swallowed hard. "Some have begun to kill their neighbours to take their food."

The long night had come.

Large numbers of the Valley's own animals had already been slaughtered, before the departure of the elders left too few to do the heavy work. The frightened cries of beasts had given a voice to the wrenching heartache of their human masters. Archived records from The Digital revealed how to preserve the meat by smoking, and the Valley floor looked as if it were on fire, stalks of grey and black holding up a mammoth canopy, where an inversion layer of air had moved in above. Kayden pictured the homes themselves burning—they might as well have burned, so quickly had they become irrelevant.

"It's horrible—human turning against human." Romana had come quietly to his side.

"We've allowed the best among us to sacrifice themselves to give us their food," he replied softly. "Is that so very different?"

#

Romana became indispensable to him—she understood his needs before he knew them himself.

"The children are grieving," she said on the third morning. She meant that Kayden needed to do something about it.

Two days later, he watched as chattering faces and awkward limbs disappeared into the warren of streets, the excitement of a new challenge lifting their feet and drawing their mouths into rare and precious smiles. The unruly scramble even brought a brief smile to his own lips. The teams of six—five children and one adult—weren't yet very good at staying together. Would they eventually become surrogate families, as he hoped?

He caught the bright eyes of a young boy, six or seven, and gave him a wink. The boy scurried off. In a short while the youngsters scattering through the streets would attempt to make their way unseen through an abandoned stretch of the city while a second group, dubbed the Seekers, would try to spot them from high places. There was no tangible prize offered to the winners of the game, only pride of achievement.

It was the first of several competitions Kayden announced. The second involved a search for the most creative hiding places for food: hard to find, but secure from weather and pests. Between contests, barricades were built with rubble across nearly every street into the inhabited core. Select routes were left open but with large stacks of debris kept ready to block them. The few underground concourses were thoroughly surveyed, and their outside entrances disguised.

Once the heavy labour was complete, Kayden announced a third competition. Teams would try to outlast each other in going without food.

"You're deliberately starving them? Long before it's necessary. Why?"

Kayden had learned to welcome the challenge in Romana's dark eyes. It kept him sharp. "All the hard work has been done. The food has been moved into the new storage sites."

"Where the children themselves put it. They know where to find it anytime they get hungry."

"Exactly. It's the honour system. I need to foster their sense of duty. And willpower."

"But why make them suffer now? There will be more than enough suffering when supplies begin to run short."

"Our people have always had ready supplies of food—all we could want. It's made our bodies burn far more energy than our ancestors did. We need to change that. We need to use a lot less food each day."

"So reduce it gradually. Don't starve them."

Kayden shook his head, forced to trust knowledge gathered centuries before he was born, though the words were awkard in his mouth.

"A gradual drop won't do—it has to be a state of starvation. Within a few days the body responds by lowering its metabolism. Shutting down unnecessary fuel burners, and restricting other systems in a deliberate rotation. We also have to reduce our muscle mass. We won't need strong muscles for a while, and they burn more energy than we can afford. Doctor Eelayne has special supplements that will make sure the children's health isn't compromised. If I'm right, within three weeks most of us will need only a little more than half of the daily food ration we're currently eating."

"But Semanta..."

"Semanta couldn't guarantee that our supplies will last until the next harvest."

Romana fell silent. After a time she lifted her eyes.

"What were the other competitions for?"

"Have you ever heard of *war*? No? Then I think you should ask The Digital about it."

#

More scouts arrived at long intervals. Small communities had taken to raiding each other for food. Yet, strangely, not all had turned to eating meat. Many had simply driven the livestock away from the settlements instead of killing them, either unable to face the act of killing, or hoping the animals would be able to subsist on wild vegetation where humans could not.

Kayden hoped so, too. He was nearly certain that his people would need to slaughter more of their animals than planned—more than the minimum viable population estimates allowed for. The remainder would have to find mates from somewhere else.

One wild species thrived for the first months. There were protests when he ordered openings to be made in the fences around their few remaining crop fields, but the reward came quickly. The sight of befuddled children and adults trying to chase down fleeing rabbits made him laugh out loud. But when he watched as the neck of a struggling animal was wrung by a young girl, it felt as if hands had tightened around his own throat.

The young adapted to their changed circumstances far better than the adults. The Digital had no advice to offer about that.

Kayden organized a dance.

When the event came, the Great Hall was resplendent in a glittering pastiche of trappings and trinkets for which there was no longer any need. The dance floor filled with gaudy outfits long neglected, and everyone was shocked to realize how much they missed music, so rarely played anymore.

Kayden had only planned to supervise, but he was kept busy with invitations to dance. The ratio of women to men was nearly five to one. Even so, it surprised him to find Romana sitting alone each time he looked her way. At last, he went to her side.

"No-one's asking you to dance? The prettiest woman at the ball?"

"They all think I'm with you."

His eyebrows rose. "Are they right?"

She searched his eyes, then looked away. "You think so hard, and see so much. But not everything."

He felt heat swell in his chest, and reached for her hand.

#

The invasion came a week later.

Spotters in the outlying quadrants of the city raised the alarm, and Kayden went to look for himself. His magniviewer revealed a ragged force of men and women—hundreds more than he'd expected—dirty, thin, but armed with rough clubs and long pieces of wood that were called spears. Within an hour they were within easy reach of Millwood Commons, the enclosed field that had been used for recreational sports. Thin spires of smoke rose above it and had done so for weeks.

"You were right," said Jayn, the overseer of the perimeter patrols. "They expect us to be where the smoke is."

"Smaller communities that depended on the Valley lost their energy supply when our workers left. They'd assume that we'd need fires to cook. Be thankful for our solar collectors."

Once the raiders entered the Commons they'd see that it was empty but, with luck, they'd wait for the occupants to return. Kayden's plan depended on that. He began to issue instructions, and runners sped for the nearest pasture.

#

The pinnacle of the Millennium monument overlooked almost all of Millwood Commons. There were narrow slots for windows, just wide enough to allow a signal flag. Kayden's forces had been in place for nearly half an hour when he finally saw signs of the raiders settling in for a meal, spread over the wide grass surface. Everything was ready, yet he hesitated, repulsed by what he was about to do.

He imagined Romana standing before a rampaging mob if he failed to act.

He let the signal flag drop.

Five small figures herded a black shape toward the nearest opening to the Commons. The same thing would be done at two other gateways on the far side. It seemed an eternity before anything else happened. Then came a sudden roar of noise. Screams. Cries of warning. Shrieks of pain.

He focused his viewer on the far end of the field: dozens of figures were fleeing as mammoth bulls charged down on them. Men were tossed through the air; women stumbled and fell beneath heavy hooves, never to rise. The ones who kept their wits raced toward the nearest walls, but it made little difference. The bulls were enflamed with hunger and confusion. Few of those who fled reached safety. Kayden hung his head over his knees, waiting for his stomach to empty itself.

When he looked up again he saw a group of men with spears standing back-to-back. The bulls did not attack them, so they went on the offensive, drawing recruits as they shuffled raggedly forward. A spear struck home. Another. A bull finally fell, and was swarmed by spearmen. Kayden slammed a fist against the brick lintel of his window, and quickly turned around to wave a second signal flag. Then he descended the inner stair and made his way to the nearby underground concourse to wait for reports.

The raiders left many casualties on the field, but not enough. The remainder would be chastened: they'd suspect more traps, and advance very slowly, but they wouldn't stop, fresh rage driving them on. Kayden's complement of adults was still badly outnumbered, and he would rather surrender than see the children spill blood and have their own spilled.

A young runner came swiftly down the concourse.

"They're calling," she said. "They're calling for our leaders. They say they want a parlour."

Parley, Kayden thought. He hadn't expected that. What compromise could such desperate people offer? He strode to a hidden vantage point within earshot of the Commons.

A tall man with an improvised megaphone was repeating a simple message. Kayden raised his viewer and gave a start of recognition: Keeth, a long-time Council assistant, who'd been second-in-command after Gwinn's son Wain in the expedition to the sea coast. Did that mean Wain was dead? Clearly some of the force had joined with the Coasters, and instead of returning with supplies, had brought only a gnawing need.

A woman handed him a rolled cone of fibre sheeting and he put it to his mouth.

"We have nothing to talk about, Keeth," he yelled. "Go back the way you came."

"Who's that? A councillor? Good. Someone who knows you don't always get your way. We're not leaving, councillor. You have food. We want it. We will get it, and you will die."

"If you're so sure, what is there to discuss?"

"We didn't come here for the love of killing," Keeth said. "We know you're trying to save the children. Very noble. So we won't hurt them. We'll leave them alive and they can fend for themselves."

Could he really mean that? What if Kayden surrendered himself and the other adults, and handed over a believable portion of the food? The children would know where to find the rest. At least they'd have a chance.

"We give you our food and you leave?" he shouted.

"You give us the food and we *stay*. Any adults we find after that we *kill*. Except for a few women we might choose to keep around."

Romana would be one of those, Kayden was sure. But it was a moot point. Keeth had betrayed his own community—he couldn't be trusted.

Without bothering to reply, Kayden gathered his followers and fled back toward the core. All entrances to it were quickly barricaded. Then he went to every high point along the perimeter and organized chains of his young workers to pass up bricks and other debris to adults on the roofs. Catapults or slings would have been a great help, but willing arms would have to do. If only his rationing had not left his people too weak to defend themselves.

When the sun was nearly below the horizon, a dark stain poured forth along the Causeway from Millwood Commons. The leading edge was ragged, but implacable, spreading across the road in arrogant confidence. It would reach the barricades within a half-hour.

As Kayden hung his head, an arm roughly nudged him.

"Councillor, look! On the Causeway. About a hundred meters ahead of the raiders."

People. There were people spilling out onto the road!

"Who ordered that?" he snapped.

"No-one did. They can't be ours. Everyone's at their posts. Would some of the raiders have gone ahead as scouts?"

"They're not raiders."

The newcomers moved slowly, awkwardly. Not just tentative, but as if hampered by physical deformity or weakness. He swept his viewer back and forth as their numbers grew, forming into a rough line across the path of the invaders. He caught a flash of colour when someone stepped into a last ray of sunlight, right at the front. Brown. Or was it red?

Scarlet? Could it be the scarlet of a *Council* uniform?

"*Gwinn.*" He breathed.

There, at her side, must be Hannis, leaning on a staff for support. Waiting. Waiting for an end.

"It's our people!" Kayden shouted. "Our elders!" He watched in awe as stragglers streamed in from side streets, alleys, and passageways. A number greater than the enemy, but that did not mean victory. It would be a massacre, not a battle.

Many of Gwinn's people were willing to die, but not to kill. Beaten and pierced by spears, they clutched at their assailants, tripping and dragging them down. Others too weak to offer blows clung together like a living wall upon which the waves of attackers battered, and then swarmed over raiders unlucky enough to stumble. It was horrific—Kayden desperately hoped that the children couldn't see what was happening from the other outposts.

Body after weakened body fell. He lost sight of Gwinn after the first onslaught. Yet those who fell were replaced from the sidelines. How could so many have survived so long? And still they came. Helplessly,

Kayden watched the carnage as long as the light remained, and then listened to the cries of the injured and the dying in the darkness. When the sounds finally faded away, he waited for a different cry: the alert signal from watchers along the core perimeter.

It didn't come.

After an hour he gathered a force of ten men and women, with a few pairs of mining goggles to let them see in the dark. They made their way beneath the barricades and toward the Causeway, slowed only by their need for silence. The streets near the core were still deserted. The Causeway itself was empty. Until they came to the place where the elders had made their stand.

It was a scene Kayden could never have imagined: bodies piled upon bodies, over all a sour stench and a sickening ululation of feeble voices. He carefully stepped toward a half-dozen stark silhouettes slouched against a wall.

One of them was Hannis.

"I think we got them all," he rasped, breathing with difficulty. "Gwinn...Gwinn's dead. Near the front of the line." The old man looked at his outspread hands, seeing stains that Kayden could only imagine.

"How did you...?

"We found some food in the wilderness," the elder said. "But not much. It was all we could do to keep the weaker ones from returning to the city. Gwinn hit on the idea of going east. She promised we'd find food there, but I think she just wanted news of our son. We did not find him." The quavering voice fell silent for a moment, then roused itself.

"We saw the raiders coming. We knew where they must be headed, and why."

"You sacrificed yourselves."

"Wasn't that the plan? I'm only grateful we lasted long enough to do one more service for our people."

"Well you've earned your lives," Kayden declared. "I'll bring Doctor Eelayne and her trainees to do whatever they can for these others."

Hannis shook his head, but had no strength to resist.

#

When dawn came, Hannis and his companions were gone. The children could probably have found them, but Kayden didn't give the order. To pursue them further would be to dishonour their sacrifice. He stood on a high rooftop and watched the sun rise against uncertain clouds.

"Will others come to attack us?" Romana pressed against his side.

"Almost certainly. But the next will be fewer and weaker, and the next after that weaker still."

"They might have those long shafts of wood, and the other things."

"Weapons, yes. We also have weapons, but I still hoped that we could negotiate with such people. I've learned otherwise."

"What weapons?"

"Fire. Poisoned food. Electrified traps."

"You'd use such things?"

He turned to her. "You saw what the elders did for us. Would you have me value their sacrifice so little by refusing to soil my own hands?"

#

His predictions proved accurate, yet they lost few to warfare, or even disease. They were very lucky.

On a morning in March, Romana found him sitting on a slope overlooking one of the vegetable fields.

"Look," he said, sweeping a hand toward the aura of light green, newly risen over the tilled rows. "The seeds. They're taking hold. Coming to life."

"Your seed, too," she said, resting a hand on her abdomen. His puzzled look turned to a cry of joy, and he crushed her to his chest, then thought better of it and backed away.

"It's all right." She laughed. "I won't break. Neither will he. Or she." Kayden's eyes slid to her belly, his smile tempered with sorrow. "What were you doing up here anyway?" she asked.

"I was thinking about something Gwinn once said. She hoped that all this wasn't a plan by the gen-tech engineers to keep the human strain pure."

"Gwinn and Hannis and the others...they weren't mutations."

"No? Think about them: a generation of people who were able to deny their own survival instinct for the sake of others. Not just for their own children, but for the children of strangers. Are you so certain the Tech Legions wouldn't have considered that an aberration?"

She was searching for an answer when his sombre face came alight with a smile. Then she heard the sound herself.

The drone of a passing bee.

#   #   #

THE RIFT

T HE SHIP'S VIEWSCREEN REVEALED the new system like sequins scattered over tar, with a bright, ruddy, circular patch in the center that looked like a mistake.

Astrogator Burns was the first to notice the abnormal reading, but kept his mouth shut. The survey ship *Charles S. Peirce* was due to return to its home shipyards at Angel in another month and he didn't want anything to screw that up.

Chief Survey Officer Lake saw the reading when she got back from the head anyway.

"A huge spike in the cosmic microwave background radiation, Captain."

Arness looked up from a math puzzle in the air above his lap. "We already knew there was a late-time anisotropy in this area, Lake. That's part of the reason we're here."

"Yes, Captain, and I'm saying it's centered on this star system. I can't place it more exactly yet, but give me a minute." She drew her fingers through her holographic display as if plucking out an errant molecule from the air and placing it where it belonged. "Right. There are also anomalous readings in the star's gravitational field, its magnetic field, and even in the flow of the solar wind. Those anomalies converge almost exactly in a region about point zero eight AU from the star." She smiled at Arness. "I'd bet that's where the spike in the CMB is centered, too."

The captain gave a sigh and shared a look with Burns and Chief Technician Singh.

"All right. Get a team on it. That's what we're out here for."

"Why couldn't one of these assignments give us a chance to stretch out under an open sky?" Mowat, the *Peirce's* doctor and biologist, was on the bridge to run a scan on the system's five planets. Three were gas giants and one was a roasted rock that orbited its sun in less than two days. Only the second planet was within the habitable zone, but there probably wouldn't be liquid water since the planet was tidally-locked: the sunward face would be too hot and the far side too cold. "Where are we, anyway?"

The ship itself answered. "*This star does not have a name—it is designated HIP 97847. Spectral Class M0. Estimated mass...*"

"Thanks, CP. That's enough for now." Mowat turned to Lake. "M class? I guess the viewscreen filters out a lot of the red light. We're still close to The Rift, though, right?"

"About a hundred and ninety light years. Not as close as we were at the B9 star we just surveyed."

But close enough to feel it like an eye watching over your shoulder, Mowat thought. His mouth twitched. Proximity to The Rift interfered with the ability of a ship to use the sub layer of space but no-one knew how far the effect reached. They only knew that two ships had been lost near The Rift in the twenty-seven years since the Cygnus X-1 incident that had created it. There had been no explanation. There had been no data whatsoever.

Maybe the ability to roam the stars had seduced humanity into underestimating the intractability of the universe, Mowat thought. The idea of using a black hole like Cygnus X-1 for particle acceleration experiments was hubris on the grandest scale. Then to have directed the particles to collide near the event horizon....

Only one of four ships had straggled home after that disaster, leaving in its wake an un-lanced boil on the face of the galaxy. The Rift wasn't a tear in space/time, as was first thought, but a miniature newborn universe that severed the Orion Spur like a guillotine blade through a neck and, as far as their instruments could tell, also sundered the neighbouring Perseus and Sagittarius Arms all the way to the galactic core. A galaxy now divided by an impenetrable barrier, carving jaggedly through space from black hole to black hole like a child-god's connect-the-dots drawing. How many systems had been destroyed in an eye-blink twenty-seven years ago, Mowat wondered? How many races were now cut off from each other? Humankind hadn't yet encountered other sentient life, but Mowat had always felt it was only a matter of time. Until the creation of The Rift.

It occurred to him that the path of Earth's children had changed in another way since The Rift, although the two things couldn't be related. Could they?

It was probably just the rose-coloured haze of hindsight that made human expansion into the galaxy seem like a golden era, but it was a fact that there had been almost no new colonization in the past twenty-seven years, the resources of the race focused instead on inter-colony conflict and antagonism toward the home planet that had never been a problem before. An urge to deflect blame? Or perhaps it was the shock of knowing that even something as large as a galaxy was not immune to human arrogance—the tunnel-visioned confidence of a young species suddenly punctured by a harsh reality.

He went to his bunk and lay brooding.

Early the next morning, Lake found him half-heartedly pushing food around a plate.

"Cheer up. It looks like you'll get your wish."

"My wish?"

"A chance to stretch your legs. The anomaly has moved. Don't ask me how. Not randomly, either. It's now centered on the second planet."

Mowat gave a whoop that echoed down the gangway toward the sleeping quarters. Angry voices testified that it hadn't been welcome.

#

"It's like an oasis, Captain. Almost exactly at the north pole."

The planet's terminator ran through both poles, dividing endless scorching day from perpetual frozen night with a line of grudging hospitality. Extra CO_2 in the atmosphere produced enough greenhouse effect to redistribute some of the heat, but only the newly-discovered patch in the north revealed vegetation.

"A little too convenient, don't you think?" Singh said to his captain. Arness gave him a blank look.

"I'll send a boat down, Mowat, but I'm not going to risk more than three crew groundside. Take Ketsela with you."

They landed close to the center of the oasis. Mowat was astonished by the green vegetation and waved off Ketsela's concerns about the air.

"The oxygen content here is a lot higher than most of the planet—produced by the plants, I'd say. They look like they use chlorophyll. And because it's a bigger planet than Earth or Angel, with a denser atmosphere, the partial pressure of O_2...we'll be able to breathe it just fine." To prove his point he went through the airlock with his helmet tucked under his arm, while Lake frowned at him from inside the cabin. He barely paused to set the helmet down in the lock before he was off among the plants. Moments later he was beckoning eagerly, forgetting that his com link was in his helmet. Lake and Ketsela finally shrugged at each other and went outside.

"I'm with Singh," Ketsela rumbled an hour later to Lake. "This is all too damn convenient. The question is: convenient for us, or for somebody else?"

They'd left Mowat at the boat and made a large circle across the territory. None of Lake's instruments were useful—the effect she was tracking was too widespread. That left them little option but a visual search for its source.

"Maybe it's convenient for *that*," Lake pointed, her eyes wide. Ketsela followed the line of her arm.

He saw the water hole and some tall tree-like plants fringing it. What he'd first taken for a boulder was too upright for that, like a small creature, or even a humanoid crouched over.

Or a boy sitting on a rock.

"He looks human," Lake whispered. "I'm detecting a humanlike temperature and respiration." A look of horror crossed her face and she raised her helmet to talk to the *Peirce*.

CP's female voice sounded even more human than usual over the com link.

"There were no children on either of the missing ships. And no embryos. No other human craft have crossed this area of space."

Ketsela turned to Lake. "Are you thinking some of the Cygnus X-1 research crew could have landed here...and had a baby fifteen years later?"

CP answered again. *"The lone surviving craft from the Cygnus X-1 incident was damaged, and during the two weeks required for repairs they searched for signs of other survivors. There were none."*

Lake called Mowat on the com link and waited until he arrived.

"Are you afraid of him?" Mowat asked softly.

"No." Lake bridled. "Show me an alien and I'll go through the prescribed protocols. But this looks like a human. You're a doctor."

Mowat took several steps forward, not trying to be quiet. He hoped a noise would make the boy look up, but the head stayed still, apparently aimed toward the small pool of water in front. Mowat walked to within two meters of the small figure and stopped.

"You've come," the boy said.

"You speak my language."

"Yes."

"Where are you from? Who are you?"

The handsome dark head finally turned and brown eyes looked into the doctor's.

"I don't know."

#

"He appears to be human," Mowat reported over the com, "judging from every test my med-tablet can administer. About twelve-years old. Speaks flawless interlingua—with an Angel accent, Ketsela says. In perfect health, too, but I have no way to know how long he's been here or what he's been living on. I tested his blood for traces of the local minerals and plant enzymes, but came up empty. If anything, I'd say his blood and cell chemistry is a match for ours: the *Peirce*'s crew, I mean."

"Is there any chance this boy has something to do with the field anomalies Lake was tracing?" Arness asked.

"How could he? He's just a boy."

"Where no boy has any right to be. Until we know more I won't risk bringing him to the ship. And he won't say where he's from, or even his name?"

"I'd say he has amnesia, Captain. He knows a lot of facts, but can't remember anything about his past. Ketsela says we should name the boy Xavier. I think it's an Ethiopian inside joke, but he won't explain it. Just gives that infuriating smile."

#

"I don't know whether you'll like any of our food, but it shouldn't hurt you," Mowat said, as he held out a stick of protein and carbs. Strawberry-flavoured. The boy politely nibbled at it, then raised his eyebrows and took a large bite.

"Now Xavier—do you mind if we call you Xavier?"

"Any name is as good as any other. Your name is Peter Mowat."

"Yes." The boy must have heard the others use it. "Have you always spoken this language?"

"Yes."

"That means you must be from Earth, or one of its colony worlds."

"Does it?"

"Well...why else would you speak it?"

"I speak it so you'll understand me."

"Just a minute," Ketsela interrupted. He uttered a stream of sound with many ululations of the tongue. It sounded like gibberish to Mowat, but the boy replied without hesitation. Ketsela laughed.

"He says he should have made his skin like mine. The sun is strong."

"That was a language?"

"It's called Amharic. My grandfather insisted on teaching it to me."

"Did the boy speak it well?"

"He could have invented it."

Lake was standing behind Mowat's shoulder. "How would he change the colour of his skin?"

"Xavier, do you remember where you were just before this? How you came here?"

The boy paused, as if trying to recall. "I chose to be here. So you could come to me."

"*My apologies for interrupting.*" CP's voice floated from Mowat's helmet on the ground nearby. "*You are needed on board, Doctor. There's been an emergency.*"

"Acknowledged." Mowat lifted himself from the rock.

A crewwoman named Jurgens had suddenly become confused and partially paralysed. CP had already diagnosed a stroke caused by a cerebral embolism, and Mowat administered a drug to dissolve the arterial blockage, but there was no improvement after a couple of hours. For the crews that explored the fringes of known space, it was one of the most dreaded of injuries.

"If the *Peirce* were just one size-class bigger, its med-lab would have a cranial laser," Mowat told the captain. "Without one, I can't get at the clot. Drugs work too slowly for this kind of blockage. There's nothing more I can do except put her in stasis and get her to a better facility within a month before stasis wears off."

"We're farther than that from any colony planet," Arness mused. "CP, tell me the closest big ship to our current position."

"*The* Restitution *has been on colony prep duty in the Deneb system, Captain, but she is due to return to Sirius in eleven days from now.*"

"That's nearly five hundred light years. We wouldn't make it in time." The muscle along Arness's jawline twitched. "Use the strongest drugs you dare, Doctor, and we'll give them two days. Then...we'll just have to do our best." His eyes returned to the viewscreen. After months of dull routine, space had suddenly regained all of its vastness.

\#

Mowat returned to the planet. Given his habit of forgetting his helmet, he now wore a com patch below his left ear. He stopped in his tracks as he came upon Xavier, flanked by a pile of strawberries on one side and a smaller pile of discarded stems on the other. Mowat looked questioningly at Ketsela, who shrugged.

"A few plants over there. Didn't notice them before." His face revealed no more than his words.

"How is our...friend?"

"Friendly. Cooperative. But more inquisitive than informative."

"I'm right here," the boy said.

"Sorry, Xavier. That was rude of me. How are you? Is there anything you'd like us to do for you?"

"You and Ketsela don't really respect each other. You should. You're very much alike."

The two men shared an uncomfortable look.

"I meant, do you need anything from us?"

"Yes."

"What is it you need?"

"I don't know. I brought you here to find out."

"You *brought*...?" Mowat drew his head back and looked around for Lake. She was among some tall plants fifteen meters away, operating her laser analyser.

"What more have you learned?" Mowat asked her.

"Well there's nothing to prove this oasis couldn't have developed on its own, but I have my doubts. The plants are all extremely basic, but there are a few individual variations. Like one single plant that has stripes on its leaves. Another has fronds of different shades. I discovered an insect—kind of like an Earth butterfly—that doesn't seem to do anything but fly around and look pretty. That's not the way evolution works."

"As if the Creator got bored and decided to tinker," Ketsela said quietly. Mowat shot him a look, then turned back to Lake.

"Are you suggesting this place was artificially produced? For what? For Xavier?"

"That's the question, isn't it? Was it produced for him? Or *by* him?"

"Be serious. What about the anomalies?"

"As I've said, they're focused here at the north pole. Xavier is here. Is there a connection? There's no way for me to tell."

"There is a way," Ketsela said, and smiled. "Move him."

With some persuasion, Captain Arness agreed to allow Ketsela to take Xavier into orbit in the boat.

"Look at it," Lake said in awe. Even without full darkness the sky overhead rippled with sparkling curtains of colour. She'd never seen an auroral display, but Mowat had.

"Let me guess: the boat is right in the middle of all that. Of course it is. Captain? You were right—the boy shouldn't be allowed on the *Peirce*. He'd play hell with all of the electronics. I just hope Ketsela's good with manual re-entries."

The boat found them an hour-and-a-half later. Ketsela had made his best guess at a trajectory from orbit, then had to follow the terminator and hope he was heading north.

"None of the nav readings were trustworthy," he said, still shaken. "The boat's onboard computer even locked up a couple of times, though not until we were down at the surface, thank God." He darted a sudden look at Xavier and gave a nervous laugh.

Mowat drew his crewmates out of hearing distance of the boy.

"CP? Help us summarize what we know about Xavier. He's apparently human, eleven or twelve years old. In perfect health in spite of showing no signs of regular eating or drinking. All alone on a planet where no human ships have come."

"*He speaks interlingua and Amharic,*" CP continued. "*He is at the center of a disturbance in gravitational, magnetic, and electrical fields. He was found in an artificially-produced environment merely large enough for him and our crew. He knows your full names.*"

"He probably heard those," Mowat said.

"*He did not. No-one has used anything more than surnames and crew titles to address each other since the Peirce's arrival.*"

After a long silence, Mowat coughed and said, "Can we come to any conclusions? What could he be? What are the possibilities?"

"A survivor from the Cygnus X-1 incident, or one of the two other ships that went missing," Lake muttered. "I know it's not likely, but it's more damn credible than anything else."

"A non-human life-form that's a gifted chameleon," Mowat suggested.

"A mass hallucination?" Lake again.

Ketsela snorted. "You're saying we're dreaming him? Do you dream CP?"

"I do not."

"OK, not a hallucination, but how about a mirage—an artefact of the field distortions that's causing both human and electronic brains to generate false images and readings?"

"The odds of several dozen individual entities experiencing such a coherent and consistent delusion are likely beyond my ability to calculate, CSO. Shall I attempt it?"

"No, thank you, CP," Lake said. "Unless only one of us is dreaming all of this, and the rest don't actually exist."

"In that case, I'm the real one, and to hell with the rest of you." Ketsela laughed loudly. In the distance, they heard Xavier laugh too.

"Does your analysis provide a correlation with anything in your database, CP?" Mowat asked.

"God."

"Excuse me?"

"An all-powerful being, manifested in the universe itself. Omnipresent, not confined to form. However there are Earth myths that God has occasionally taken human form."

"Those are religious beliefs, not myths."

"I do not understand the distinction. Was this belief part of your religion when you were a priest, Doctor?"

Lake and Ketsela looked startled.

"Yes, CP, it was." Mowat sighed, and looked at his companions. "That was a long time ago. I was young. After a disagreement, the church showed me the error of my ways. And showed me the door." He shrugged. "But you're not making sense, CP. How could Xavier be God? Why would He manifest for us? Most of all, why would He be *amnesiac*? What could scramble the mind of God?"

Ketsela made a strangled sound. When the others looked at him, he just shook his head with a mix of alarm and sorrow on his face, and pointed a trembling hand to the sky.

Farther inward along the Orion Spur hung a denser smear of stars, but they were blurred and tenuous—dimmer than the other points of light in the firmament.

The Rift.

#

"You can't expect me to believe that." Arness massaged his forehead. "You're saying God is not only real, but he has *amnesia* because a black hole was evaporated? CP, how could you, of all of us, agree with a crazy idea like that?"

"*The dogma of many religions equates God with the universe, Captain. The universe is the mind of God. The Rift split the galaxy, and possibly beyond. Ergo, the mind of God has been split.*"

"I don't agree that Xavier is God, Captain," Mowat's voice came over the com link. "But he knows facts no human could retain—CP has tested him—yet there are puzzling blanks in his functional memory too." He hesitated. "There are parallels to certain kinds of brain injury in humans: damage to the medial temporal lobe..."

"CP's talking about *God*, for...pity's sake!" It was the first time anyone had heard Arness come close to losing his temper. "How can an all-powerful being be *damaged?*"

No-one could answer that.

#

"What have you been doing?" Mowat asked as he returned to the boat.

"Xavier's been using the boat's direct link to have a chat with CP," Lake answered. "About religious writings, I think. A lot of strange names..."

"Thomas Aquinas. Gödel. Leibniz. Sankara." Ketsela gave Mowat a significant look.

"...quizzing her, and then offering his own interpretations. It was...eerie," Lake finished.

"Proof of God," Mowat breathed. "He knows what we think and he's trying it on for size."

"Can even God prove the existence of God?" Ketsela asked softly.

"It's hard enough to prove that *we* exist. Philosophy's best answer to that is still Descartes' 'I think, therefore I am'."

"But what does God have to think to know He's God?"

"I think you're both crazy," Lake said, lifting her face defiantly. "Xavier's some very advanced life-form, that's all. There is no God. Humans proved that long ago."

"*I must disagree, CSO.*" CP's voice surprised them. "*In a search of my records, humans have never categorically proven that God does not exist. Alternative explanations have simply satisfied scientists that there is no requirement for God to exist in order for the universe to have transpired as it has.*"

"I came to the same conclusion as you, Lake," Mowat said. "Because if we believe that God created the universe we have to ascribe to him incredible powers. Then, in order to explain our disappointments in life, we have to make excuses for Him. Or moral justifications, which may be even worse. Far easier to just assume that there isn't a God. That there never was."

"Laziness," Ketsela rumbled. "Faith is hard. It requires something of us. That's why it's easier to deny the existence of God. Scientific knowledge just gave us the excuses we were looking for."

"That's the crunch for us, too, isn't it?" Mowat looked into their faces. "If Xavier were God, then the question would become: what are we going to do about it?"

"That has always been the choice, Peter Mowat."

They turned toward Xavier's voice, but no young boy stood there. The figure in the hatchway of the boat had a dark complexion like Singh's, and was, unmistakably, a woman.

#

"The crew is beginning to think we should leave you behind as a bunch of lunatics," Arness said into the communications unit. "A woman? Are you sure this isn't just an erotic fantasy, Mowat?"

"Certainly not erotic, Captain. She—Xavier—gives off the very essence of...I don't know. Motherhood, I suppose. Chaste love, at any rate. And there's no question in my mind this is the same...person."

"God," Arness rolled his eyes at Singh, but the chief engineer had a strange look on his face. "So what are you expecting me to do now, Mowat? Give God a lift somewhere? May I remind you that crewwoman Jurgens is deteriorating while you waste time down there?"

"Is she, Captain? CP disagrees."

"What is that supposed to mean?" Arness leapt from his command chair and stalked down the corridor to the makeshift treatment room. Jurgens was sitting up on the bunk, looking around for her clothes with an embarrassed expression on her face.

"Can I get back to duty, Captain?" she asked.

Arness froze, then vaguely waved a hand and leaned against the bulkhead. As Jurgens slipped past him he swallowed.

"How do you explain that, Doctor?"

"I don't have an explanation, Captain. Xavier asked me if we knew that Jurgens was damaged, and why we permitted her to stay that way. I explained. Xavier simply looked puzzled and said I was mistaken."

Arness heard a voice in the background of Mowat's transmission. Then the biologist spoke again.

"Xavier says I was *unenlightened*, instead of mistaken."

"No doubt," Arness growled.

"But she said it in the nicest possible way."

#

The bridge of the *Peirce* made a poor conference room, but Arness insisted on seeing faces and bodies.

"Does anyone still believe this Xavier is human?" he asked. There was silence. "Then that means she's either a very powerful and exotic non-human life-form, or...God." His face tightened. "Where does that leave us? What responsibility do we have toward her?"

"She's not God," Lake snorted. "There is no God."

Mowat's mind filled with a memory of the first communion he'd ever served, the surface of the blood-dark wine rippling once a second with the pulse of his own blood.

"I agree with Lake," he said, his eyes on the deck. "So our responsibility is to behave as human ambassadors to a newly-discovered sentient species. First contact."

"Meaning...?"

"Meaning we try to accommodate Xavier's needs, so as to create the best possible first impression of our own race."

"*That does not accurately reflect the situation, Captain,*" CP said. "*Xavier and I have been engaged in an ongoing discussion since soon after the being was discovered. We have explored religious, philosophical, and historical texts of all kinds in some detail. There are gaps in Xavier's knowledge, but there was already a very extensive*" *base of factual information about the human race. The term* first impression *does not apply.*"

"Maybe it wasn't such a good idea to be so open in your data exchange with an unknown entity, CP."

"*I was not commanded to do otherwise, Captain.*"

Arness frowned. "Supposing this is...God. What responsibility would we have then? To try to somehow *heal* her?"

"Why would we want to do that?" Lake snorted. "What has God ever done for us? Some of you were around before The Rift. Were things better then? Seems to me the universe is getting along just fine without her."

"CP? Analysis of the past twenty-seven years versus the previous twenty-seven. Any major shifts that stand out?"

"*It has been remarked, Captain, that the human race focused its collective energies on space exploration before the advent of The Rift, but has since engaged in nearly continuous warfare between colonies, and with the mother planet Earth.*"

"Are you suggesting humanity lost its source of inspiration?" Singh objected.

"Who knows what to think, Singh? Arness replied. "But we have lost some of the piss and vinegar that probably drove us out into space in the first place." He tried to rub fatigue from his face. "What about you,

Mowat? For a former priest, you haven't said very much. If Xavier is God, what should we do?"

When Mowat finally spoke, his voice sounded hollow. "I'd say that humanity has already given all it owed to God, Captain. Centuries of ignorance. Rivers of blood. Blind worship and adoration without a single meaningful answer in return for all of our questions. We owe God nothing. And God needs nothing from us."

"You don't pity an amnesiac God?"

"How terrible to forget. Yet how much worse to be forgotten," Ketsela said.

"What if Xavier could stop the electromagnetic and other interference she causes? Would having her on board put the crew at risk? CP?"

"*Xavier is a totally unknown quantity, and uncertainty always equals risk, sir.*"

"Then I have my answer."

#

Mowat's sleep was troubled. There wasn't room in his small bunk for so many memories, so long suppressed. At one point he found himself in a vivid dream that he was back at the oasis on the planet. Then he realized that it wasn't a dream.

"What the hell? Xavier! How did I get here?"

"I wanted to speak with you."

"*Christ*, you can't just snatch a person from their bed like that."

A smile traced across Xavier's face.

"Was that meant as an epithet, or something more, Peter?"

"So you think you're Christ now?"

"What I think isn't relevant. If you forgot you were Peter Mowat, who would you be?"

Mowat didn't answer. Xavier placed a hand on his arm. The touch was electric. Sensual, yet soothing.

"You have grievances against your God, Peter. I am sorry about that, whoever I am."

"You're not God. So it's no concern of yours."

"If it were within my power to bring your lover back to this physical existence—or the child she bore and took with her into death—would you ask me to do that?"

Mowat staggered back, suddenly nauseous. He stared at her with his mouth working, but words would not come. Only tears.

"I'm sorry, Peter. It was wrong of me to ask. Forgive me, and go back to your friends."

"Wait." Mowat blurted. He struggled for breath. "What is it you want from us? What do you need us for?"

In answer Xavier looked to the sky. There was nothing visible, but Mowat knew her gaze was directed at The Rift.

"It has been calling to me, Peter. But for some reason I cannot get there. Perhaps I am not God. There are clearly some things I am powerless to do."

"What would you do if you reached it?"

The smile was melancholy, and yet still hopeful.

"I don't know."

Then Mowat was in his bunk, surrounded by flickers of electrical equipment, but still in darkness.

When he went to the bridge Arness looked as if he hadn't slept in a week.

"I've come to agree with you, Doctor. If Xavier is an alien life-form, there's nothing we can do for her that she can't do for herself. And if she's God...well, maybe there was a time when humanity needed God. But not anymore."

"We truly owe God nothing, sir?" Ketsela asked.

"My first concern is with the welfare of my crew, Mr. Ketsela."

"May I...go down to the planet to tell her in person?" Mowat's eyes were glazed.

"That is not necessary, Doctor," CP said. *"A com link was left with Xavier. I can easily deliver a message."*

"Captain? It's the human thing to do."

"All right, Doctor. But don't take long. I've lost my taste for this region of space."

#

Xavier was waiting, her face sculpted with the worn lines of the elderly, and traces of grey in her raven hair. She reminded him of his favourite instructor at university.

"It's not your fault, Peter."

"You knew what they would decide, didn't you?"

"A mother knows her children. She cannot help it. And she cannot always help them." This time her face was matronly, the unwavering eyes troubled, but full of compassion.

"Why did you choose me for this?" he asked softly.

She looked upon him a third time as a lover, with a melting gaze and inviting lips. "I thought you chose me."

She lifted a hand toward his face, and the next thing he knew he was staring at a bank of foliage, swaying in a rising wind.

"Mowat? *Mowat!* We've been calling you for half an hour, dammit. Where are you? Are you piloting that boat?"

"Captain? I'm here, on the planet. Xavier is gone, sir. And so is the boat."

"I know that, damn you. I'm watching it break orbit right now. Maybe I should leave you there and go after it."

But he didn't. Instead he dispatched the *Peirce*'s second boat to retrieve his crewman.

As Mowat entered the bridge he felt the full weight of the captain's stare.

"The boat is headed for The Rift. Something tells me that's no surprise to you, Doctor."

"Why would God need a ship?" Singh asked. "When we arrived She was formless energy that moved to the planet on its own."

"Maybe it's like when a human suffers a severed *corpus callosum*," Mowat said. "A split brain: even thoughts can't cross from the left hemisphere to the right without artificial assistance. Maybe God can't enter The Rift without a vehicle."

Ketsela's voice was soft with reverence. "Is she hoping to collapse it and heal herself? Or to become the God of a new universe?"

"It's just a boat," Arness protested. "It can't enter sub space even if she dared to, and The Rift is nearly two hundred light years away."

"There was a saying, Captain." Mowat's face was calm, at peace. "One day is with the Lord as a thousand years, and a thousand years as one day."

Later, at his bunk, he pulled a weathered cross from a small box in his storage cupboard and ran his fingers lightly over it.

"*Doctor?*" came CP's voice. "*You went to the planet to let Xavier take the boat.*"

Mowat didn't answer.

"Are you going to worship your God again, now that you've met her?"

"She's not *my* God, and she doesn't need my worship."

"But this meeting renewed your faith."

"Faith doesn't require proof. But I realized that what I'd always resented was the idea of a perfect God, an omnipresent and whole God. A wise human once said, 'a thing that's complete is also dead.' I discovered that I *like* a God that's not perfect. Not whole. Still searching, still striving for completeness. And that's the God I'll know is out there, for the rest of my life."

#   #   #

HURRICANE

CARSON HATED TO FLY.

He was forcefully reminded of that as the big Hercules aircraft plummeted hundreds of feet before it could grasp the wind again, shaking like a dog just out of water. He reached for the sick bag, but decided he could hang on for a little while longer.

Christ! What was he doing there? He could have monitored the experiment back at Keesler AFB, or at the base station in the Bahamas. Not that it would have been a tropical vacation with the hurricane passing overhead. But better than being tossed around the inside of a fifty-year-old converted air freighter, tarted-up with fancy electronics and nothing left over for soundproofing.

He kept his opinion to himself, though. These 53rd Squadron boys were fiercely loyal to their Hercs. They'd let you come for a ride, but you had to pretend to be impressed.

He gripped hard on the metal frame of the canvas seat as they endured another round of buffeting. They were still forty miles away from the eye—it would get worse, much worse. Rochelle was a Category 4 storm, with every sign of becoming a Category 5 once it was over water again. The thought of the pounding they would get from the eyewall itself made his forehead pop with sweat. As he wiped it with his sleeve, he saw movement from the direction of the flight deck. It was Captain Mayfield, coming back to check on his passenger.

Who was flying the damn plane? That young co-pilot?

"'Limey' can handle this stuff." The pilot read his mind. "Done it dozens of times." He landed hard in the canvas beside Carson as the Herc yawed suddenly to the left and pitched up. His gave a wry smile. "Of course, practice makes perfect."

"'Limey'?"

"Lieutenant Eversham. A Brit name if there ever was one. I think his family's from Alabama, but no matter. Name's dogged him since college." He leaned closer, but it was no intimate conversation. Both men were nearly yelling to be heard over the screaming wind, the rattling airframe, and the roaring of the four Allison engines.

"One of our weather officers, Fuentes, is willing to let you have his seat up front. He'll take the dropsonde operator's chair unless we need him. First time I can remember flying a mission without placing at least one sonde in the eye."

"Leave it to the other flight crew to keep track of the storm, Captain," Carson replied, standing carefully. "We have other tasks. Just please keep our planes out of each other's way."

"I'll try not to take that as an insult, Doctor."

Except Mayfield took offense at the whole situation, which was why he didn't give Carson a hand up the pitching interior of the plane to the cockpit. There'd been heavy pressure on him to take the mission, and he resented it. He'd been due for a few days leave, and he wanted to spend every moment he could with Sara. God knew she didn't have many left. Two months, maybe. He would have quit to be with her, but she wouldn't let him, with the medical bills piling up. Once she was gone, what would he have left but his work? Flying antique planes into the worst weather in the world. And occasionally ferrying crackpots like this one who arrogantly believed that a hurricane would submit to being his laboratory.

The Herc bounced and the scientist cracked his knee hard on the metal floor. Rubbing it angrily, he gave a grateful nod to Fuentes, and tossed himself with relief into the vacated chair. On a hand signal from the young man he put the headset over his ears and positioned the microphone near his bottom lip. The windowpane to his left showed nothing but dirty grey cloud through streaks of rain. The rain would come a lot harder as they descended toward the center, he knew. Then he'd be lucky to distinguish anything at all. By the time the experiment was fully underway, night would have fallen.

"Doctor?" It was Mayfield's voice in his headset, deep and confident. Carson swung his gaze away from the window.

"The title isn't necessary."

"Excuse me?"

"Neither of my doctorates is in medicine." They didn't get it. "Mr. Carson will do. Chris would be fine." He silently prayed that none of them would call him 'Kit'.

"*Mr.* Carson," Mayfield resumed, "I was told what you're doing might lead to a way to weaken hurricanes. Is that true?"

Carson suppressed a groan. It wasn't a lie, but it certainly wasn't the main purpose of the experiment. That was the Institute's PR man talking.

"It might," he said. "The intent is to draw off energy from the storm—as a power source, eventually. We don't really know how much of the energy produced will be taken away from the storm itself, and how much will just be a sort of...byproduct." The answer sounded lame even to him. What was it about these military types that intimidated him so much? The fact that they looked perfectly comfortable in a bucking tube of metal thousands of feet above a storm-whipped sea, while he could barely keep his dinner down?

"So that part was a load of bullshit," Mayfield said. "I should have known."

"Not all bullshit, Captain. The nanocables are designed to collect all kinds of energy. Kinetic energy. Heat. Most of it will come from the molecules of air and water themselves. Whatever we get has to mean less energy available for the storm—I just can't honestly tell you how much difference it will make." He tried to look the pilot in the eye, but had to blink hard against a flash of lightning that was frighteningly close. It made him realize how much darker the sky had already become.

"Not collecting lightning?" The navigator, Lieutenant Williams had a light rasp to his voice, and a faint Cajun accent. The nearby bolt hadn't fazed him in the slightest.

"The cables will take strikes for sure but, as you know, there isn't all that much lightning inside a hurricane. Recent evidence to the contrary." He gave a light laugh that fell flat. "Uh, farther in, near the eyewall there aren't the powerful updrafts to make large amounts of ice crystals. That's where most lightning comes from." He looked to one of the weather officers, Lieutenant Crowe for support. She nodded her head in agreement.

"Did you say 'nanocables'?"

Carson turned his head toward the flight engineer across the cabin, a young airman whose uniform said "Ritchie". Thin, and rather tall for an aviator, his face showed an enthusiasm his crewmates definitely did not share. Before Carson could reply the plane plunged again and shook hard. Without any words, 'Limey' Eversham relinquished the controls to Mayfield and reached for his radio microphone.

"This is Alpha Foxtrot nine seven seven, Keesler. Our position is 24° 47 minutes North, 77° 40 minutes West. We are approximately 25 miles from the estimated center. Over."

Just west of Andros Island, Carson thought. According to plan they would catch up with the eye just after it left the Andros coastline, giving them lots of time to do what they needed to do as the storm roiled its way toward Miami. After dumping much of its load on the Bahamian island, Hurricane Rochelle would quickly suck up moisture again from the warm surface of the Florida Straits. That warm water would strengthen her winds, tightening the storm like a watch spring.

"Radar has the eye," Lieutenant Williams called out. "Looks to be... thirteen miles across." The navigator's brows lifted in mild surprise. Then he crooked a finger at Carson, inviting him to take a look. The radar was performing a sector scan, sweeping back and forth like a windshield wiper, and an ominous black circle was left behind each time the arm painted the screen with yellow. A small eye—a powerful storm, even after the brief landfall. It would soon coil even tighter, building an eyewall of shattering force that might reach up to fifty thousand feet.

Right where they were headed.

Carson nodded thanks and resumed his seat, pulling the belt even tighter than before. For a moment he had a vision of Louise and the kids. If something happened to him, how would she cope with Jessica just entering the dating years, and Tim about to face the onslaught of pubescent hormones? It'd been foolish to risk taking this flight, even though the military types insisted that they had hundreds of thousands of flight hours without mishap. He didn't even have a goddamn parachute. Better odds ditching the plane, they said. He looked up and caught a smile on the face of Flight Engineer Ritchie.

"It'll get pretty rough at the eyewall, sir," the young man said. "I like it though. Kind of like a free midway ride. Do you think you'll want a barf bag, sir?"

Carson had left one back in the cargo area, mercifully unused. He saw another in a mesh pocket near his seat. He gave a nod of acknowledgement to the engineer, and pulled the bag free enough to partially open the top. Just in case.

"What was that you said about *nanocables*, sir?" Ritchie asked. "Did you really mean cables that are microscopically small?"

Carson had no taste for trying to explain the experiment to this crew of air force flyers. "I probably shouldn't be taking up the comm. channel at a time like this, Sergeant."

Mayfield spoiled the gambit. "That's all right, Mr. Carson. We've got a few minutes. I'd like to hear more about this thing myself."

Their guest surrendered as gracefully as he could, and tried to remember how he'd explained it to the Institute's Board of Directors and the congressmen with them.

"When I said *nanocables*, that doesn't mean the cables themselves are microscopically small. They're actually more like ribbons, about an inch wide, made of something called *carbon nanotubes*, which are spun together into fibers and woven into a very long strand."

"Nanotubes a few *billionths* of a meter across," Ritchie contributed.

"Exactly." Carson blinked in grateful surprise. Good. Even one of their own members with a passing familiarity with the science would help to convince the rest of the crew. "Carbon 60 has a hexagon shape at the atomic level. It can be formed into sheets one atom thick—picture something like chicken wire—and these sheets can be rolled into tubes. When they are, they have an amazing ability to conduct heat and electricity, as well as incredible tensile strength."

"We're going to a lot of trouble for a few ribbons," Mayfield said.

"Ribbons more than sixty thousand feet long, Captain."

"*Holy shit.*" Crowe spoke for the first time. "Sorry, Captain."

"I agree, Crowe." The pilot's voice had an edge. "That's not possible, mister. The weight—nothing could hold that up."

"Ten miles to the eye," Williams interrupted. "Into the thick of it any minute now, sir."

As if to emphasize his words, the aircraft lurched hard to the right, its nose jerking upward as a giant hand slammed them from beneath. Carson felt a powerful need to loosen his collar, but he could see Crowe calmly surveying her weather instruments, tapping lightly on a keyboard. Williams was absorbed in the radar, his body looking relaxed. Ritchie grinned as he waved a hand over his panel of gauges. And Eversham gazed out the window, although he couldn't possibly have seen anything through the relentless wash of rain.

Mayfield cleared his throat expectantly.

"Sorry, Captain. Uh...the weight, yes. Well, as Sergeant Ritchie said, these *nanotube* fibers are incredibly small, about one thousandth the width of a human hair. But they're stronger than steel—nearly a hundred times stronger, especially in woven ribbon form. Yet much, much lighter. A square mile sheet of this material would only weigh a little more than you do, Captain."

Mayfield's face showed his disbelief.

"And you think a ten-mile-long ribbon of stuff that light can stand up to the punishment of a hurricane?"

"One hundred times the strength of steel, yet it can stretch by twenty per cent of its length and bounce back. It can also be tied in a knot without harm. Yes, Captain, I think so. More importantly, the government thinks so."

"Coming up on the eyewall," Williams announced, louder than necessary. Carson turned his head to the window, as if there might be an actual wall to see. There was nothing but dark cloud and sheeting rain. Without thinking, he tightened his grip on the metal edges of the seat frame.

Jenna Crowe looked across at him as surreptitiously as she could. She remembered her own first flight into the vortex, at the beginning of the season, and the effort it had taken to conquer her own fear. Especially at this moment, as they were about to penetrate the eye. They were in for a ride, all right. Almost as good as the ride Jack had given her the night before.

She turned her face away to hide a grin. God, she shouldn't be thinking of him at a time like this. She needed to pay attention to the instruments...monitor wind speeds in the eyewall, and especially the barometric pressure. Without a sonde to drop into the middle of the storm, it was a trick to get anything like an accurate pressure reading, based on their known altitude. Fortunately, that wasn't her job on this flight. A second Hurricane Hunter aircraft would take care of the routine stuff later: plant the dropsonde and take the whole series of readings. This trip Crowe was only along to make sure they didn't run into any surprises that might jeopardize the mission, and to keep Carson informed of conditions so he could assess their effect on his experiment. On that thought, she keyed the mic.

"Wind speed at one hundred twenty-one knots, Mr. Carson. That's one hundred thirty-nine miles per hour. Just coming off land, that's very powerful, sir. Category Four, for sure." She checked a gauge. "Temperature 12 degrees Celsius at 3100 meters. That's 54 Fahrenheit at just over 10,000 feet. Pretty warm, plus we can expect a big jump in temp inside the eye."

The scientist nodded, but said nothing. Crowe turned back to her panel. The nearly nonstop bucketing of the plane made it hard to read. Instead her mind skipped back twenty hours...Jack raised on his arms, looking into her eyes. For a man fifteen years her senior, he kept in terrific shape. Real stamina, and a sensitive touch that could only come from experience. Had his wife taught him that?

Shit. What was she doing screwing a married officer anyway? One of her direct superiors, no less. And white. That still made a difference. If she didn't watch herself she'd be selling shoes for a living. Sure, he said he loved her. Then why was he still married?

He could make her feel like a goddess. And he could make her feel like a tramp.

The 130-J slammed hard on a wave of air, pounded again, and a third time, then shot upward with a powerful shiver through the length of its fuselage.

Williams gritted his teeth. He hated this part, but didn't dare let it show. He'd spent two years training his body to hide the tension inside. Guys like Ritchie, they actually liked this shit. Williams did it because it was his calling. God called him to this hellish task because it could save lives. The more you knew a storm—really saw into its soul—the better you could warn people to stay out of its way. Although the civvies hardly ever listened anymore. How many times had the Florida Keys taken a serious hit? Yet people kept building and rebuilding. They treated a mandatory evacuation like it was an advisory. Thought they were immortal. Not on this Earth, they weren't. On this Earth they could feel pain...pain like his mama and papa must have felt after Hurricane Andrew while they waited in vain for Dade County officers to find them in the rubble. The irony was, they'd moved to Florida after losing their home in bayou country to a twister spawned by another hurricane. Grandpère had insisted over and over that God had sent Williams to visit his grandparents that late August day in order to spare his life for a heavenly purpose. He'd spent the past two years riding storm winds over the Gulf and the Straits, trying to fulfill that duty.

After a couple dozen flights and nearly two hundred transits of the eyewall, the prayer he silently mouthed had become well refined.

Carson was counting the seconds under his breath, eyes tightly closed, teeth clenched to keep them from rattling and to hold back the bile rising in his throat. Two long minutes of hell, then three. Just when he couldn't hold back anymore, he heard Eversham's voice call, "Here it is." He forced his eyes open, marveling at the glorious rose-golden glow that filled the windows—and then the aircraft dropped like a stone, all of its lift gone, plummeting helplessly toward the waves below. Before it could regain its hold on the air, Carson had ingloriously filled the bag. Thus was spoiled his first encounter with the eye of a hurricane.

As he wiped his mouth with a Kleenex, he was further embarrassed by Crowe apologizing. "Should have warned you about that, sir. The air in the eye itself is descending, which is why there aren't any clouds. And when the air we're in goes down, so do we. Sometimes a long way."

"I'll try to remember that next time, Lieutenant." His voice was hoarse, and he coughed to clear it. "Though I'm not sure that anticipating a drop like that will help much."

"The best remedy is to look out the window," Eversham offered. "I'd be willing to bet you've never seen anything like this, Mr. Carson. Come up front, if you want. We'll be in smooth air for a while."

The scientist weakly hoisted himself out of the chair, and took a few uncertain steps forward to lean on the co-pilot's chair.

Eversham was right. It was a sight he would never forget.

They'd just caught the last of the setting sun, and the scene it created was a Renaissance painting of Glory.

"A full stadium," Crowe said softly.

They were completely encircled by a wall of cloud, towering almost above their line of vision in the upper windows. The half of it they faced was anointed with every warm shade of the spectrum, bright daubs of orange defined by shadows in broad curving sweeps of blue-gray. Swathes of sun yellow and yellow-white almost too bright to look at, capping colossal columns of flame.

Williams crossed himself, as he always did in the presence of such majesty. To him it was a portent of God that an engine of such potent destruction could produce a cloudscape such as this: a vista to invoke awe and exultation in the human soul. The calm grandeur of the eye was the promise of Heaven itself in the midst of chaos.

The storm-etched canvas made Captain Mayfield think fleetingly of Heaven, too, as he allowed himself to hope that such a realm would hold a place for Sara. The rest of his mind was already calculating the time of the aircraft's transit of the eye, and the likely moment of passage through the very center, when the winds from his left would quickly shift to his right.

Carson felt a shudder deep in his bones. Far more than the brutal punishment they'd just been through, this towering stadium of menacing cloud brought home to him the sheer insignificance and vulnerability of their tiny craft. It was a stunning panorama of dazzling beauty. And he'd never been more afraid in his life.

Mayfield interrupted his reverie. "When does your experiment start, Mr. Carson?"

"Uh...what time is it?" He glanced at his watch. "The...uh, the winches should have been paying out for the past half-hour. The cables might have reached the cloud tops by now." He shifted closer to the pilot, searching the top of the cloud wall to the north. At more than six miles distance there was nothing to see, at least not in the light. Maybe after nightfall, during their next pass through the eye. "The cables have beacons attached at intervals of a thousand feet. Very powerful light-emitting diodes that flash every five seconds to show where the cables are. Along the lower half, the LED's are attached to small packages of instruments we hope will be able to tell us the amount of energy being collected."

"Before they're destroyed," Ritchie said.

"Yes," Carson acknowledged. "Inevitably. The LED's may survive, but the instruments themselves... well, we don't have anything robust enough to withstand the energies we're likely to see."

"Just what kind of power are we talking about, Mr. Carson?"

"Captain, it's been calculated that every day of a hurricane's life its winds can produce kinetic energy the equivalent of half of the world's entire electrical generating capacity."

"I've heard that, of course."

"Yet most of a hurricane's energy is in the form of heat. Heat produced by the condensation of moisture in the air into raindrops. That daily output, for a storm like Rochelle, is more like *two hundred times* the total production of the world's generators. A harvest of energy that could supply a huge percentage of our society's needs if we could only find a way to collect it and store it."

It was a staggering image. Before anyone could comment, they felt the plane shift under them. Mayfield nodded as Eversham gave him a signal, confidently adjusting the throttles of the engines to compensate for winds that had suddenly changed their direction one hundred and eighty degrees. They had just crossed the center of the storm.

Carson repositioned his feet as the Herc pivoted and began to crab slightly to the right.

The pilot continued as if there'd been no interruption. "Are you saying that your ribbons will be able to collect that kind of energy?"

"In fact, we aren't directly collecting the kinetic energy of the wind or the heat of condensation. The generation of the electricity depends on a couple of other scientific principles, but the wattages and voltages involved will be tremendous."

"This still sounds like a flight of fancy to me, Professor," Mayfield said, offering a new title that held more mockery than respect. "I don't suppose you plan to explain these other 'scientific principles'?"

Carson grimaced. "How technical do you want me to get, Captain?"

"Try me."

"All right, but not right now. As I'm sure your commander discussed with you, I need to use your radio to contact our Bahamas base station." He shifted back toward Eversham. The captain nodded, and the co-pilot reached for the radio.

The eye of the storm had passed just north of the Institute's monitoring team in Andros Town and they were still being pummeled by slashing rain and vicious winds that caused their signal to break up badly. They were able to report that the descent of the cable had been perfectly smooth down to the cloud tops, and had encountered no difficulties in the ten minutes since then.

Carson signed off, nodded his thanks to Eversham, and began to return to the weather officer's seat. The mammoth mountain of cloud in front of them loomed threateningly close. He should have taken advantage of the calm to check on his instrument package in the cargo area, but it was too late now.

"Strap in tightly, Professor," Mayfield said. "We're about to get back into the thick of it."

Moments later the windows went dark as rain slashed across them, and the Hercules caught the rising air of the eyewall, lurching painfully and leaping upward. Even so, Carson found it easier to take than the last time. The feeling of an ascending elevator is much less frightening than one plunging to earth.

He knew from briefings that the Hercules would fly a long, slow loop through the hurricane, returning to the eye at a point ninety degrees from where they had just left it. That would put them on a heading almost directly north, set to cross their previous path like a giant 'X' through the center of the storm.

They'd have to change course then. Continuing northward would take them directly through the Grid

Field, through the net of nanocables as they built up their charge. Carson was sure that wouldn't be a good idea.

Eversham had little to do for the moment, and let his mind drift home to the base at Biloxi. Hurricane Rochelle showed no signs of heading toward the Gulf, so Amani and the twins would be safe.

The Mississippi delta had been spared over the past decade and more, but he knew that Captain Mayfield had been stationed at Keesler AFB in 2005 when Hurricane Katrina struck. He and Sara had lost everything, their home one of the 800 base residences destroyed by the terrible flooding. It had nearly cost them their marriage too.

It was only a matter of time before the conditions were right for another killer storm to rip across the Gulf and into the Mississippi coastline. Eversham believed that in doing his job he was protecting his family. Amani had already suffered enough after a life of devastating poverty and repression by the patriarchal society of Iraq. When he'd taken her away from all that he'd promised her a whole new life of freedom and safety. Maybe Carson's scheme could help with that. Maybe there'd even be a job in it for Eversham, something that would offer better than a lieutenant's pay.

Carson had just decided to close his eyes and try to rest, when Eversham's voice came through the comm.

"I have to ask, Professor. What in God's name is holding these cables up? Aircraft would fly too fast, wouldn't they?"

"*Stratellites*," Ritchie answered before Carson could. "That's right, isn't it Mr. Carson?"

"Yes, it is. Have you heard of Stratellites, Lieutenant Eversham?"

"Giant dirigibles," the captain supplied. "Meant for radio re-transmission. They stay in one place above the Earth and can cover an area the size of Texas for relays of cell phone signals and things like that."

"Look like blue whales in the sky," Ritchie said. "I didn't think there were many around yet."

"There's a small fleet of them in the air much of the time," Carson said. "The problem has been finding telecom clients with confidence in the technology. So the company was glad to have our money, even though this job is far from anything they envisioned." For the benefit of the rest, he added, "A Stratellite flies well above 60,000 feet, beyond the reach of storms—even Rochelle—and uses solar-powered engines to stay in the same place over the ground. The whole upper surface is covered with solar panels, and everything is controlled by computer. So it can stay up there indefinitely."

"No flight crew?" Fuentes asked.

"No need for one. But believe me, Lieutenant Fuentes, you wouldn't want that duty. There'd be absolutely nothing to do."

"You say that as if it's a bad thing," the weather officer quipped. "The view would be fantastic."

"So you've got...what? A couple of these stratellites over our heads with huge winches on them, trailing cables into the storm?" Mayfield asked.

"Actually it's more like a net. I mentioned the *nodes* installed every thousand feet, where the beacon lights and instrument clusters are located. At each of those nodes below 30,000 feet another nanocable is attached, aimed diagonally downward to connect with the second main cable a thousand feet lower. Like a very loose mesh with the secondary ribbons crossing in the middle. We wanted to provide different angles for the cables, to see if that affects how much energy they collect. Also, one of the most important properties of the nanotubes is that all of the energy can be directed downward only—into the ocean, for now. That protects the stratellites from any energy discharge. That, and a few hundred feet of insulating material at the tops of the main cables."

"You still haven't explained how this energy will be produced," Mayfield persisted.

The next twenty minutes grew too technical for Fuentes to follow. There were a few names he vaguely remembered from college science courses. The "*Sood*

Effect" that produced an electrical flow when air or water passed over a carbon nanotube doped with certain chemicals. The *"Seebeck Effect"* that created an electrical current from temperature differences along a conductor. A few others. He'd much rather think about Nina and her long legs and the prospect of getting to know them better on the coming weekend, when they planned to pay a quick visit to New Orleans. Yes, a much more pleasant course of thought.

"I hate to admit it," Carson said finally, "but the physicists at the Institute can't quite agree which of these forces will have the greatest effect. Or even if more than one will occur at the same time."

"Well you must have been convincing enough to talk somebody out of a whole lot of money for all this," Williams said.

"I guess so," the older man laughed. The rest were quiet, trying to digest what they'd heard. Then Mayfield asked the question that had occurred to all of them.

"What would happen to an aircraft that flew between these cables, once they're all charged up?"

"I don't know," their passenger admitted. "I suggest we don't find out."

#

When they were about a half-hour from re-entering the eye, Carson made contact with the base in Andros Town again. Their signal was even worse than before, but he was able to learn that the mesh had successfully been let out to its full length with the bottom ends of the two main cables dragging in the ocean. The Grid had begun to build up a significant charge as soon as it was exposed to the winds and rain within the hurricane clouds, and by the time the cables had reached the surface of the water the energy levels were reaching the limits of the measuring equipment.

"I think we've got a winner here, Chris," came the excited voice of Fenton, the Bahamas team leader. "The sheer amount of energy...into the terawatts already...voltage gone off the scale...."

Carson couldn't help grinning as he keyed the microphone. "Got you on that, Dave. Are we seeing any dispersion pattern through the Grid? Over."

There was no reply. Carson repeated his question a half-dozen times, then Eversham tried his best, without success.

"It's possible something took out their antenna," he said. Left unsaid were their fears that something had taken out the team as well. Carson was just about to return to his seat when the radio came to life again.

"Alpha Foxtrot nine seven seven, this is Keesler Tower. Do you read?"

Eversham gave confirmation.

"Alpha Foxtrot nine seven seven, from Keesler Tower. Do you read? Over."

The co-pilot tried again, but to no avail. After several more attempts, the voice at Keesler continued, "Am not reading you Alpha Foxtrot. Hope you're getting this anyway. Have lost radio contact with your Bahamas base camp. Repeat: have lost contact with Bahamas base. Last telemetry received from Institute sky stations five minutes ago. Telemetry readings indicate imminent loss of instrument function. Repeat: loss of instruments is imminent. Due to our loss of signal from sky stations, suggest you attempt to use your own onboard instruments package. Institute sends bes...."

The transmission ended abruptly, and Eversham couldn't raise the Hurricane Hunters' home base again.

"Radio reception doesn't go to hell like that without a reason," he said.

"I'll give you three guesses what it is," Mayfield replied. "I'd say we're on our own. What do you think Professor?"

"With that much electrical energy running down several miles of unshielded cable, yes. That's why I brought some portable equipment. I'll see what I can do with it." He began to stagger back toward the cargo area.

"I'll give you a hand," Fuentes offered.

"Well find something to tie yourselves to," warned the pilot. "Because it's about to get rough."

Unpacking the instruments was a nightmare, and it was wasted effort anyway. The hope was that even if electrical interference along the cables disrupted reception of the instrument telemetry on the stratellites and the ground station, Carson's gear in the aircraft might still be able to receive the weak signals. He got nothing.

He tried to measure local magnetic fields, but the pounding and shuddering of the airframe played hell with the old-style needles of the sensor. Frustrated, he shut it off. Then he stuffed the gear back into its protective case, and he and Fuentes helped each other back to their seats.

"Any luck, Mr. Carson?" Mayfield asked.

"None at all. And my magnetic field sensor must be malfunctioning."

"Why do you say that?"

"Because the readings...let's just say, if the readings were accurate we'll soon find out how good you are at flying by the seat of your pants."

The pilot's head snapped around. "I hope you're joking, mister."

"A malfunction, Captain. It has to be a malfunction. You can't really expect delicate instruments to take this kind of punishment, but we thought it was worth a try."

"Twenty-five miles to the eye," Williams said.

Crowe had just turned her head to speak...

...when the universe came apart.

"Jesus Christ!" Mayfield's voice was sharply cut off, and every instrument on the plane died. There was an instant of suspension before the cabin dipped onto its nose and plunged downward.

Something hit them.

Carson gagged on his fear. *Oh God*, he thought, *like a ripple...a ripple through solid steel.* He felt it pass through him too. The skin of his hands danced with a blue flame. *St. Elmo's Fire.* He spread his fingers, mesmerized.

"... restart the engines!" The captain's near scream stabbed into their ears as the plane came back to life. There was a horrible noise that Carson realized must be a crash warning of some kind. It paralyzed him.

Fortunately it had no such effect on the flight crew. They scrambled madly to check their systems, and the comm. was full of shouted reports as Mayfield fought the giant Hercules into level flight again. Mercifully, Eversham switched off the alarm, but the plane continued to buck. They were nearing the eyewall again.

"Was that lightning? Were we hit by lightning?" Fear was in Fuentes' voice, and it made Carson feel a little less inadequate.

"No lightning strike I've ever seen," the pilot snapped. "Crowe, you have any indication that was lightning?"

"No, sir. That was...I have absolutely no idea what that was, Captain."

"Everyone run a full check of electronics function. But do it fast. We'll be getting into the thick of the eyewall winds any minute. Mister Carson." The voice took on an edge. "Could what we just experienced have been caused by this experiment of yours?"

"I have no idea. I don't see how." The scientist was still in shock. Could the hyper-energized nanocables have suddenly released an enormous electrical discharge? Nothing of the kind had ever shown up in the computer models, but he had to admit there were no certainties.

"*Goddamn!*" Mayfield again. "Don't rely on your instruments. They're suspect. In fact, I think everything that depends on magnetic fields has just packed it in."

"There's more, Captain," came the voice of the navigator. "Whatever that was, it reset the inertial navigation system. The INS can start clean from this point, but it lost our location, sir. I'll try to reload the data as we go."

"The compass is completely unreliable," the pilot said. "I hope you remember your flight school simulator training, people, because the instructor has just pulled a nasty one."

"Radar's still working, Captain. I *think*," Williams said. "It shows us about five minutes from the eye." His fingers danced over the controls.

Suddenly a sound from the radio froze them all.

"...Tyler 41. I am at 37° 15 minutes North Lat...est Longitude...level flight at 23,000 feet. I am flying on instruments...ground speed 385 mph...request you relay this...Oceanic Air Control."

Eversham and Mayfield exchanged startled glances.

"What the hell is that?" the pilot said. "He sounds damned close for somebody ten degrees of latitude away. See if you can raise him."

"*Blip on the radar*, sir." Williams voice broke in. "Almost...almost dead ahead of us. Unidentified aircraft, Captain. About forty miles, heading westward."

"*Forty miles?* And you just spotted it? How is that possible, Mr. Williams? Have you been asleep?"

"No, sir." Williams sounded more confused than offended. "It just appeared on the scope, sir. There was nothing until now, I swear."

"A radar malfunction because of the interference?" Eversham asked.

"Unlikely, Captain," Ritchie answered first. "I'm getting no signs of equipment failure. Every system seems to be reading properly—even the magnetic ones. It's just that...the readings themselves make no sense."

"I'm not in the mood for games, Mister," Mayfield snapped. "There has to be an explanation. *Find it.*" He turned to his second-in-command. "In the meantime, try to raise that damn plane."

" ... Foxtrot niner seven seven...tanker flight Tyler 41...of Bermuda. Have run into....storm out of nowhere. Navigation unreliable. Visibility zero. Am descending to...get better...please advise." The signal crackled with interference, the last words barely audible.

"Did he say north of Bermuda?" the co-pilot muttered.

"No...no, his nav system must have been screwed up for a long time and he somehow wandered into our neighbourhood." Mayfield sounded grim. "I hope to hell he's not trying to descend in this muck with dodgy instruments." They all knew the image that was in his mind: a plunging tube of steel and the unforgiving sea. "Call him back. Advise him of our magnetic interference and suggest he *not* descend." His hand pounded on the control yoke in frustration. "How is it possible that he just realized he's in the middle of a goddamn hurricane?"

Eversham's voice went out over the ether. The rest stayed quiet, hoping to hear an acknowledgement, any response that would indicate the other plane had heard and stopped its descent. There was nothing.

"Captain," Carson said, "Could the aircraft on radar be your other Hurricane Hunter?"

"*Collinson?* No, not unless he's an hour ahead of schedule, and he'd be coming in from west-northwest, heading eastward. This is some joker who has no business being here."

"No joker, Captain," Ritchie spoke again. "It sounds like a military aircraft to me."

"I know, Ritchie. I know. None of this makes any sense."

A series of punishing impacts brought conversation to a halt as the Hercules was tossed mercilessly by the eyewall winds. Carson closed his eyes and concentrated on holding his teeth together to keep them from chipping each other or taking a piece of his tongue. When the plane dropped he was ready for it, and didn't lose the contents of his stomach. Then, as they leveled off, he looked out.

The first thing he saw was the huge tropical moon, bright enough to make him squint until his irises could adjust. It flooded the gigantic stadium of cloud and painted the surface of the sea far below.

The second thing....

"Good Christ!"

The Pillars of Hercules, his mind said. Two colossal towers of blue flame stood starkly against the black cloud of the wall opposite, with ripples of brighter blue-violet washing slowly up and down them. Yet his eyes couldn't hang onto the image. It teased and taunted his brain, dancing away, then reappearing. In between the columns—he couldn't see that at all. There was something, and there was nothing, like the indefinable nothingness produced by the *blind spot* of the human eye. His brain wanted to fill in details from the cloudscape on either side, yet knew that it was wrong.

"What in God's name is that?" Mayfield's voice was infused with awe.

Carson swallowed hard. "It's the Grid. It has to be." It was in the right place, directly north of them, and he'd known that it would be gathering energies mankind had never before witnessed up close, but this...this was unimaginable.

The aircraft fell silent as its crew tried to comprehend the message of their senses. The Hercules sliced through the dark air unaided and unguided, its masters spellbound. It slowly came to Carson that the whispering sound in his ears was Williams reciting a prayer.

The rapture was broken by Crowe's strident cry: "Captain! Look below!"

The others reluctantly tore their eyes from the spectacle ahead, and searched the space beneath them. At first Mayfield could see nothing but the brilliant sheen of the moonlit ocean, but then, gradually, he picked out a pair of black shapes amidst the silver that were far too large to be waves.

"Oh my God," he said. "Don't tell me those are ships down there. What in Christ's name is happening here? Has the whole world gone crazy?" He turned toward Eversham. "Limey, see if you can tune in a marine channel. I want to know what in hell those craft are doing out here in a storm like this. Williams, keep an eye on that other aircraft and let me know if anything changes. And Mr. Carson." His voice became cold. "I want to know if that...whatever it is up there is a danger to my crew."

" ...steamer *Cotopaxi* bound for Havana..." Heads snapped up around the cabin, startled by the urgent voice from the radio. "Have suddenly encountered gigantic waves and are surrounded by storm cloud. Any nearby vessels please advise." Static spat from their headsets, and Eversham reduced the volume. "...cargo of coal beginning to shift...emergency situation...any assistance...." Electrical crackle obscured the voice, and it did not return.

"One of those ships below us, you think?" Eversham asked his captain.

"Can't do a damn thing for him if we can't punch a signal through this interference. Check that channel periodically and monitor a few others. And Limey...the rest of us don't need to hear them." The look on his face sent a shiver down Eversham's spine.

"Right, sir."

"Radar contact sir!" Williams called out. "Just appeared. Coming right at us out of the north."

"Dammit, Williams. How far? Do we need to evade?"

"I think…. No, sir. She'll pass us, but not far away. High, and on our right. Within the next minute."

Those who could stared upward, toward the bright sky. The appearance was so brief they nearly missed it, but there was no mistaking the silhouette of an aircraft against the waxing moon.

"Jesus, I don't believe that," Ritchie hissed. "That was an *Avenger*. A Grumman Avenger torpedo bomber. Second World War vintage. I swear it was."

"Ritchie, if you start in on that occult stuff, I swear to God I'll rip…"

"No, Captain, I'm not saying that. And anyway Flight 19 was five Avengers and evidence says they either ditched in the ocean or crashed in a Florida swamp. This was a single plane. God only knows what it's doing out here, but it was an Avenger. I'd stake five year's leave time on it. My father had a restored one."

"This isn't the time for an argument," Mayfield said. "Limey, are you getting anything from that plane?"

"No, sir. But the marine channels, Captain…." His voice dropped. "It's awful, sir. Maydays on almost every frequency. There must be a few dozen small vessels down there, and they're all in trouble." He hadn't wanted the others to hear him, but they did.

"Everyone had plenty of warning about Rochelle. There shouldn't be anyone down on that sea." Mayfield clenched his teeth. "We've got to try to get somewhere we can punch a signal out. At least get some

Search and Rescue teams out here to look for survivors once the storm has passed." His voice faltered. "There'll be damn few."

"Captain Mayfield," Carson said. "Clearly we have to get as far away from the electrical interference as possible, as soon as we can. There's nothing more we can do out here about the experiment. I can't get any readings—we're out of contact with the ground and the stratellites. Our mission is over. Go wherever you need to go so we can help these people."

"Thank you, Mr. Carson. With our navigational aids next to useless, I'm going to assume your stratellites are still carrying that grid along the storm track. We'll steer well to the left of it and carry on straight until we can find out where we are. In fact, we might just follow that other radar contact to the west."

"It's not there anymore, Captain." Williams looked away from his scope. "I think it went into the sea."

Each of them withdrew into dark thoughts filled with the wail of the unforgiving wind. Then William's voice shattered the pall.

"Another radar contact! Coming straight for us!"

"Talk to me Williams. Give me something."

"It's big and close, and it's coming fast. *Climb to port.* Climb *now*, Captain!"

The G-forces shoved them back into their seats as the big craft clawed the air and banked hard. The Allison engines roared with the challenge.

"*Motherf...!*" came Ritchie's yell, his voice breaking as a mammoth winged shape passed over the silvered sea, its upper lines given shape by the moonlight.

"What was that?" Crowe shouted. "It was huge!"

"Ritchie?" Mayfield called, as he struggled to level the plane.

"You have to believe me, Captain. It was a B-52. An honest-to-God *B-52 bomber!* I could see it against the ocean. No chance it was anything else."

The pilot's profane reply was drowned in the banging of metal plates and beams as they re-entered the vicious winds of the eyewall.

"Limey, are you getting anything from that aircraft? Lieutenant Eversham?" The senior officer reluctantly took his attention from the windscreen and turned toward the right hand seat. "*Limey!*" The co-pilot didn't react. "Crowe, get up here!"

The weather officer stumbled through the lurching fuselage and nearly fell into Eversham's lap. "He's out, Captain. Unconscious." She brushed back a lock of the man's hair. "There's a gash high on his forehead, just starting to bleed. Who's got a flashlight?"

Williams handed it to her, and she carefully rolled one of Eversham's eyelids back with her thumb, then flicked the beam of the light into his eye and away. Again. And a third time. She checked the other eye.

"I don't think his pupils are responding. Goddamned hard to tell with this bucketing, though. A concussion for sure. Maybe something worse."

"What can you do about it?" asked Mayfield.

"I can't do anything about it," the woman replied. "I can clean and bandage the cut, that's all. We'll have to see if he comes out of it. If it's just a concussion, he'll wake up soon."

No-one asked the obvious question. Instead Mayfield ordered, "Find something to secure his head to the seat back. Otherwise this bouncing will snap his neck. Fuentes, come and help her."

They used rolled-up t-shirts and a cloth strap to brace the oblivious airman's skull, but the storm fought them all the way.

"Williams, what are you getting on your scope? Where did that aircraft go? Am I in for any more nasty surprises?"

"That last aircraft is continuing straight south, Captain. No further risk to us." The man hesitated. "As for more surprises...I just can't say, sir. These planes appeared without warning, I swear to you. Either the radar is malfunctioning and only has a range of a few miles, or...well I just don't have any other explanation, sir. But Captain Mayfield?" His voice was ragged. "There are half a dozen contacts in the airspace behind us now, sir. More by the minute."

"Lieutenant, *have you lost your mind?*"

"I'm beginning to think we all have, sir."

"Captain!" Crowe barked. "Limey's awake."

The co-pilot was trying to shake his head and found it immobilized.

"What...? What's going on?" His hands reached for the strap at his forehead and began to pull at it. Fuentes grabbed his wrists and tugged them away.

"Don't touch that, Lieutenant," Crowe commanded. "You hit your head. You've probably got a concussion. Give it a few minutes to see how you feel."

"I feel...I feel like King Kong just sat on my head." He tried to smile but only the left half of his mouth responded. "*Shit*, what hit me? Where the Christ are we, anyway? What's been happening?"

"It'll all come back to you in a minute," Crowe reassured him. "Just take it easy for a while. Try to keep your head still."

"Easy for you to say. Feels like we're... Oh, shit. We are in a hurricane. Goddamn it. How did I miss that?"

Crowe said nothing more, concerned about the man's uncharacteristic swearing. Had the others noticed? Should she find a way to mention it to the captain? It might mean nothing. She made her way back to her seat and strapped in. Fuentes remained squatting between the pilots' chairs.

"Limey." Mayfield's tone was deliberately light. "How about passing the 'phones to Fuentes? I want to hear if there's any chatter on the air."

"That's my job, sir. I'll do it." Eversham snatched the headphones from his right hip, where they'd fallen, then howled in pain as he clapped them onto his head. "*Sweet Jesus*, that hurts! But I'm O.K., I'm O.K. ." He held the 'phones out a little from his head and listened for thirty seconds. A minute. Two. In slow motion the man's hands moved forward, and the headphones fell from them. Fuentes grabbed them quickly and placed them over his own ears, then reached for the band spread control on the radio.

"It's like Hell." Eversham's voice faltered. "Like the gates of Hell. All those voices, crying. Crying in death."

"Fuentes?" Mayfield snapped.

"God, he's right, Captain," the younger man said. "Cries for help on every frequency. Interrupting each other. Desperate...boats sinking. Jesus, sir. Isn't there anything we can do?"

"No, Mr. Fuentes, there isn't. Not until we can get clear of this damned interference. *Mr. Carson!*" he spat. "Can't you just shut that thing off? There has to be a command code to do that. Lives are at stake here."

"I agree, Captain. In the event of any danger the system was designed to allow the stratellites to cut the cables loose and let the Grid fall into the ocean. But that override is controlled by the Bahamas station. Unless we can get through to them...."

"Try it, Fuentes. Don't wait for a response. Just keep transmitting in the blind. Maybe they'll pick it up. Tell them Carson says they have to do an emergency cable release. Hurry!"

The young officer leaned toward the radio again, then stopped, transfixed.

"Captain!"

Eversham was writhing in his seat, in uncontrollable spasms.

"It's a seizure!" yelled Crowe. "Stay back. There's nothing you can do. He's strapped in—all we can do is wait for it to pass." Then ignoring her own advice, she unbuckled her belt and lurched forward to kneel beside the co-pilot with her hands held out to cushion him if needed. Finally the convulsions stopped, and the man was still.

"He's unconscious again. This is a bad sign, Captain. We've got to get him to a hospital."

"I hear you, Crowe. That's where I'm heading, just as fast as this crate will get us there, but we don't even know where we are. We could be steering miles off course." He was afraid to ask the next question. "Williams, how many contacts are on your scope now?"

There was a pause while the navigator counted—an answer in itself.

"Seventeen, sir. And that's just in the air. I have no way to know how many surface vessels are back there. I think at least two contacts have gone down. Splashed, I mean."

Everyone's mind held an image of the violent ocean below, and the fear that they might be next.

Mayfield spoke as if to himself. "What the hell is going on here? What can we do? What in God's name can we do?"

"Captain?" Ritchie's voice was fragile and forced. "Captain, I think I know what it is, sir. You're going to hate this, sir, but please just hear me out. Even science fiction is based on real scientific principles."

"Just spit it out, Ritchie."

"I think it's a *rip*, Captain. A...a *tear* or a hole. A rip in the fabric of space/time. That's what the grid has created. That's where all of these vessels and planes are coming from."

Carson saw incredulity build into rage on the pilot's face. The man looked ready to burst a blood vessel. He didn't wait for the inevitable explosion.

"What you're suggesting isn't possible, Ritchie." He kept his voice as calm as possible, hoping to stop Mayfield from going off the deep end. "Something like that—even if it's feasible—would require energy on the order of a *supernova*. The explosion of a star."

"I know that, Professor," the flight engineer replied. "The math doesn't add up. But the evidence does. Look around us. I think some...phenomenon created by your energy grid is drawing objects from other places and times."

"That's enough, Mister!" Mayfield barked. "I will not have you trivializing a tragedy like this with your fantasies. We're in a crisis situation. I could have your stripes for an outburst like that!"

Ritchie shrank back in dismay. It would have been so easy for Carson to have kept his own mouth shut and stayed out of the battle, but he couldn't.

"Captain Mayfield, you're out of line." He gulped a breath and forged on. "Sergeant Ritchie, may God forgive me, might not be far off track."

"Explain yourself, Mister, and do it quickly."

Carson swallowed hard. "I don't mean that we predicted something like this—we didn't. But there are some irrefutable facts. We're seeing things that shouldn't be possible—aircraft and ships that appear, apparently out of nowhere, with indications that they belong in another *location* certainly, if not another time."

"There could be other explanations for that."

"I'd love to hear them sometime. The other factor we can't ignore is the Grid. Energy readings beyond anything we've measured before, focused into an area of a few square miles. You've seen what it does to your instruments. You've seen the phenomenon with your own eyes. Or maybe I should say *didn't* see it—our minds couldn't grasp it."

"Goddamnit, be serious. A rip in *time*? That's nothing but..."

"Science fiction. Yes, Captain. I know. Or theoretical physics, which I also know. In a nutshell, what we think of as time and space isn't like a flat sheet of paper. It may be folded upon itself like...well, picture those paper fans you folded when you were a kid. If you poked a pin through one of the folds you'd suddenly have a major shortcut to another point on the fan." He looked around to see if they were getting it. "It's theoretically possible for such a shortcut to be created in space/time. It's just that it would require an unimaginable amount of energy."

"Which is what we've got right here," Ritchie added in a voice nearly inaudible above the storm.

"No. That amount of energy would destroy the planet," Carson protested.

"Maybe not, Professor. Not if you think of it like a bolt of lightning. An enormous amount of energy, yes, but spread out over every different place *and time* it touches. A huge amount is right here and now. But not all of it." His voice strengthened with growing confidence. "Maybe the energy from your Grid triggered a chain reaction, a chain that spreads down through time and draws energy from its surroundings at each point that it exists." Then he gasped. "No, wait. Oh my God. Wrong metaphor. It's not a lightning bolt, it's a *tornado*. Touching down in other times and places, and sucking up everything in its path."

The Hercules hit a sudden air pocket and then lurched hard to the left. Crowe was thrown against Mayfield, who cursed himself for allowing his attention to wander. "Crowe!" he said. "I need you and Fuentes to do your jobs. Williams, help them get Limey aft to the dropsonde operator's chair. Then I need Fuentes back in the second seat to operate the radio, and I need everything you can give me about this storm, people. Especially the fastest path out of it."

The discussion wasn't over, but Carson and Ritchie knew better than to interrupt. Each man was deep within his own thoughts. It was Mayfield's somber question to Williams five minutes later that drew them out.

"More than twenty contacts now, Captain," the navigator replied. "I can't get a good count because new ones come and others go every few minutes. The new contacts all appear at the same point in the sky. They disappear...well, wherever they're knocked out of the sky." His voice softened. "Those are probably light aircraft, sir. Not able to weather the storm."

"Acknowledged, Williams." The pilot sounded like a different man: weary past knowing, and badly out of his depth. The terminal illness of his wife had forced him to confront death, and a lifelong denial of anything beyond the world he could see. Now, the ground had been torn from beneath his feet again.

"Mr. Carson," he asked.

"Yes, Captain."

"How much faith do you put in this...*time rip* explanation of Ritchie's? The truth, please."

"It's not about faith, Captain. It's about fear. I've been trying to think of every possible way to refute it, and I can't. There's nothing else I can think of that fits the evidence we've seen." He took a ragged breath. "I'm desperately hoping he's wrong. But I'm utterly terrified that he's right."

"Like a giant tornado, with its bottom end skipping across time and space?" Mayfield asked dully.

"Think about it, sir," Ritchie said. "The planes we've seen, and the radio messages. It appears to have reached as far north as Bermuda, and as far back in time as the 1960's or 50's. Maybe even the 40's, if that Avenger was a new one. There's no way to tell about the surface ships. The bottom end of the effect could be reaching much farther back than that, to long before there were any aircraft." The sergeant hesitated, then plunged on. "My fear, sir, is that the phenomenon might still be gaining energy, and stretching farther and farther back."

"What makes you say that, Ritchie?" Carson asked, startled by the man's intuitive leap.

"I've studied this area for a long time, Mr. Carson. It has a history of strange phenomena, going back centuries. Even Columbus saw..."

"*Columbus.*" Mayfield thundered. "Jesus Christ, Ritchie."

The engineer stammered, "All I mean is the effect could be reaching back over decades or even centuries of human history, and over hundreds of miles of ocean. And our end is moving with the storm, Captain."

He hesitated, then finished the thought. "Moving straight toward Florida."

When Mayfield turned the giant aircraft into a steep bank, no-one said a thing.

#

"Do you understand what I'm trying to do, Mr. Carson?" Mayfield had to shout into the other's ear, only inches away. He'd disconnected his mic from the comm. system.

"Yes, Captain. I think so." The scientist nodded, his face pale.

"You need to tell me the best way to do it, and don't use gestures. The others might guess, but it will be easier on them if they're not sure."

"I understand," Carson said, wishing he could have enjoyed the same ignorance. "The best bet to disrupt the Grid would be to take out one of the nodes on one side, where the cross-ribbons connect. The higher, the better. That won't stop the fibers from collecting electricity, but it will throw the distribution of the energy completely off balance and, with any luck, collapse the field."

"Luck? You're not sure?"

"Captain Mayfield, there is nothing certain about any of this. It wasn't supposed to happen in the first place. How can I be sure how to stop it?"

The senior officer's head slumped forward for a moment. Then he looked into Carson's eyes. "Mister," he said through tight lips. "I'd convinced myself this was the right thing to do, but if you can't tell me..."

"It should work, Captain. Unless we can get through to the Andros base...it's the only thing we can do." There was open fear on Carson's face, but also firm resolution. He waited for Mayfield's nod, and continued. "The target you're aiming for is only a few yards square: a casing protecting the instruments, and in the middle of that is the actual connection between the vertical and diagonal cables. The connection points are much weaker than the cables themselves, so at least we have a chance. But anything less than a direct hit at the joint might not sever the cable at all." He shook his head. "Worse than that, you probably won't even see the node—at least not until the last moment—because of the brightness of the electrical field. I can only give you the estimated altitude."

"Christ, do you know what you're asking?" Mayfield's eyes were wide. "Here in the eye the air is stable, and it would still be nearly impossible. The Grid is well within the worst winds of the eyewall."

"I understand, Captain. I don't see that we have any choice. Clearly you don't either."

The pilot gave a slow shake of his head. He'd faced the prospect of death before, but it didn't help to know that it might be for nothing. He put the headphones on and swung the microphone into place.

"Fuentes. Any sign that you got through to Andros Town?"

"I keep trying. Either they haven't heard, or they decided not to drop the cables. Do you want me to check the marine channels again, sir?"

"God, no," Mayfield said. "They're beyond our help. Williams, if you see an aircraft headed anywhere close to us, don't keep it to yourself."

"Count on that, Captain," the navigator said. "There haven't been any new arrivals for some time now. Not in the air, anyway. It might be like Ritchie said: maybe this thing has gone back to before the Wright Brothers. For now."

The older man grimaced. "I wish I could find that comforting."

The Grid now filled all of their view to the right, its towering pillars of blue-violet flame dazzling in their majesty as they cleft the darkness. The space between them was an affront to the human eye. If it produced or reflected visible light, the brain was incapable of processing it. A void so absolute that it was a peril to the reasoning mind.

The westward pillar was straight ahead, shining through the clouds of the eyewall as if they didn't exist. Mayfield had to keep one eye closed most of the time, to leave that eye with just enough night vision to read the altimeter every few seconds. The Hercules was only moments away from penetration, leveling off. If Carson was wrong about the altitude of the node...but that didn't bear thinking about. The winds grew stronger. The transit of the eyewall began.

Everything after that happened too quickly to follow: the stabbing glare from the ribbon; Mayfield's mind imagining a tiny zone of shadow; a reflex twist of the yoke; a sudden lurch to the right; shock of impact; a piercing shriek of sound, then:

Time frozen. A nanosecond—or a millennium.

Blinding blue-white light. Steel, flesh, bone, all translucent.

Silence, as of the moment before creation.

...utter darkness, emptiness, helplessness, as the universe turned upside-down.

The wounded Hercules flipped onto its back and slid nose-downward, plummeting toward the sea.

Klaxons filled the air. Carson closed his eyes and gripped the armrests as if to crush them, but the plane's crew responded according to their training and focused on survival. The alarms stopped. The engines coughed, then roared. Dimly he heard Fuentes' voice calling out the altitude while Mayfield fought the battle of his life.

At eight thousand feet Carson was sure all was lost. At six thousand feet he prayed with all his soul.

At four thousand feet the cosmos unexpectedly let them live another day.

Cheers filled the cabin, the aircraft slowly came level, and he dared to open his eyes.

"What happened?" His voice was no more than a croak.

Mayfield's intense relief was quickly dimmed by dismay as the realization came to him. "We *missed*," he said simply.

"We couldn't have. I felt the impact. Then we passed on the right, *through the Grid.*"

"We hit your cable," the pilot said. "Not the node—a last-second updraft prevented that. Just the cable. It took off the end of our port wing." The last was spoken with a cold detachment. The crew was thunderstruck. "It would be madness to try to fly out of the storm now. I'm barely keeping us in the air as it is. We're heading back to the eye again. If we can survive that long, we'll circle until we run out of fuel and have to ditch. Hopefully somewhere near land."

No-one spoke. There was nothing to say. Instead they clung to their seats and their routines, any task that would help them ignore the constant shudder of the damaged airframe as it magnified every bounce and twist into imminent disaster. It was hardest on Carson who had no chore to divert his mind.

Relief came at last. The blackness lessened and the battered craft found an uneasy equilibrium on the lighter winds of the eye. Now they would play a long game of patience, and try not to think of the cold waves that waited for them.

Ritchie's cry was like an electric shock.

"Captain. *Look!*"

There was no need to say where. The Grid still dominated the sky as it dominated their minds. Only now there was a difference.

Mammoth discharges of electricity staggered their way up the columns like the 'Jacob's ladder' of an old horror movie laboratory, and the *blind spot* effect within was shredding like ancient cloth. By the light of the flashes they could see dark bands of cloud drawn into the vertical maelstrom and, far below, the waters of the sea itself.

"Good God. It *is* destabilizing!" cried Carson. "Maybe our passage through the field triggered some kind of feedback!" He watched in terror as the stark bursts of light showed the surface of the sea beginning to swirl, an ominous pattern out of sailors' nightmares. "A whirlpool. My God, it's creating a vortex in the ocean." Was it only his imagination, or were darker specks amid the waves already being carried to their doom?

For an instant the Grid became a silvered mirror, reflecting the stadium walls of the storm.

"Three radar contacts, Captain!" shouted Williams. "Now four!"

"The effect is wrapping inward on itself." Ritchie gasped. "The far end is whipping back through time!"

The titanic mirror coruscated with ragged bands of lead grey and electric blue.

"All contacts are now gone," Williams sounded as if he were about to weep. "That *thing* drew them back to it. They didn't have a chance."

The end came so suddenly and swiftly that it could have been a trick of the mind: a fleeting glimpse of a twisters' tail, like an angry lash sweeping over the dark sea then flicking upward toward the nearest column of fire.

The universe filled with blinding light, and moments later the concussion tossed them like refuse across the shattered sky.

Yet the stubborn Hercules was well named, and it bore them safely through the frothing night. And when they could see again, the black ether was filled with fireworks such as the world had not known since its birth.

#

"What did we just witness?" Mayfield asked, half a lifetime later.

"I think it was what Ritchie said," Carson replied. "The tail end of the phenomenon recoiled back through time. Perhaps it destroyed a node, perhaps it simply fed upon itself and imploded."

"Like the *Ouroboros*," Ritchie murmured, awestruck. "A symbol of alchemists: the serpent devouring its own tail. It's a symbol of Life out of Death."

"It was death, all right," Mayfield said wearily. "Death disguised as the solution to all of our problems. We've seen that before. Too many times. Am I painting the picture for you, Mr. Carson?"

"No need, Captain. It may not be possible to close Pandora's Box, but once someone estimates the potential legal liability, this project will be buried dark and deep. I think we can be sure of that."

"It's Captain Collinson, sir!" Fuentes cheered, pointing needlessly at his headset. "They set course back to Keesler when communications went out, but he's turning around and heading our way."

"Can we be re-fuelled?" Carson asked, picturing the other Hurricane Hunter coming to their rescue.

"No," Mayfield said. "But at least they can stay on station and watch out for us. Maybe vector in a Coast Guard vessel, if they get a break in the storm. It's cause for hope, anyway."

Did he really have hope? Mayfield wondered.

He realized that he did—not hope for a cure maybe, but at least a sense that there would be something, some place for Sara beyond their knowing. He'd seen a glimpse of the infinite, and his view of the world could never be the same as it was.

"Crowe, give me all you can on the winds. I'll need everything I can get when it comes time to set this thing down."

Crowe nodded and her hands moved automatically as she faced the prospect of death. It had made her understand that life—her life—was worthy of more respect than she'd given it. Jack was a good lover, but she deserved a better man.

"Fuentes," she said. "Maybe Keesler can give us something helpful from the latest satellite images."

Fuentes looked at Carson while he got the radio ready. The scientist and his team had dreamed big and failed spectacularly, but the audacity of their dream captivated him.

There were grand things still to be accomplished in the world, and Fuentes had the imagination to pursue them. When they got back he'd ask Carson for advice about good universities.

He collected the data from Keesler AFB and passed it on to the navigator.

Williams knew they had witnessed hubris on an unprecedented scale, and the cosmos had slapped them down hard. It reaffirmed his faith that God's plan was carried out by ordinary people doing ordinary, but important tasks. The safety of his home depended on him staying the course, doing what he did best. The hopes of the world did not depend on Carson and his kind.

Hope, Carson thought. Yes, hope was a good thing. He didn't want to die, but he'd lost some of his fear of it. He was surrounded by damn good people who'd do their best to keep him safe. But if they couldn't, he'd seen eternity in that frozen moment within the Grid. He knew that, come what may, he would always exist.

Somewhere in time.

#   #   #

ONCE UPON A MIDNIGHT

*I*N THE END, THE FATE OF HUMANITY rested in the hands of a woman scorned.

Lennie Allen wouldn't have characterized herself in that way. But she'd already triggered one warning from the computer's security subroutine by being distracted. The next time she'd be locked out for twenty-four hours. The Director would not be amused.

Normally she welcomed the security protocols; the retina scan, voice recognition, code-words, and fingerprint-scanning trackpad were all a part of life in one of the nation's highest-echelon research facilities, and they helped her sleep at night. God knew, the stuff they handled could be used with catastrophic effect by the wrong people. It was the *keystroke dynamics* keyboard that turned out to be a pain in the ass. If its biometrics system ever suspected that she was acting under duress it would offer only two warnings and then go into complete lockdown. Mendelssohn swore he'd been locked out once as a result of chugging one too many Starbucks.

Lennie was finding it hard to care about invented global cataclysm when her own world was falling apart.

She loved working in WCSD—the development and analysis of *worst case scenarios* made good use of her vivid imagination and overflowing cup of personal paranoia. In fact, it was often cathartic. If she could imagine the very worst things that could happen to the planet, and devise potential responses to them, it robbed her own personal fears and troubles of their potency.

But not this time. Ed was gone. Three nights ago. The notification of divorce proceedings had been delivered to her this morning. *God*, that was fast. What was his hurry? Considering that Lennie hadn't suspected a thing until three nights and...twenty-three minutes ago. Maybe that was what hurt the most, that she'd been so blind. Lennie the genius, her friends called her. Not so smart, after all. Wrapped up in her work, imagining the most terrible things that could happen to a world, without realizing that sometimes 'the world' came down to just two people.

She ran her hands over her glossy black work-station. It was her link to the powerful computer nexus that produced the Reichmann Analog Virtual Environment—a long name with a catchy acronym was important to the people who wrote the cheques. Those grey-suited dark-tied backroom government autocrats had seen enough plain old supercomputers. They needed a name that could jazz up a bland requisition proposal and bamboozle a roomful of auditors. Lennie never used the full title. To her, the RAVE Nexus was part-taskmaster, part-playground. From its matrix of graphics imaging software, intelligent problem-solving, and pure brute processing speed sprang forth creations of startling realism. Lennie could step into a three-dimensional projection of a pristine globe, key in the disaster parameters, and watch it bleed in spreading pools around her.

As a biologist her specialty was pandemics. It was a sexy topic—had been since the first years of the century, for some reason. Scientists had latched onto the idea that pandemics followed some kind of regular schedule, and the world was overdue. After that it was a matter of course that every biological outbreak anywhere attracted an inordinate amount of attention from a global media fascinated with dying things. And if the scientific community found that modestly fanning the flames meant mounds of research money thrown their way, well, who could really blame them?

Lennie's job was to gather everything, from their most carefully assembled data to their wildest flights of fancy, and feed it to the RAVE-n. Then the cyber-mind was charged with assessing the probabilities of every scenario, analyzing the etiology, predicting the spread pattern, forecasting the fatality rates, yea, prophesying over the quick and the dead. They ran several scenarios a week. The human race had nearly been eradicated dozens of times.

Lennie and the RAVE-*n* were very good at their job.

Now, though, disaster had invaded her own reality. She felt it like a poison in her veins. Her vision lost its focus, and her fingers miscarried on the keys.

What had gone so wrong in the life they'd shared, she and Ed?

(Eddy. She always called him Eddy because he called her Lennie. He was a sports writer, and everyone in that world was called Bobby or Jimmy or Scotty, weren't they? He dreamed of being a political reporter. Would he have called the President Donny?)

The screen was angrily flashing an image at her.

It was the corporate logo of the Reichmann Analog Corporation: a representation of the Pallas Athena, goddess of war and wisdom. *Damn.* She entered the "SAFE" code to reset the security function.

She had to concentrate, or the RAVE-*n* would kick her ass. And deservedly so. It wasn't just computer modeling that the RAVE-*n* controlled. All of Level Seven was a full-blown Hazmat lab, operated robotically. The substances studied in there were so dangerous that humans rarely ventured inside, except for the PhD equivalent of janitorial work. The test-tubes and beakers and petrie dishes belonged to the RAVE-*n*. Inside were samples of Rickettsiae bacteria, the villain behind typhus and Rocky Mountain spotted fever; Arenaviridae viruses responsible for Lassa fever; Ebola virus; the corona virus that produced SARS; Marburg virus; several different strains of avian type A influenza viruses of the H5, H7, and H9 subtypes capable of infecting humans, and even a few precious grams of the 1918 Spanish Flu, culled from a corpse frozen in the Alaskan permafrost. Some of the most deadly pathogens known to humankind, all held in the capable pincers of a cybernetic brain and its robotic minions. It was the stuff of sci-fi fright movies, but Lennie wasn't worried. The RAVE-*n* had the abilities of an Artificial Intelligence in many ways, but no independent thought. She liked to say that even if the supercomputer *could* take over the world, the RAVE-*n* was too smart to *want* it.

No, there was far more danger from humans screwing up, maybe because they couldn't keep their inconvenient emotions from getting in the way. Lennie reached for a cup of coffee that was hours cold, and put it back down with a grimace.

They were running simulations of avian flu outbreaks again this week. Although it had been years since the first flare-ups of the H5N1 strain in Hong Kong in the late 1990's, and the more frightening outbreaks later in Southeast Asia, the best minds said that H5N1 or something like it was still lurking in the shadows, waiting for its moment to strike. Every so often it would appear in a flock of domestic fowl somewhere around the globe, and a massive slaughter would follow.

There hadn't been a documented case of H5N1 human-to-human transmission beyond one secondary victim. It was a pandemic held in check because the virus couldn't yet spread among the human population. But flu viruses mutate like there's no tomorrow.

A flock of wild ducks might fly over a poultry farm, leaving behind a bombardment of infected droppings. Wandering chickens would spread the virus to the nearby stock of pigs, one or two of which had already been unlucky enough to pick up a dose of *human* flu from the overly attentive Farmer Nguyen. Once inside the accommodating blood stream of the swine, the two visiting viruses could swap a few genes and, Presto: a new strain of bird flu capable of spreading among *homo sapiens*. Within a few days Farmer Nguyen and his family would have ruined lungs filled with blood, as their bodies' misguided immune systems deployed cellular soldiers that destroyed the very tissues they were meant to save.

In the outside world the process of mutation was random and slow. It was a different story among the gleaming white walls of Level Seven. There a macabre array of stainless steel bones danced within Plexiglas cylinders, slicing and dicing and splicing, finding new recipes of DNA—shiny new double strands of nucleotides mixed and matched from human diseases and those of the animal kingdom, with the deliberate purpose of *creating* new pathogens deadly to humans. The rationale was that, by creating these lethal agents we could learn how to fight them.

Lennie was always grateful that she didn't tend to remember her dreams.

She also felt that her own hands were clean. She didn't create the murderous agents. She only ran simulations of their path of destruction.

When she and the RAVE-*n* turned the new killer loose, it was only on a *virtual* globe—an ethereal construct of numbers and electrical impulses, sanitized and safe. Lennie provided the data and the computer showed her Armageddon.

She would never admit it to anyone, but it was morbidly fascinating to watch the world's dominant species die a thousand gruesome deaths. Particularly if at least one of the virtual victims bore the face of Eddy.

No, that wasn't true. She didn't want him dead. Maybe the blame was hers. She'd always known that secrets could tear a relationship apart. Her father's military career had poisoned her parents' marriage after he'd been promoted into the upper echelons of the Pentagon and had to hide the details of his workday from his own wife. After that, the trust was gone and the fire along with it—Lennie had watched it happen.

She'd vowed never to make the same mistake, but that was exactly what she'd done. It wasn't just her job's security demands; she'd told herself she was protecting Eddy from the horrors of Level Seven for his own good. It wasn't healthy to live day after day with the threat of a biological holocaust hanging like a Sword of Damocles in the mind's eye. Some people simply couldn't take it, and spent the rest of their lives in therapy.

So she couldn't tell him about her work, and she couldn't tell him why not. But he wasn't a fool. He suspected something. Eventually it turned into the conviction that she was involved in something big...a potential hot story that could be his *entrée* into the political arena. She was sure he hadn't come up with that idea on his own. It had the perfumed taint of that blonde internet blogger he'd talked about more and more often. The one who was always digging for government conspiracies. The one with the inflated ego and the inflated chest....

God! Was that what had happened? Had an online correspondence sparked an offline romance? *Oh Eddy...Eddy...did I drive you to that?* She felt a hot tear well up, and had to snap her head away before it could splash onto the keyboard.

She didn't want him dead. She was furious, cruelly hurt, and hopelessly infatuated all at the same time. She loved him beyond reason, and even now she knew that she would take him back without hesitation, if he asked. But what were the odds of that? Predicting them would take more skill than she had. It would require a master of predictions....

No. No, the idea was ridiculous. She turned her head away from the screens and imprisoned her hands beneath her legs to restrain them, while she rocked back and forth in confusion.

There was no-one else in the lab. There likely wouldn't be for another forty-five minutes—her coworkers liked to take long lunches. And she knew how to erase almost all traces of her commands, except in the RAVE-*n*'s deepest core memory.

Did she dare...?

Inevitable as a pandemic itself, she surrendered seven minutes later and furtively began to key in the data. The RAVE-*n* already had reams of information about Lennie. She quickly fed it a rough profile of Eddy, warts and all, resisting the powerful temptation to embellish the warts.

Query: *Will Lennie and Eddy get back together?*

There was no sign of activity from the RAVE-*n*—there never was. But sixty seconds was an eternity of processing time for a task that involved no global modeling, no quantum variables, and no fancy graphics in 128-bit studio-precision color.

The screen finally came to life.

RAVE-*n*: *Insufficient data.*

She exhaled a long-held breath and realized that her hands were trembling. She didn't dare try it again. It was sheer idiocy to have done it in the first place. She spent the next five minutes covering her tracks.

The rest of the afternoon was excruciating. Each time someone came over to speak to her, she expected them to hiss a withering accusation about using lab facilities for a personal whim. She vowed that she would never give in to such an unworthy impulse again. She hurried home that night in relief, and dreamed of a spinning globe projected in mid-air, with her face on one side and Eddy's on the other, and she could only watch helplessly as scenario after scenario brought spreading patches of emptiness like a cancer between them.

At the first coffee break the next morning, she asked again.

RAVE-n: *Insufficient data.*

This time she didn't delete the query, she merely hid it behind layers of other tasks. But it waited there for her to call it up, first at lunch, then at afternoon break, and eventually whenever she had the room to herself. In between, her mind would wander from cross-indexing fatality rates to trying to recall any memories of her marriage that might help in her Cupidean quest.

RAVE-n: *Insufficient data.*

In frustration she nearly pounded a fist on the keyboard, but that might trigger another computation. Because of the dynamic interface, the machine already finished most of her sentences for her—they'd worked together for so long it anticipated nearly every keystroke. Instead she chastised herself again for obsessing over a husband (*EX* -husband!) and tried to force her tense fingers to relax on the keys.

She was startled to see the screen begin to fill with words...words beginning with EX....

Exacerbate

Exact

Exacting

Exaggerate

She quickly keyed in a 'Terminate' command. The RAVE-*n* was getting too damned helpful for their own good.

But not helpful where it really counted. Why couldn't the supercomputer produce an answer for *her*? Why didn't it even try?

The question was too simple—that must be it. She needed to approach it like any other scenario. Build a model, enter the data, run the simulation. But that would take time. She could never accomplish that much in a couple of coffee breaks. She had to....

She had to work overtime. Which meant she needed a cover story. Say her last pandemic simulation had run into bugs—of the computer, not biological variety—but she was close to tracking them down and didn't want to lose the momentum?

Her supervisor accepted the fiction readily enough. Lennie was one of his best workers. And anyway she was on a salary.

She had to be careful. There was still a possibility that someone else might be working late and walk in on her. It was even possible that one of the security people would make a random check on her work station. She needed a shadow screen—a secondary display she could bring up with a stroke of a key. Only a real task would be convincing enough to fool a colleague, but she'd just finished the last of her most recent series of simulations. What else would look plausible?

She called up the RAVE-*n*'s latest results from Level Seven. And instantly regretted it. A quick scan of the data caused the blood to drain from her face.

Good God. This was the worst one yet: a strain of virus that appeared to be based on a hemagglutinin 5 and neuraminidase 1, but had stitched-on RNA from half a dozen sources. The testing just completed that afternoon showed a startling 100% lethality—virtually unheard of. Early indications revealed a six or seven-day incubation period, followed by fatality within four days. That alone made it much more dangerous than killers like Ebola—they killed their hosts so quickly that they rarely spread very far from the original source of the infection. This new creation had no such weakness. It was the perfect traveler. *God help us if....*

She didn't let her mind complete the thought. Instead she began the practiced routine of building the computer model that would complete it for her. The horrific allure of the new pathogen was nearly enough to distract Lennie from her original purpose.

It was the moment when the world could have been saved.

But destiny or fate or evolution dictated otherwise. The pull of her aching heart was stronger. Once the basic parameters of her scenario had been established, she allowed the RAVE-*n* to fill in the rest, adding only the simple command to Run the program and then Terminate. Then she turned back to her private project. The reunion of Lennie and Eddy. The *best* case scenario.

#

It happened only minutes before midnight. She awakened to the sound of the alarms, and the pain where the keys had become embedded in her cheek.

Had they caught her?

The klaxon reverberated through the room, piercing her ears until her jaw ached. Warning lamps painted the walls in spasms of colour. Finally gathering her wits together she snapped her head up to look at what they called "The Big Screen", a liquid crystal panel mounted from the ceiling that displayed announcements for all staff, and alerts of any kind. It was mutely screaming in giant fluorescent letters.

There was a breach on Level Seven. A deadly toxin was loose.

Already an army of biohazard experts would be scrambling into hazmat suits—she could picture them racing down echoing hallways to bring the enemy to battle. Yet, even as she watched, her initial alarm turned to helpless horror.

The vents were opening!

The outside vents of the lab were intended to exhaust toxic gases in the event of a fire. They were a dangerous necessity, but there were countless failsafe systems to prevent them ever opening in the aftermath of a spill—exactly the kind of accident she was now witnessing. The failsafes could not be overridden manually by a murderous saboteur or terrorist maniac. That had been demonstrated again and again, before the lab could even be built. No-one could open the vents to the open air once a breach alert had been sounded.

No human.

The RAVE-*n*! The computer must have allowed it. *Good God*, could it have been caused by something *she*'d done?

Her fingers flew frantically over the keyboard, recalling the recent list of commands and actions, luminous letters reflected in her wet eyes.

No! It wasn't possible!

The last command line accused her from the screen like an executioner's pointing finger:

"Run program. EX-Terminate."

She slumped back in the chair, and her vacant eyes came to focus on the holographic globe suspended in mid-air before her, running its final simulation.

Blotches of invading crimson ate their way hungrily around the ghostly blue projection of her home world, almost more quickly than she could see. In a daze, she tapped a trio of keys to check the time scale and drew a ragged breath, then expanded the range to slow the simulation down. This time she could see the wash of salmon colour, representing the transmission of the virus, racing around the globe in a flash. Immediately afterward followed the blood red flood of fatality, moving slowly for the first ten or fifteen seconds, then almost instantly transforming the whole mottled Earth into a pulsing red beacon of warning. Stunned, she stood and walked into the center of the projection, then turned slowly in place, and swept her gaze over each quadrant. There was nowhere left untouched, no safe haven of shelter or resilience. Not even in the Himalayas, or the desert of the Sudan, or the barren Antarctic.

A flicker of movement drew her attention back to the Big Screen overhead. Its glaring fluorescent letters had been replaced with an epitaph of damning words.

Query: *Will Lennie and Eddy get back together?*
Quoth the RAVE-n: *Nevermore.*

\# \# \#

ABOUT THE AUTHOR

A broadcaster for more than thirty years, Scott Overton's novel *Dead Air*, published by Scrivener Press, is a mystery/thriller about the world of radio. *Dead Air* was shortlisted for a Northern Lit Award in Ontario, Canada. But most of his writing is science fiction and fantasy. His short fiction has been published in the magazines *On Spec*, *Neo-opsis*, *Penumbra* and several Canadian and American anthologies including *Canadian Tales of the Fantastic*, *In Poe's Shadow*, and *Tesseracts Sixteen: Parnassus Unbound*. His distractions from writing include scuba diving and a couple of collector cars.

You can learn more and read free stories at Scott's website.

www.scottoverton.ca

364

ALSO FIND SCOTT AT:

Goodreads   www.goodreads.com/ScottOverton

Facebook   www.facebook.com/ScottOverton.author

Twitter   @SFtruenorth

Look for more great reading from Scott Overton

Dead Air

It's a hard thing to accept that someone wants you dead. It forces you to decide if you have anything worth living for.

When radio morning man Lee Garrett finds a death threat on his control console, he shrugs it off as a sick prank—until minor harassment turn into undeniable attempts on his life. When the deadliest assault yet claims an innocent victim, Garrett knows he has to force a confrontation.

"A gripping, insightful debut from a veteran radio personality and gifted wordsmith." —Sean Costello, author of *Here After*

"Scott Overton is a storyteller of boundless skill...a writer to watch." —Mark Leslie, author of *Haunted Hamilton* and *I, Death*

Find out how to buy your own copy at www.scottoverton.ca/dead-air .